Miss You Once Again

Kelly Baugh

So thankful to my critique group girls! You're the best :)
Kelly

Printed in the United States of America
First Printing, 2015
Hot Chocolate Press
Fort Collins, Colorado

http://HotChocolatePress.com

Cover Design by Kerrie Flanagan

ISBN-10:0-9910626-8-X
ISBN-13:978-0-9910626-8-3

DEDICATION

This book is dedicated to my family (past, present and future) and my friends who are like family (you know who you are!). Without your support and encouragement, this book wouldn't exist. Families are wonderful, crazy and messy, but they are the most beautiful thing on earth. I love you all and thank God for you every day.

.

ACKNOWLEDGMENTS

First and foremost I would like to thank my critique group; your insights, suggestions and encouragement gave me the courage and will-power to finish this book even when I wanted to throw it out the window: Ellen, Helen, Kerrie, LeAnn, Carol, Liz, Jenny and Sally (who I know is smiling down from above).

I also want to thank my Nana and Mama Jean for being the strong Southern women the characters of this book are modeled after. I'm so thankful you gave me a different flavor of life when I was a child and my summer visits to your homes created memories I still treasure. Nana, I wish you could have read the hard copy, but hopefully you get your own version up in heaven.

Kerrie, thank you for being a publisher and editor extraordinaire, encouraging me in my writing and life (and rescuing me in my accidents). Working with you has been nothing but a joy.

Lastly, I want to thank my parents, my sister, my husband and two children. The gift of a life lived with each of you inspires me to write, even if what I express isn't a fraction as beautiful as what I get to experience with you.

CHAPTER ONE

I just can't understand why, of all the clothes in my closet, I would be in this ugly cardigan and dumpy wool skirt?

I mean, when you're dressing for an occasion, you consider your audience, the climate, the statement you want to make... it's much more complex than most people ever realize. In this situation, for example, I'd either wear a suitably dramatic piece, like my vintage riding costume I picked up on a trip to London, or maybe something more appropriate to the climate, but with a flair. Outdoorsy, with a Dr. Zhivago–type theme.

Yes, that last one. I could have a full-length leather duster with matching fur mittens, boots and hat. Maybe one of those dramatic ones with the ear flaps. It would be absolutely darling. I don't know if I could carry it all off at my age, but half the battle with that sort of thing is having the right attitude.

'Course, I would be a little overdressed, I realize as I study my granddaughter. All she's got on are some dusty jeans, a vest and a dingy white shirt. As always, she looks frumpy and unmemorable. She's not making use of any of the assets the Good Lord gave her. Those skinny hips are

just the type designers love. I watch her at work, wondering once again why I'm here.

All I can say is this isn't the first time I've wanted to shake her until her teeth rattle...but it is the first time I've had that inclination floating on the side of a cliff.

"Calm down, Steve. Relax and take a deep breath," Lee ordered from the top of the limestone cliff where she braced Steve's climbing rope. Late afternoon sunlight highlighted flecks of mica on the rock face.

"I can't do it!" Steve shouted again from where he dangled below her.

Lee sensed his rising panic and knew he was close to losing control. "Yes, you can. You've already made it up 90 feet. Don't tell me you can't make it just a few more."

"I really can't. I'm going to rappel down." Steve's voice shook. "It's not that big of a deal."

"It's a big deal to me!" Lee kept her voice light despite her burning forearms. "No one gets left behind. It's time to man up and finish the climb so you can enjoy the sunset with all the others."

"Fine. One more try," Steve agreed after a pause. The rope moved, then went slack as he finally grabbed onto the side of the mountain. The cry of a lonely hawk filled the air, and Lee let out a sigh of relief.

"I'm over the hard part now!" Steve shouted a moment later. "Guess it wasn't that bad after all."

"It never is," Lee murmured under her breath before calling, "Great job, Steve! Almost done."

"Sorry about panicking before." His voice, now calm, floated from below her.

"No worries. You pushed through your fear just like you needed to," Lee said and Steve's head popped into sight. She held out her hand and pulled him the last few steps onto the top of the cliff. "Now enjoy your reward." Lee gestured to the 360° view of the San Juan Mountains that surrounded them: snowcapped peaks and shadowy valleys bathed in the late afternoon sun.

Lee wound the length of Steve's rope, but paused when she heard a shout. Nick, one of her employees, ran toward her with a phone in his hand.

"Hey, Lee," he said. "Your dad called while you were finishing up with this guy. You need to call him back—it sounds like there's an emergency with your grandma."

Lee's heart began to thunder in her ears. She grabbed the phone and tried to dial out, but she couldn't get enough of a signal for the call to go through.

"What did he say?" she asked Nick, hitting the redial button again and again.

"That it was important and you needed to contact him. Something with your grandma. Look, Lee, just go," Nick said. "I can get the group back into town. The guy from Texas can help me drive. He'll have the time of his life going through the canyon."

"You sure?"

"Yes. Now go so you can find a signal," Nick said.

Lee waved a thank you over her shoulder and ran down the dirt trail in the direction of her Jeep.

She continued redialing as she sped down the canyon's dirt road. Finally, the phone began to ring.

"Snowy River Internists, how can I help you?"

"Hi, this is Lee. Is my father around?"

"Oh hi, Lee, this is Susan. I think he's just finishing up with a patient. I'll let him know you're on the line and transfer you to his office."

Lee's stomach filled with dread. Usually Susan was so chatty Lee had a hard time even breaking in to ask for her father. Whatever was wrong, it was serious.

"Hello, Lee." Her dad's deep voice replaced Susan's. "I'm afraid I have some bad news about your grandmother. Nana's passed away."

Lee let her foot off the accelerator and coasted to a pull-off on the side of the road.

"Hello, Lee? Are you there?"

"Yes."

"Are you okay?"

"Yes." She closed her eyes against the gathering tears.

"I'm sorry, Lee." She heard her dad shut the door to his office. His voice was gentler now. "You know Nana and I didn't always get along well, but—"

"How did it happen?" Lee traced the steering wheel with her finger.

"Her heart gave out, apparently. The doctors say she didn't suffer, which is good. She died in her sleep."

"Was she at home?" Lee had a hard time keeping track of her grandma's busy travel itinerary.

"Yes, she had just arrived. Back from Rome or Paris or wherever she was. Jenny even talked to her on the phone the night before."

"I'm glad she got to say good-bye." Lee knew her sister would be heartbroken at Nana's death. They'd always been close. "Is Jenny okay?"

"She's...doing as well as can be expected. Her doctor says she thinks they finally have Jenny's blood pressure under control, but she's on complete bed rest for the next two months until the baby is born."

"Maybe I'll try to call her."

He hesitated. "So Lee, I know now's not the best time, but you and I need to discuss the arrangements of settling Nana's estate."

"Her estate?"

"Yes, it's going to take some work. You know how gargantuan her house is, filled with all that junk."

"Dad, it's not junk." Lee felt tired. "Nana loved fashion and decorating. She had different interests than you."

"Whatever. We just lost a partner here at the practice and I don't have time to go deal with her things."

If only her mother were still alive, Lee thought. She would have made sure all of Nana's treasures were treated with the love and respect they deserved. "What about Mark or Jenny? Can they help?"

"Lee, I just told you Jenny's on complete bed rest."

"I'm sorry. Of course she can't go." Her mind numb and battered, Lee felt a creeping dread as she asked the next question. "What about Mark?"

"Mark?" Her dad snorted. "Mark would have less of a clue than I would about what to do with your grandma's... stuff."

"But could he at least help?"

Impatience radiated through the phone. "He just dropped out of college last month to become a yoga instructor. He's barely responsible enough to manage his own life, let alone someone else's."

There was a moment of silence before he continued. "Here's the deal. You're going to have to be the one who goes to Eden Grove and settle your grandmother's estate."

"Dad! I've got—"

"Lee, I'm sorry, but I know I can depend on you. I don't think it'll be that big of a deal. Take most of her stuff to the secondhand store. Maybe keep a few mementos for yourself and your sister. Put the house on the market. That's it. It should take a week or two, max."

"Dad, I've got my own business to run!" Lee cried into the phone.

"I realize that." His voice exploded in her ear. "But what do you want me to do, Lee? I'm up to my eyes in work, your sister's pregnant and your brother's an irresponsible—" he paused and took a deep breath, "well, we both know what your brother is. So that leaves you, Lee."

It always does! A little voice in her head cried even as she heard herself conceding, "If that's the way it has to be, then I guess I can...figure something out."

"Good. When's the soonest you can get there?"

"Well, there's going to be a funeral right? I assumed at least we'd all go down for that?"

"No, no funeral. Nana didn't want one. According to her lawyer, she asked to be cremated. They've already taken care of that at the funeral home. Her only other request was to have her ashes scattered by your grandfather's grave. You can pick them up from the lawyer's office when you get there."

"So it's really just me going down to Eden Grove?"

"Yes. When is the earliest you can be down there?"

"I guess...maybe in four or five days?" Lee tried to calculate, but her mind was racing through the fall/winter schedule at work and whether her employees would be willing to take over more responsibilities. Would she have to hire a third person?

"I'll be more than happy to pay for your ticket."

"Ticket?" Lee said, still trying to tear her mind from her business. "Oh, but Dad, I'll have to drive."

"Drive? Why on earth would you drive?"

"Because of Charlie, of course."

"Charlie? No, that's ridiculous, Lee. It's more than a two-day drive to Mississippi from Durango and you can't do that by yourself. You need to fly. Make some other arrangements for your dog."

"No, listen," Lee interrupted, her temper having finally reached its breaking point. "I'm willing to make this sacrifice. For Nana. But Charlie and I will be *driving* down there and that's final."

"Fine," came her father's voice, tinged with ice. "Whatever, just get down there as soon as possible. I'll talk to you later." The line went dead and Lee glared at the phone for a moment before flinging it across the car. It bounced off the door and clattered to the floor.

"Thanks, Lee, I appreciate your help. I know it's a lot to ask, but I really need you." She leaned her head back to study the twilight stars from the open top of her car. "Oh and don't worry, I'll be there in a few days to help you sort things out. I'd never want you to do this all on your own."

And then, all the anger melted away, replaced with emotional exhaustion. "Why is this my job?" Lee asked the deepening darkness around her. She shook her head and covered her face with her hands. A sob ripped through the quiet of the deserted mountain road and the crickets, who were just beginning their nightly chorus, paused at the sound.

CHAPTER TWO

As she lay in her bed a few hours later, Lee studied the ceiling above her. Charlie, seeming to sense her distress, had not left her side since she'd come home, not even for his dinner. Stretched out on his side next to her, the dog leaned back every once in a while to give her a companionable lick.

A gentle night breeze blew through the gauzy curtains in Lee's bedroom. The scent of late roses from her yard filled the air, but Lee barely noticed.

"I can't believe Nana's gone," she whispered to the air around her. "She can't be."

Nana had been bigger than life in so many ways, and by no means a traditional grandma. While her friends' grandmas taught them to bake bread or cookies and hosted Thanksgiving dinners, Nana pierced Lee's and Jenny's ears and bought them their first bikinis. She taught them to drive a stick shift in her bright red convertible and how to sweet talk their way out of a speeding ticket.

Nana, as the head of the fashion design department at Eden Grove University, used to take trips to Dallas, New York and even Paris to buy her on-trend wardrobe. Her

Christmas presents were so ahead of the fashion curve that Lee and Jenny usually tossed them to the back of their closets. It was only when they reached high school that they recognized Nana's gifts for the treasures they were and became the envy of their friends.

She was the type of grandma that everyone admired, the type of grandma who guaranteed outrageous fun, especially since her escapades usually involved the breaking of some household rule. She was not, however, the type of grandma who fostered deep relationships. Her jet-setting lifestyle and masses of friends and work colleagues precluded most of the one-on-one time necessary for a deeper bond with the more introspective Lee.

*And now she's gone. I always thought there'd be time for that deeper conversation. The one where we'd really share our hearts with each other. But now...*Lee's stomach knotted at the thought and she fingered the sapphire drop Nana had given her on her sixteenth birthday.

"Every woman needs a classic piece of jewelry, Caralee," Nana had instructed her, ignoring her granddaughter's six-year insistence that everyone call her *Lee.*

"You're a woman now and it's time you started dressing like one who knows what she's worth." Nana gestured to Lee's cut-off shorts and tank top.

"I've told you before, people don't dress up here like they do in the South."

"Nonsense." Nana dismissed her with a wave of her hand. "Just because people are ignorant and uninformed is no reason to act like them."

"So you're saying that not wearing couture, or at least designer labels, is a sign of ignorance?"

"Exactly!" Nana motioned for Lee to lift the hair off her neck so she could fasten the new necklace. "And no granddaughter of mine is going to grow up without knowing how to look fabulous."

She'd turned Lee around to face her once more. "There." Nana touched the drop, an uncharacteristic look of tenderness in her eyes. "You know my grandma gave this to me on my sweet sixteen."

"Really?" Lee said. Of the two granddaughters, Jenny had a much closer relationship with Nana. Why hadn't she given it to Jenny instead?

"I knew it belonged to you, darling," Nana answered as if reading her thoughts. She pulled Lee into a hug. "You and I are more alike than you realize."

"What?" Lee asked, intrigued, but then Nana pushed away and began to gather the discarded tissue paper.

"Besides, you have the Abney family eyes." Nana turned. "Of course you had to have the sapphire drop to match your baby blues. I'll come up with a topaz or citrine for Jenny on her sweet sixteen. To compliment her hazel eyes."

Remembering the exchange brought a fresh sting of tears. Roughly, Lee brushed them away. Charlie whined.

"It's okay, boy." She turned over and buried her face in his neck. "We'll be okay. We always are."

Overwhelmed by the details she needed to organize before she left for Mississippi, Lee struggled to get to work the next day.

When she walked in the doors of Play Harder, Nick followed her to her office, peppering her with questions.

"We can talk in a bit, Nick. Right now, can you go help Cassie get the climbing group checked out?" Lee needed a minute to steady herself.

"Yep, no problem." He returned to the front of the store and ushered the 12 returning climbers to the counter.

Lee sat at her desk, calming all the thoughts reeling through her mind before going out to greet the customers. "How did you enjoy the Watch Crystal climb?" she asked a couple as they handed in their helmets, ropes and hardware.

"It was amazing!" the woman answered without a second's hesitation. "The north face climb was really intense—"

"But once you got to the top," her partner interrupted, "the view was insane!"

"Yeah, it really is," Lee nodded. "I'm glad you enjoyed it and I hope you climb with us again."

"Oh definitely." The woman handed Nick the last of her gear. "Your guide was wonderful. She had great suggestions, but she also let me figure out things on my own."

"Cassie's one of the best climbers in town." Lee glanced toward her guide, who chatted with some other satisfied customers. "I'm really lucky to have her."

Cassie smiled over at Lee and waved, but continued debriefing her clients. Lee exchanged a few more pleasantries and then moved back to her computer. She was working on the company's website, updating it with pictures from the summer's climbing, backpacking, jeep and rafting tours. It always gave her customers a thrill when they checked out the website and found pictures of themselves advertising Play Harder's services. Some of them had been returning to Lee's outdoor adventure outfitter in Durango for years.

"Still working on the computer, huh? You've become such a corporate drudge." Lee felt a hand on her shoulder. She looked up to Cassie's smirking face.

"We can't all spend our days playing on rocks, Cassie," she shot back. "*Someone* has to make sure we actually get customers tagging along on these trips so *someone* can pay for all the playing."

Cassie pulled up a chair and sat down next to her. "Want to show me what you've got so far?" She pulled out a bag of almonds and her sports drink.

"Not right now." Lee took a deep breath. "Actually, I need to talk to you and Nick for a minute if you've taken care of everyone."

"Is it about your grandma?" Nick's voice came from behind them.

"Um, are the customers gone?" Lee asked, steeling herself for the conversation to come.

"Yeah, the last one just walked out the door."

Lee stood up and leaned against the desk. "I'm really sorry to drop this bombshell on you two, but I'm going to have to leave town for a few weeks. My grandmother just passed away and I have to go close up her home."

"That's awful!" Cassie jumped out of the chair and engulfed Lee in a hug. Lee hesitated and hugged her back, trying not to give in to the tears that had been burning behind her eyes all morning.

"Just tell us what we can do," Nick said. "Whatever you need, we're here for you, boss."

"Absolutely," Cassie agreed. "My schedule's pretty open for the next few weeks until the snow starts falling. I'm sure Nick and I can work out the tours and office hours between us."

"Really?" Lee felt the tension in her shoulders release a few degrees. "I can also try to hire a temp to do some of the in-store stuff."

"What about my sister?" Nick offered. "She's helped before during the busy times. I can see if she'd be able to answer phones and do office stuff in the mornings."

"That would be great. I have so much to get organized and customers are already calling in to book for skiing trips and ice climbing."

"Leave it all to us." Cassie squeezed Lee's hand one more time. "We're old pros now." Lee nodded. The two had worked with her for almost five years. She knew Cassie and Nick were more than capable of running things. Still, she hated asking for their help.

"Why don't you head home to pack," Cassie suggested after the three of them worked out a few more details.

Lee grabbed her bag and headed to the door. "Call me if you have any other questions. And don't forget to spray down the helmets," she said as she pointed to Nick. "And finish uploading those photos," she called back to Cassie.

"Just go, boss," Nick waved. "We've got it all under control."

If only I could say the same, Lee thought and waved one last good-bye.

CHAPTER THREE

"One to two weeks?" Lee said as she and Charlie stood on the sidewalk in front of what appeared to be an overgrown haunted house. "More like one to two months!" Charlie whined and nosed Lee's hand, seeming to understand and absorb her horror.

She'd arrived too late in the evening yesterday to see anything more than a large, shadowy impression when she and Charlie had driven past it on their way to a hotel. Nana's guest room bed with feather duvet and pillows beckoned to her through the long empty spaces of New Mexico, Texas and Oklahoma but she knew it was too late to pick up the keys from the lawyer's office.

Now, armed with the keys she'd retrieved that morning, Lee wasn't sure that she should have left the hotel. No longer the lovely antebellum home she remembered from her childhood visits, the property in front of her made her double check the address even though she knew it was Nana's.

The overhanging porch and eaves were in need of a power wash to get rid of a thick coating of spider webs and wasps' nests. It looked like it could use a new coat of paint as well. The most glaring problem, however, was the overgrown jungle surrounding the house.

Lee shook her head. "I can't believe this, Charlie. It looks like something from the Amazon rainforest! Why would Nana let it get this bad? Usually she was so immaculate about everything—her clothes, her home..."

She took a deep breath, opened the gate and walked toward the front door. Charlie trotted next to her on his leash. Leaves and branches tangled around her calves as she got closer to the columned front porch. A thread of a half decayed spider web swept across her face. Brushing it off, she fumbled with the key and inserted it into the lock. It took several jiggles before she felt the bolt disengage.

She looked down at Charlie. "Ready, boy?" Charlie lowered his ears and whined. "Yeah, me too," Lee said and pushed open the door.

Unlike the outside of the house, the inside still echoed with Nana's grandeur. Despite a few dust bunnies and cobwebs, the downstairs rooms with their formal Louis XVI furniture, silk wallpaper and highly polished wood floors still spoke of Nana's taste for opulence. Lee felt some of the tension in her shoulders relax. As she passed the staircase with its ornate banisters, she swore she could almost smell Nana's Chanel No. 5 perfume.

"This isn't so bad. It looks like it always did except a bit dusty." Lee's footsteps echoed in the empty house. She bent to take off Charlie's leash before walking back toward the kitchen. With its soapstone counter tops and dark cherry cabinetry it looked just as exquisite and unused as ever.

"Oh, I never cook for myself." Nana's voice popped

into her head. "I've been on a steady diet of hors d'oeuvres most of my life. There's barely any cleanup and even if you get them from the freezer section of the grocery store, you still look like you hired a caterer."

Lee chuckled and ran her hand over the empty counter, but her laughter froze as the reality that she'd never really hear Nana's voice again shot through her. The thread of disbelief, the hope that someone as vibrant as Nana couldn't really be gone, died and Lee absorbed the emptiness of the house around her.

"Oh Nana." She laced her fingers across her eyes and leaned to support herself on the counter. "I never got to say good-bye. Now you're gone and...and." Charlie padded over and placed a paw on her left knee while Lee struggled with the tears that had clogged her throat for the last 1,400 miles.

She stumbled over to the far side of the kitchen and grabbed a paper towel to wipe her nose. "The back's even worse than the front!" She gasped, looking out the rear window at overgrown grass and kudzu that consumed the rear yard. She turned back to Charlie. "And I'm supposed to get this place ready to show and on the market in a week or two? There's no way!"

Lee's stomach roiled, and weariness joined grief as she contemplated the task ahead of her. She felt her eyes just beginning to burn again when she heard a noise and spun around. A slender older woman with a frizz of salt and pepper curls regarded her from the doorway.

The woman's face broke into a sad smile. "Caralee? Sweetie, do you remember me? I'm your grandmother's friend from down the street?"

"Miss Bobby? Of course I remember you!" Lee wiped her eyes and nose with the paper towel.

"That's right. I didn't hardly recognize you when you pulled up. I've been keeping an eye out for one of you girls or your daddy since Nana passed." Miss Bobby shook her head and frowned. "Let's go sit in Nana's front room and catch up."

When they were settled Miss Bobby continued, "Honey, all of us here in Eden Grove are just sick to death about Nana's passing." She reached over and patted Lee's knee. "Even though her schedule kept her busy, she was like family to everyone. We all loved her." Tears came to Miss Bobby's eyes and she reached into her sleeve for a tissue. "I don't know what we're gonna do without her."

Lee's throat swelled with grief. "Thanks, Miss Bobby. That means a lot."

"Oh sweetie, just call me Granny Bob." She laughed brokenly and wiped away her tears. "I think you're a bit old for the *Miss* now and that's what everyone else in town calls me these days.

"Well, the doctor told me that Nana passed away in her sleep," Granny Bob continued after a moment of silence. "And I think that's a real shame."

"What?"

"Why, Caralee, she was such a drama queen, you *know* she would be disappointed by the conventionality of her passing. I think she would have preferred something a little less vanilla, don't you?" Granny Bob's eyes were full of tears again, but she was smiling.

Lee laughed. "You're absolutely right, Miss— Granny Bob. What would she have liked instead?"

"Well, in her younger years, perhaps a dramatic fight with a dark, handsome stranger?" Granny Bob said and wiped her nose one last time.

"Or maybe a mysterious death linked to a treasured jewel she picked up on one of her trips?" Lee said and the two of them chuckled.

"Even if that's what she would have preferred," Granny Bob said after they quieted, "I think she was real blessed to go peaceful-like. I pray it's the way I go too." She paused and looked at the room around her. "So what are y'all fixing to do with Nana's home? Are your daddy or sister headed down here soon? It'll be real nice to see them."

Lee's hands tightened into fists. "No, it's just me."

"What?" Granny Bob's voice bordered on shrill. "So you're dealing with *all* this? On your own?"

"I guess, yeah, I guess I am." Lee looked around, her stomach clenching again. "But I don't think my father had any idea how rundown the place had become."

Granny Bob, still shaking her head, answered, "Yes, Nana didn't give it a whole lot of attention these past few years. I mean the inside still looks nice, but I never knew her without a cleaning service." She ran her fingers over the light dust on the coffee table. "But the outside..."

"Yes, what happened to the outside? The last time I visited was a while ago. It was all manicured lawns, hydrangeas and tulip trees."

Granny Bob started to speak, but hesitating, closed her mouth in a tight line.

"What happened? Please tell me."

"Caralee, you've got to understand what a huge expense and undertaking a house like this is. And your grandmother was a bit more forgetful in her later years. She always had a gardener to take care of the outside, just like her cleaning service for the inside. But in the last few years I think she just forgot. She didn't notice things like she used to. I don't know, maybe it was the money too?"

"Didn't the neighbors care?" Lee asked thinking of her Gestapo-like HOA back in Durango that regularly created new restrictions and punishments for the homeowners.

"Oh no, of course not, honey! We knew Nana was just getting older. She needed a little grace."

Lee smiled, trying to picture her HOA responding the same way.

"But, honey, don't you tell me that you're taking care of Nana's things all by yourself. Surely you have a husband? Boyfriend? Friend?"

Lee shook her head at each of these options. "Just me." She tried to meet Granny Bob's eyes, but failed.

"Well, bless your heart." The anger in Granny Bob's voice died and Lee felt despair threaten to overwhelm her again.

Granny Bob looked around, her gaze falling on the large window that offered a view of the bedraggled front yard. "What we need is a battle plan. Let me take you out for some breakfast and we'll figure this out. The Good Lord doesn't want a person to shoulder something like this on their own."

Lee felt tears prick at the back of her eyes and gratitude flooded her. "Okay, let me just grab Charlie's crate out of the back of my Jeep and I'll get him locked up before we take off."

A few minutes later Charlie was settled in his cage with a bone in Nana's old mud room. Granny Bob wrapped her arm around the small of Lee's back as they walked out the door. "Let's go to Dot's Diner. They've got the best pancakes for miles. Nana and I always went there for breakfast on Saturdays."

"Sounds perfect."

Even though I'm happy as a lark about being back home, I can't deny there's a part of me that hoped all this was a dream. I guess I assumed if I saw my house again, I would wake up and all this trailing around with Caralee would have been a strange nightmare. One I'd finally shake off then laugh about with Bobby.

Bobby.

As I sit on the banister and watch Caralee and her drive away, there's a little pang in my heart, or the place where my heart used to be, I guess. I would give anything to go off with the two of them and have a nice long visit. Bobby and I have eaten at Dot's more times than I can remember, starting when we'd save up our pennies to go share an ice cream sundae after school. Now she's taking my granddaughter under her wing, just like she takes everybody. A natural mama, that one. I suppose I could follow them, but I think it would be more painful to see what I'm missing.

So, like I said, one part of me was a tiny bit jealous that they were going off to Dot's without me. Another part is madder than a wet hen that there's a giant, HAIRY dog in my house. A dog! It's enough to throw me into a conniption. He'd better not scratch my restored hickory hardwood floors. I spent a fortune on those. Over my dead body would I have allowed a dog in this house.

Well, come to think of it, I guess that's what happened.

The Good Lord knows I've been a regular church-attending Baptist my whole life. This isn't what my Sunday school teacher Miss Clarence taught us about mansions in heaven and streets of gold when I was a little girl. And even though Pastor Garwood was a bit more reticent on the subject, I think he'd be just as surprised as I am.

What on God's green earth am I doing floating around here?

CHAPTER FOUR

Buttery, sweet wonderful exploded in Lee's mouth as she took the first bite of her pancakes. Sinking back into her chair, she closed her eyes and enjoyed the fluffy, maple syrup–covered pieces of heaven.

Initially, she'd tried to protest that she didn't *do* dairy or meat, but Granny Bob waved away her protests.

"Honey, you're in Mississippi. If you don't *do* dairy or meat, you're gonna die. You can go back to your Yankee, hippie diet when you get home."

Lee laughed. It was exactly like something Nana would have said, *Yankee* and *hippie* being synonymous with any place outside of the South.

"I guess I can make an exception," Lee said as she studied the menu. *In for a penny, in for a pound,* she decided and ordered eggs, sausage, and buttermilk pancakes.

"No grits?" Granny Bob eyed Lee over the rim of her coffee cup.

"Not yet. You've got to break me in slowly or I'll die of indigestion."

"All right," Granny Bob agreed, "but next time I'll expect more of an effort."

The two ate their meal and Lee felt herself relaxing in Granny Bob's familiar presence.

She had many memories, mainly from when she was younger, of summers with Nana, Granny Bob, and their assorted grandkids. Lee's mother had died when she was only four, but her father still brought the children to his mother-in-law's home in Eden Grove during the summers, especially when they were younger. They spent weeks at a time banging around Nana's house, which seemed like a mansion, and explored her large backyard, marveling in the wonder of horny toads, fireflies and sweet tea, none of which they had at home.

The days were filled with unsupervised adventures in town and rambles through the neighboring woods and farms. Lee, Jenny and Mark were free to roam almost anywhere they wanted in the small town. All in all, her visits to Eden Grove ranked as some of her favorite summer memories.

"Now I don't want to poke my nose into your business too much, but I'm not real happy about your relatives leaving all this on your plate. For that matter, I'm not impressed with Kathryn either. Can you imagine her not ever getting around to writing a will?"

Lee sat up straight and forced a smile on her face. "I'm here now, and I'll get this figured out. Don't worry about me."

"Honey, I *will* worry about you and don't you tell me otherwise." Granny Bob searched through her voluminous purse while motioning to the waitress. Locating her notepad and pen she blinked up at Lee. "All right, let's think on what you need to do."

An hour later they'd filled several sheets of paper with all the tasks that would occupy the days ahead. Granny Bob and Lee discussed contacting the local antique dealer, Realtor, consignment shop, jeweler and the university fashion department.

"You know a lot of Nana's clothes should probably end up in a museum instead of a closet," Granny Bob said as she studied her list. "She once told me that she had some original pieces from different budding designers' first fashion shows. She bought them when she worked in New York and they were still nobodies. But she told me she knew as soon as she saw those clothes walking down the runway that they were destined for greatness. Boy, could she call fashion.

"Anyway, she bought those way back before she inherited the big bucks from her daddy. And who knows what other treasures are tucked away in her closet. I mean closets." Granny Bob shook her head, a fond smile curing at her lips.

"Would someone from the fashion department know what to look for? Because I'd be completely lost." Lee took a sip of coffee.

"Well of course, honey, didn't your Nana train all of them? She probably even showed them some of her things. But you make sure to keep a few of the real nice pieces for your sister and yourself."

"I'm not sure I'd recognize a *nice* piece if I saw one." Lee gestured to her cut-off shorts and tank top.

"Hmmm, maybe not." Granny Bob, dressed in an immaculate sweater set and khaki shorts, surveyed Lee's outfit with dismay. "But you still need to make the choice where those things end up. It's what your Nana would have wanted."

The waitress stopped by their table and asked if they needed a refill.

"No, thank you, Cherise. Now I hear your boy's playing football this year for the university. You tell him Granny Bob is hoping he'll help get us have a winning streak this year."

"I'll tell him," Cherise said and filled Lee's coffee.

"How does the team look so far? Does he think we'll have a good season?"

"Them's the coaches right behind you," Cherise gestured to the two men at the corner of the restaurant, "so I'll just say that he sure is tired when he gets home at night."

"But he's keeping up on his studies?"

"Yes ma'am. He's there on a scholarship so he'd better." Cherise laughed and moved on to the next table. Lee smiled. She'd always loved how everybody knew everybody here.

"Now," Granny Bob continued, "the biggest challenge ahead that I can see is Nana's yard."

"You're right. But I have no idea how to get started. I mean I helped landscape my own yard, but I think I'd need professional grade equipment to make a dent in that jungle." Lee ran her hands through her hair. "Maybe I should just leave it as is and discount the asking price on the house? Let the buyer take care of that mess?"

"Well, I must admit that was my first thought too," Granny Bob said, "but then I got to thinking about how sororities and fraternities have been buying up houses on our street, us being so close to the campus. I don't particularly enjoy having so many young folks roaming around our once quiet street, but, " she paused and tapped her notebook, "I think you could get a pretty penny for Nana's house if the outside reflected the beauty of the rest of her home."

"A sorority?" Lee tried to picture Nana's now empty house alive with giggling girls.

"And you know, I think your grandma would have liked that, what with the university being the place she spent the last 40 years of her life." Granny Bob continued, "I'll call up Roger Dorset and the Stricklands and ask how much they got when they sold their homes. They lived just down the street for years and years before they moved to those new condos up at Lake Montikata."

"But that still doesn't solve the problem of how I get the yard fixed up." Lee worried the drop on her necklace.

"Now don't you carry on about that. I know just the man for the job." Granny Bob threw a few bills on the table and stood up. Lee tried to protest, but Granny Bob insisted it was her treat and that Lee could take her out next time.

"Now then," she continued when they were outside the restaurant. "We'll just head on back to Nana's and you can unpack. Don't you worry about making any of these calls until tomorrow, and I'll send the landscaping man around first thing in the morning."

Hopping into Granny Bob's shiny Cadillac, Lee leaned her head back against the seat in relief. She hadn't felt this at peace since before she heard the news of Nana's death.

After Granny Bob dropped her off with a big hug and promises of contacting the right people, Lee surveyed Nana's house from the curb.

"I think we can do this," Lee murmured with a quiver of hope battling against the despair she'd felt earlier that morning. "Maybe even in a way that would make Nana smile."

SMILE, the child says?

I changed my mind and followed Bobby and Lee to Dot's, and I must say, I wish I hadn't. Do the two of them really think I'd smile about having all my designer clothes, jewels and antique furniture divvied out like some church jumble sale?

That Pauline Trigère dress alone must be worth a fortune. I got it when Bergdorf Goodman featured a portion of her first New York fashion collection, when she was fresh off the boat from Paris.

I should have written a will, should have left specific directions with what to do about all my treasures. I kept meaning to of course. But like my daddy always said, the road to Hell is paved with good intentions.

And another thing, Bobby's right, as always. That girl shouldn't be doing all this on her own! How can Daniel put all this on Caralee's shoulders? What can he be thinking?

I feel a whisper of reproach, from where, I have no idea. But it sets me to thinking.

Truth be told, I suspect I know exactly why Daniel's so hesitant to return here. It's hard to revisit a place where you fell in love if that loved one's gone. Isn't that just the way I feel about New York City?

Caralee's daddy, Daniel, and I always did butt heads, especially over my sweet Cecilia. Pulled between being my daughter and Daniel's wife, poor Cecilia didn't exactly have an easy time between the two of us. Gentle as a dove, she spent her short life trying to make peace, even though Daniel and I were like oil and vinegar. That man drove me...well, I don't want to be ugly.

God's honest truth, I know Daniel loved my Cecilia with all his heart and visits back here dredged up feelings that tore him apart. Sometimes, when he didn't know anyone was looking, I could see the pain so raw in his eyes, it would take my breath away at the suffering I saw there. I also know he pushed those feelings down deep, to hidden places so my grandbabies could know me and see where their mama grew up.

I respect him for that, even if I still didn't much care for him.

CHAPTER FIVE

Her mind still spinning with the events of the last few hours, Lee went on a quick tour around the perimeter of Nana's backyard to make sure it was safe for Charlie. She tried to ignore the kudzu and focus on the fence. After she'd made a few repairs with an old hammer she found in the shed, Lee let the now howling Charlie out of his crate.

"Oh hush up, you big baby." She gave his nose a kiss after she let him out of the crate. She filled the largest container she could find with water, a Le Creuset Dutch oven still in its original packaging. Lee couldn't help but smile at Nana's unused extravagance.

"Here you go, boy," she said as she toted the makeshift water bowl onto the deck. "Make sure you drink lots of water!" she called after Charlie, who'd already found some unsuspecting squirrels and cardinals to chase.

Lee left the French doors cracked open and wandered back into the house. A sudden wave of drowsiness hit her when she entered the den off the kitchen. A fairly committed vegan back in Durango, Lee felt almost drunk as the combination of butter, cream and other forbidden delights churned their way through her pristine digestive tract. Dot's had not offered the gluten-free, meat-free, dairy-free, raw and plethora of other options she was used to seeing on menus in Colorado.

Lee pulled Granny Bob's list from her purse and collapsed on the couch, but the words swam before her eyes. Promising herself that it was only for a minute, she let her eyelids drop. In just a moment she'd start looking it over and schedule out the coming days.

When what seemed like only seconds had passed she jolted awake, but the sunlight on the floor told her that many hours had passed. She stumbled from the couch and walked back into the front room, searching for a clock.

"Two o'clock?!" Her raspy voice broke into the empty home's silence. Lee stumbled over a rug, disoriented by exhaustion and emotion. "I've been asleep for—" but the words caught in her throat as she noticed the wide-open front door.

Had she left it that way? Her heart began to hammer in her chest. Was someone in the house? She backed into the den and then up against the wall, looking for something to protect herself with. Her hand grasped at the bronze poker by the fireplace. Slowly, she advanced back to the front of the house, cringing as the wooden floors creaked with her weight.

Another thought shot into her adrenalin-revved brain. The back French doors were still open too—a perfect way for Charlie to escape into the streets of an unfamiliar town. Caution forgotten, she raced down the hallway crying Charlie's name. A shadow appeared at her left and instinctively she swung at it with the poker.

"What in the— Watch it, Caralee!" Disarmed by the shadow knowing her name, Lee lowered the poker, but raised it again when a large male form staggered toward her. She made to swing again, but the shadow-man protested, "Wait, wait! Caralee, it's me! John Hunter. Remember?" Cradling his side, he held out one arm in supplication. "Remember John Hunter Fairchild—Bobby's grandson?"

"Jon-Jon?" Lee gasped and dropped the poker. His face was hidden by the now crooked baseball cap.

"Yes. I mean, no, not anymore." He let out a deep groan of pain. "I think you broke my rib. Maybe a few ribs."

"I'm sorry, John, but I was looking for Charlie. I saw this shadow and the front door was open." Then she remembered. "Charlie!" She catapulted the rest of the way to the backyard. When she finally spied her shaggy husky lounging under a large magnolia tree, Lee almost cried in relief.

"Thank goodness." She collapsed at the kitchen table, taking a few shuddery breaths.

"No, I'm fine. Don't you worry about me. I'll just drive myself to the emergency room. Bye now." John Hunter appeared from around the corner, cradling his left side.

"Oh please forgive me, John, for hitting a stranger who had entered my home uninvited."

"What? Just wait a—"

"A stranger," Lee ignored his protest, "sneaking around in dark corners and leaving doors open."

John made his way across the kitchen and towered over her. "Oh I get it, I'm the bad guy here." His dark eyes crackled with anger that matched her own.

"Was that ever in question?" Lee grabbed the table edge with white-knuckled fingers.

"It's not like Granny called me up, begging me to come over and help out at Nana's. I'm just a menace to society roaming through people's homes." He took a deep breath to continue, but wincing in pain, he raised his shirt again to study the now darkening bruise near the bottom of his ribcage.

"Granny Bob?" A seed of dread began to unfurl in her stomach. She forced her eyes away from John Hunter's raised shirt and undeniably impressive abs.

"Yeah, Granny Bob. I got a message on my phone earlier today about 'poor, sweet Caralee trying to take care of Nana's house all by herself.'" He dropped the shirt and pulled out a chair next to Lee. It squealed in protest and he eased himself into it. "You seen 'poor, sweet Caralee' anywhere? I sure don't."

"John, maybe I shouldn't—"

"And who's Charlie? Some sorry fool you've drug down here?"

"Charlie's my dog. And since you left the door wide open, he could have escaped." John rolled his eyes but she continued, "We just finished driving 25 hours to get here. We're in a strange city, in my dead grandmother's house. If he'd escaped I'd probably never see him again and...and..." Lee's usual steely veneer failed her. She dropped her head into her arms on the table and began to bawl.

"Caralee, don't."

"Just go away, John!" She bellowed from the cocoon of her arms, humiliation burning through her. "Get out of here!" She flinched as she felt a hand tentatively pat her back.

"Oh c'mon, Caralee. Hush now, don't cry. I'm real sorry about losing my temper."

"I said go," Lee cried, her voice nearly unintelligible.

"It's just you nailed me real good. That's some arm you've got there. Hush now, Caralee, everything's gonna be fine."

"It's Lee now, not Caralee," was all she could think to say. She peeked out from under her arm. He'd taken off his hat and his wavy dark hair fell across his forehead.

"Okay then, Lee, now why don't you wipe those pretty brown eyes—"

"They're blue."

"Those pretty blue eyes and let's start over." He moved away and returned with several paper towels.

Lee grabbed one and stormed toward the bathroom. "Just give me a second."

The cold water she splashed over her face helped soothe her flushed skin and tumbling emotions.

"You need to calm down," she ordered herself as she took in the swollen red eyes, blotchy skin and sleep-tangled hair.

In the medicine cabinet she found a brush and some

L'Occitane lotion, along with the other delicious toiletries Nana always stocked in her bathrooms. Lee freshened herself up as best she could, but refused to put on any of the makeup that beckoned her from the cabinet drawers. "I'm not trying to impress Jon-Jon, after all," she muttered and slammed the drawer shut.

She surveyed herself in the mirror again. Better. She stood up straight and pushed her hair back over her shoulders.

"You're not a kid anymore," she whispered to her reflection, "and John Hunter isn't the leader of your little gang. You're here to do a job, and Granny Bob asked him to help for some reason. Go out there and find out why. Act like the articulate, professional adult that you are." She nodded at her reflection and marched out of the bathroom.

John Hunter leaned against the kitchen counter holding a bag of frozen peas to his side. "You all right now?"

"Yes, I'm fine," she brushed off his words, "but what about you? Should we get you to the doctor? I've got my Jeep out front. I could drive you."

"Yeah, I wondered who that souped-up thing belonged to," he said. "I was admiring it before I came in and got attacked by a crazy wildcat." His dark eyes twinkled with laughter.

"I thought I locked the front door. I'd been asleep."

"Hey, don't worry about it." John shot her a grin.

"Oh, I'm not worried about it." Lee took a deep breath

and crossed her arms. "And it's not a good idea for you to barge into people's homes uninvited."

"Not this again." He threw the bag of peas on the counter. "Here's the deal. I did not barge in. I'm one of the caretakers for Nana's house. She gave me a key. The place is so overgrown that I assumed you must be staying at a hotel. I let myself in to see the extent of how bad Nana's house was. I didn't expect..." His voice trailed off into a mutter.

"What's that?"

"Nothing."

After a few moments of tense silence, Lee spoke. "So if you're the caretaker, why is this place such a dump? Why did you have to check to see how bad it was?"

She saw his jaw clench. "I've been out of state for over a year. I figured Nana had hired someone else while I was gone. Appears she didn't."

"Caretaker, huh?" Lee felt the rumblings of aggression draining away. "So what are you? Like a helper for the elderly?"

"No, I own a landscaping business. I was helping around Nana's house as a favor to her and Granny."

"Oh." Lee's anger deflated like a popped balloon. "I guess that makes sense." She paused and took a hesitant step in his direction. "So did you want me to drive you to the doctor?"

"No. I'll be fine."

"Are you sure?" Her emotions jumped in a whirlwind of anger, shock and now contrition. "Or maybe I could find you some witch hazel?"

"Witch hazel?"

"You know, for the bruise?"

"No thanks. I don't care about the bruise, just the ribs underneath."

"Then maybe we should go to the doctor and get it X-rayed?" Lee grabbed at her keys.

"No. I said I was fine." He ignored her concern as she had ignored his earlier. "I'll go this afternoon if it's still bothering me."

Lee dropped her keys back on the counter. "Maybe we could chat about Nana's house later? After you're feeling better?"

John reached for his baseball cap and pulled it back on. "Maybe, but only if we meet on neutral ground. Don't wanna give you another chance with that poker. You might bash my head in next time."

"Listen, John, I'm sorry. Could I..." she searched for something, but came up blank.

John Hunter studied her face. "Well, I wasn't going to say anything after our little interlude here, but Granny did invite you over to her place for dinner. She wanted me to help you figure out everything that needs to be put right in Nana's yard."

"Are you still going to invite me?" Lee asked after a long moment of silence.

He rolled his eyes. "'Course I am, Bean Pole. Granny wouldn't be too pleased if I didn't deliver her invitation."

Bean Pole. She'd forgotten that one. "What time

should I come?"

"She said six, but I'll only let you through that door on one condition." He turned and walked toward the front of the house.

"What's that?"

"You leave that poker behind." He slammed the door behind him.

Lee followed him and locked it.

The timing here seems just a little too coincidental. John Hunter coming back into town at the same moment as Caralee, who has only breezed through here every few years since she reached adulthood? It's enough to make you wonder.

And the way those two were at each other's throats—it's been like that since they were little ones. They've been playing and fighting together since they were babies and all through their childhoods. Caralee was such a little tomboy that she loved running around with John Hunter and his gang whenever she would come to visit. I think she enjoyed the break from having to be mama to Mark and Jenny. When she was in Eden Grove I took over the mama role, as best I could, and Caralee got to be the child that she so often had to deny.

Caralee was tall for her age and skinny as a rail, that's why everyone around here called her Bean Pole. She'd wander through the woods, go fishing, canoe around the lake, whatever those boys were doing, she'd do just as well. As I recall, there was a time one of the boys tried to play the 'you're just a girl' card with Caralee. It was Charles, I believe.

She rewarded him with a cow pie in the face.

In the main, she was friends with all of them: Grant, Charles, Rusty, and Wade, but John Hunter was her special friend. Bobby and I wondered many a time if something stronger might develop between the two of them when they grew up. But then that last summer she came here...nothing was the same after that visit.

Now they're practically strangers. I suppose they won't ever be much more than that, despite all of my and Bobby's wishing.

Still, would it have killed her to put some concealer under her eyes and a little mascara on her lashes? When she ran to the bathroom, I followed her and kept trying to grab her hands and put them in my makeup drawer. It didn't work, though. I find myself a little less forceful than I once was.

Guess I shouldn't be too surprised, but I sure as heck wouldn't face that handsome John Hunter looking like some mess.

CHAPTER SIX

"Wish I didn't have to do this," Lee muttered to Charlie as they walked toward Granny Bob's house a little before six. Her *attack* on John Hunter with the fireplace poker and tearful breakdown ran through her mind as if on instant replay. The sting of embarrassment was still sharp and fresh.

If she hadn't been worried about offending Granny Bob, Lee would have grabbed a quick snack and fallen into bed as soon as possible. But Lee remembered well the rules of Southern hospitality. No matter how tired or embarrassed she was, it wasn't an option to refuse Granny Bob's invitation.

The tension in her shoulders eased as the Fairchild house came into view—it was almost as familiar to her as Nana's. Memories flitted through her head like scattering leaves. She remembered the time she and Tammy, John's sister, almost caught Granny Bob's kitchen on fire trying to make homemade donuts. Then there was the time Lee, Mark and Jenny spent the night in a tent in the backyard with John Hunter and Tammy. John's ghost story was so scary that Mark started screaming and Granny Bob came out in her nightgown and slippers. After chewing them out, she ordered them to fall asleep immediately. No one dared disobey.

The memories began to trip over themselves: long hot afternoons spent sipping lemonade and flipping through comics in Granny Bob's den, playing Marco Polo in the local pool, the smell of freshly baked cinnamon rolls tickling her nose as she woke up in Tammy's room after a sleepover. She almost expected to see a small Tammy and Jon-Jon come tearing around the side of the house with their old blue Heeler, Spark, in fast pursuit.

She stood at the front door now, motionless. Charlie wagged his tail and gazed up at her, his blue eyes winking in the evening sun. He whined and stirred Lee out of her reverie.

"Sorry, buddy. I was back in 1985." She stood up straight and knocked on the front door.

"Coming!" She heard Granny Bob's distant voice.

"No, I'll get it, Granny!" John Hunter's voice came through the door this time. It was louder. The door jerked open and before her stood John in his full high school football regalia, including the helmet.

"Hello there, Cara—I mean Lee." His eyes crinkled behind the mask.

"What on earth are you doing?"

"Just making sure I was prepared if you came armed. You know Granny's not as young as she used to be. I don't think she could handle herself as well as I did."

"As well as you did, huh? You screamed like a little girl after I hit you." It was so easy to fall back into the easy banter of their childhood.

"Excuse me, ma'am. I believe you remember wrong. I was—"

"John Hunter, what in the Sam Hill are you doing in that getup?" Granny Bob's voice came from behind John's hulking, football-clad frame.

"Just fooling around with Lee." He smiled and pulled the helmet off.

"Well, get out of the way and let her in." Granny Bob shoved him to the side and held the door open.

"I had to bring Charlie with me. I hope you don't mind?" Lee gestured to the dog who eyed John Hunter with a cocked head.

"Mind? Of course not. This is a dog house remember?" Granny Bob let Charlie sniff her hand. "Is he friendly?"

"Yes. Just a little aloof sometimes."

"Sounds like someone I know," John Hunter shot from the bench where he took off his jersey and pads.

"Hush up, John," Granny Bob ordered without turning around. "Now you two come on in. Supper's still a little ways from being ready." She ushered Charlie and Lee to the back of the house and its sunny kitchen.

"Is your backyard still fenced in? I can let Charlie out there."

"Oh, just whatever he wants, honey. Yes, it's still fenced it. Just got it replaced last winter when some of the branches of that sycamore blew down and crashed through the old one. We had to cut the beauty down."

"Not the big old sycamore? The one we had the look-out tower in?" A rush of unwanted memories flooded her mind. She peered through the window to confirm that the giant was truly gone. Seeing the reality of its absence filled her heart with a dull pain.

"Yes, I'm afraid so." Granny Bob put a tray of dinner rolls in the oven. "I know you kids loved that tree and it broke my heart to cut it down. It had a lot of laughter stored up in those branches."

"It was a beautiful tree." John's voice came from right behind Lee. "Some of the most important times of my childhood were spent up in those branches." Her neck prickled and she sensed his gaze on the back of her head, but she refused to turn around. Instead, she leaned over to adjust Charlie's collar.

"Well, it's still a lovely backyard." She ran nervous fingers through the fur on the dog's neck. He pulled away and Lee opened the half door to let him outside. "I notice some other changes out here," she observed. "Look at that gorgeous flower bed. I wish I could get my yard in Durango to look this nice."

"You like it?" Granny Bob smiled as she stirred a saucepan on her old gas range. "John Hunter redid everything for me after the broken sycamore made a mess of things. He and some mighty fine looking boys worked back there for days and days getting all those new flower beds planted. They even created a little re-circulating stream out there that wanders around."

Granny Bob took a taste of the sauce. "Not enough

salt. John Hunter, you take Caralee out there and show her around while I finish up with supper."

"No, I'd rather stay and help you if I can," Lee said, not ready to face the memories that awaited her beyond Granny Bob's back door. "Please, can't I help you in here?"

"No, you can't," Granny Bob replied. "Didn't you tell me at Dot's restaurant that you don't eat dairy or meat?"

"Oh well, you know. I stay away from them most of the time."

"Stay away from them," Granny Bob chuckled, "like they're some kind of monsters. Well, this meal is chock-full of the two, so I don't expect any help from you. Just for you to eat it and not complain." She winked at Lee. "Now get out there and look around at John Hunter's hard work."

"Yes, ma'am." Granny's tone made Lee want to march.

"I'm not going to bite you, Lee, if that's what you're worried about," John said as he followed her out the door.

"I'm not worried about anything," Lee answered. She took a deep breath and forced a smile. "One thing's for sure, I've missed that smell."

"What smell?" John asked.

"The one that comes in the evening here in the South. I've never smelled it anywhere else. It's, I don't know, cozy."

"Cozy?" John snorted and bent to pluck the spent blooms off a hydrangea.

"Well, it is. Or different from Durango anyway." She

grabbed at a twig tangled in her sandal strap and snapped it in half. "I think it's the humidity. And probably all the trees? Maybe some of the leaves rotting too."

"Tell me what Durango smells like."

"It depends. If the narrow gauge train has rolled through town within the last hour, it smells like coal smoke. If it's just rained, it usually smells like pine pollen, fresh and sharp. Down by the river it smells like dried algae or wet grass."

"Do you notice smells everywhere?" He brushed his hands off and stood.

"Yes."

He took a step closer to Lee. "You know what I smell right now?"

"What?" Her heart tripped as she studied his face and recognized glimpses of the boy she'd known.

"Wet dog."

"What?"

"Yeah. I think your dog got into the stream I made back here. Let me show you."

For the next half hour he walked her through Granny Bob's yard, explaining the work he and his crew had done.

"I never knew you were interested in landscaping, John," Lee spoke as he ended his tour. Charlie came and sat at her feet. She stroked the soft velvet of his ears and tried to ignore his wet smell.

"Took me a while to figure it out too," he said. "Tried some other stuff before I settled on it, but none of it suited."

"Like what?"

"Well, I worked in a bank in Nashville for a while." He rolled his eyes. "Not for me *at all*." Lee chuckled in agreement. "Then a buddy of mine back here in Eden Grove invited me to help out with contracting work. He remodels all the old houses around here. Actually, you know him. It's Wade, remember him?"

"Yes."

"So I started helping him with all these remodels, but I never wanted to do the inside work. Only the outside stuff. 'Course, there's always more work on the inside of these old houses." He gestured to Granny Bob's home and her neighbors' on either side. "But anyway, I started offering some suggestions about the yards from time to time. Wade kept taking my advice and the homeowners seemed to really like my ideas. Eventually it got to where the outside stuff was keeping me busy, so I started my own business. Wade and I still work together a lot. We both love these old homes."

"Did you go to a horticulture program?"

John nodded. "Yes, ma'am. Got my undergraduate and master's up at the University of Tennessee in Knoxville. Once the work here in Eden Grove became more full time, I split my classes, doing some online so I could work here. Then I'd go stay with a buddy of mine up in Knoxville for the classes I could only take on campus. Wade's been real helpful about managing my business when I'm up there."

"So when did you finish all your schooling?"

"Well, I'm actually working on my doctorate right now." He kicked some mulch out of the grass and back into the garden. "I've been up in the Ashville area for about nine months researching traditional uses and folklore of plants and herbs indigenous to the area. I knew it was time to head back here so my business didn't get too neglected. Also, I need to start making some headway with my dissertation, and there's no place I work better than my own home."

"Surely you don't need a doctorate to landscape, though. I mean, you've obviously got the knowledge and the gift." She gestured to the garden around her. "So what's the doctorate for?"

"Well, I haven't told many people this, but I'm thinking that maybe I could get a job at the university level. I know the horticulture department here in Eden Grove needs some new blood. The main emphasis is still the agriculture side of things, but I'm hoping I could shake up the department a bit. Maybe get some landscaping design courses up and running or classes on the historical uses of plants, folklore and stuff."

"I had no idea you loved plants so much." Lee ran her hand over the blushing Crepe Myrtle blossoms next to her.

John shrugged. "Well, that's why I was real ticked off with how bad Nana's yard looks. It was one of the first places I even *noticed* the plants around me. Do you remember that old gardener she used to have?"

"Was it something Lewis?" Lee tried to drudge the memory from some forgotten place.

"Yeah, Bob Lewis. He was such a master. In the summers after you'd head home to Colorado I'd just hang around in your Nana's backyard because..." He paused and Lee looked up from the flowers.

"Because why?"

"I just, I would hang out in that yard to get a little peace and quiet. You know how crazy Granny's house could be. I started asking old Mr. Lewis about the how and why of your Nana's yard. He'd tell me all the scientific answers but he'd also give me all the old stories of the plants. I think that's what made them come alive for me."

"Like what? Give me an example," Lee said.

John looked around the garden and gestured to the vine growing up along Granny Bob's lattice fence.

Lee followed him to it. "So what do we have here, soon-to-be Dr. Fairchild?"

"It's a honeysuckle," John said as he brushed a bloom and released its sweet fragrance into the air. "First, you gotta take a deep smell of the flowers."

"Amazing," Lee said as she inhaled the blossom's perfume.

"Now pay attention to your dreams tonight. You're gonna dream about your true love—the one who'll never leave you." He smiled and gave her a wink. "And I don't mean your dog over there." They turned to Charlie who was nosing his way through Granny Bob's hostas.

"Hmm, I think this wise old honeysuckle might have a small problem with supply and demand," Lee said and pulled the blossoms close again.

"What do you mean?" John asked.

"In my dating experience there's hardly enough faithful, true loves out there to satisfy every girl who's ever smelled a flower." Lee released the bloom and it sprung back to the lattice, dropping petals as it went.

John laughed. "Someone sounds a little bitter."

"I'm not bitter, just realistic. And perfectly happy with my life, the life I've created."

"Perfectly happy, hmm?" John walked away, along the edge of the garden.

"Yes, I own an outdoor adventure company." Lee felt a surge of pride as she always did when she thought of Play Harder.

"Outdoor adventure company? What the heck is that?" John knelt to brace some dangling sweet potato vines.

"Summer and winter, it's a resource for outdoor enthusiasts who want to challenge themselves by tackling and mastering the world around them," she quoted directly from her brochure. "We offer extreme hiking and camping tours, rock climbing and off-roading adventures in the summer. During the winter there's ice cave camping, back-country skiing, telemarking, along with our newest activity, ice climbing."

"Sounds like there sure are a lotta bored people with way too much money in Durango," John commented without turning from his work. "Do people really pay you to run them around like that?"

"Yes, they do." Lee gave him a tight smile.

"Huh." John glanced at her. "Guess it's always interesting to see what people will spend their money on."

"Are you saying that what I do is a waste of money?" Lee asked.

John shrugged his shoulders.

"Well, we can't all spend our days prancing through the honeysuckle and smelling the flowers," Lee threw back at him. "Maybe some of us are too busy running businesses and paying taxes." Lee felt a jolt of annoyance. She'd just parroted one of her father's favorite phrases.

John gathered the weeds he'd been pulling and walked over to dump them by the garden shed. "I guess I just don't understand why you can only enjoy nature if you're risking your life."

"Because excitement and challenge, they add something to being outdoors. I love feeling like I've conquered the impossible."

"Nature's where I let go of my impossibles. Guess we just have a different take on that sort of thing." John shook his head. "There's one thing we agree on though."

"Oh?" She didn't try to keep the sarcasm out of her voice. "And what could that possibly be?"

"It's a shame that old sycamore is gone."

Lee froze. Was he teasing her? Testing her? What did he mean? "It was a lovely tree." She hoped that was neutral enough. "But you cut it down?"

"Had to. It got diseased, which is why all those branches broke off in the storm. There just wasn't anything we could do to save it." John studied the air where the massive branches had once arched. "Broke my heart to cut it down." His eyes returned to her face. "I slept up in the lookout the night before we did it."

"Did you really?" Lee's heart skipped a beat. "I bet you barely fit up there."

"Well, my feet did hang off the edge, and I was mighty happy to climb down in the morning." He looked up once more and chuckled. "Yep, lotta memories in that tree. I hated to say good-bye." He shrugged and walked back toward the kitchen door.

The shadowed stump of the sycamore caught Charlie's interest and he sniffed about the rotting wood.

Lee tucked a strand of stray hair behind her ear. She'd thought the hardest thing she'd have to do in Eden Grove was take care of Nana's estate. If only John Hunter had stayed in Ashville for a few more weeks, she found herself wishing. He complicated everything.

CHAPTER SEVEN

After a feast of ham bake, cheese grits, fried okra and chocolate chess pie, Lee realized that she was not going to be allowed to do *anything* on her own while in Eden Grove. Even eat.

"Now honey, I want you over here every night for dinner with John Hunter and me," Granny Bob ordered. "With all that you have to do, you're gonna be too tired to make yourself dinner at night."

"Granny Bob—" Lee tried to protest, but John beat her to it.

"Granny, I've got my own place. Contrary to what you think, I can take care of myself." He leaned over to squeeze his grandmother's hand.

"I know, John, but you'll be working on Nana's yard full time these next few days, so you won't have energy to make dinner either."

"Full-time?" John looked at Lee.

"Um, maybe," she said, "that is unless you have other jobs lined up. I could look for someone else."

"No, I told you I've been outta state for a few months, so I don't have anything lined up at the moment. But why all the rush?" John cut himself another piece of pie.

"I'm trying to settle Nana's estate as quickly as I can," she said. "I need to get back home."

"Why?" John asked. "I thought your boyfriend was already here." He gestured toward Charlie who was camped out under the table.

"Hmmm." It wasn't the first time she'd heard that joke. "You laugh, but he's certainly more faithful and well-trained than any boyfriend I've ever had."

"He's faithful 'cuz he dies if you decide to stop feeding him."

"Oh, stop it." Granny Bob smacked his knee. "Now John Hunter, you clean up these dishes while Caralee and I get to work in the other room."

"Yes, ma'am," John said, whistling as he began to stack dishes.

Lee tried to get Charlie to follow her and Granny Bob to the living room, but he stubbornly refused to leave the delicious smells and stray crumbs that still beckoned from the kitchen.

"Now come on in here, honey, and look over this list I've been working on." Granny Bob handed her a sheet of paper.

Lee took a seat on the couch next to Granny Bob and began to read through it.

Furniture: Sarah Beth Jamison—antique dealer; owns consignment shop
Secondhand Shop: Matilda Smithen; drop off area behind store

Cleaning Service: Xander and Jennifer Jones service Kathryn used last 20 years
Jewelry: Blake Etherby—owns jewelry pawn/consignment shop
Realtor: LaTanya Renault—Eden Grove Realty; one of Kathryn's former students
Handyman and Painter: Dirk Mattesson—friend of the family
Banker: Dwayne Twiford—First National; Kathryn's current banker
Lawyer: Mary Clarksford—Wallace, Clarksford and Schmidt; Kathryn's lawyer

Granny Bob completed the list by consulting her cell phone and adding each person's phone number and address.

Although the enormity of the task and all the details she'd have to pay attention to left Lee's mind spinning, she felt a huge weight lifted off her shoulders at seeing this first step completed.

"This is amazing, Granny Bob. I can start making calls tomorrow. You've saved me hours of time and work."

"My pleasure, honey." Granny Bob finished the list and took a sip of her eternally present sweet tea. Then she settled back into her recliner. "I used to work up at the Chamber of Commerce, so it was easy to get everything together. The town hasn't changed that much since I retired."

"Now you and John Hunter just need to get your heads together so he can show you the magic he's gonna work on the outside of Nana's house," Granny Bob said. She fell silent and cocked her head. "I don't hear any more clattering from the kitchen. Why don't you check if he's all done and y'all can come in here and discuss the yard."

Lee walked into the kitchen and surveyed the pots and pans on Granny Bob's drying rack, the wiped counters and swept floor, but John Hunter was nowhere to be seen.

"I guess he left." Lee ignored the flutter of disappointment in her stomach. "I didn't see him in there or in the backyard."

"Hmm," Granny Bob answered, her attention now focused on the nightly news. "I'm sure he'll wander back in after a while."

Unsure of what to do, Lee sat back down on the couch. She looked at the clock. If John wasn't back in half an hour, she'd head back to Nana's house and make an early night of it.

After about 20 minutes John Hunter burst through the front door. "I ran back to the house while you and Granny were talking so I could show you a few mock-ups from my last couple of projects," he said, gasping to catch his breath. "One of them was a house with a yard real similar to Nana's. I altered a bit of the sketching so I could show you something of what I'd suggest with her yard."

Lee looked down. "Oh, I guess I didn't realize we'd quite agreed..."

"Well, it's up to you, of course." John shuffled the rolls

of paper in his hands. "I'm not pressing my services on you, but I am one of the only landscapers in town, outside of the grounds crew for the university."

"Why doesn't John just show you his work?" Granny Bob suggested as she picked up her knitting.

"Sure, I think...I think that would be fine," Lee said, already worried what her father would think about little *Jon-Jon* doing most of the work on Nana's house.

John unrolled the plans on Granny Bob's coffee table and weighted down the corners with four coasters. As he talked, Lee relaxed when it quickly became obvious just how good he was. He showed her a mock-up with Nana's existing trees, large shrubs, flower beds, and pathways along with an overlay that showed his new plans for the yard.

Lee studied the list of plants he'd suggested for Nana's yard and floating dollar signs replaced her initial excitement. "John, this looks beautiful, more than beautiful, but I don't think I can afford all this. I'm sorry. You're obviously gifted at this but I—"

"Now don't you worry about the money." John set his pencil down. "We'll get that figured out later."

"John, besides my little place in Durango, I've never landscaped, so I'd only be guessing as to the cost of all this." She gestured to the plans. "But the plants for this project alone must run into the thousands of dollars. I just can't manage that."

John brushed back the hair that had flopped over his forehead. "I've thought about that already, Lee, and I'd be willing to do this project at cost. I'll cover my labor and planning. For Nana," he spoke over Lee's objections. "I told you she was the one who got me started in this business. And what's a few weeks out of my life compared to the happiness she gave me by letting me find my calling in her yard."

"Well, I can't argue with that," Lee said. "But even if you do all this for cost, the fact remains that I can't pay for the plants, let alone all the landscaping materials. And what about your workers? Surely you're not going to do all this on your own?"

"Can't we take that cost out of the price you get on the house?" he asked after considering for a moment. "Like defer my payment until her home sells?"

"Would you be comfortable with that?" she asked.

"Sure. I've done it before with people I know I can trust and houses that seem like they'll sell real easy. I know Nana's house won't have any problems if we can get the outside looking as nice as the inside," he assured her.

"I'll just have to run that by my dad first," she answered, feeling her stomach clench at the thought of that conversation.

"Then you'll need some air-tight specifics and an estimate." John grabbed his iPad from his briefcase. "I know your daddy, and I wanna make sure you got everything you need before you call him."

Lee leaned back and gave a weak laugh. "That's right. You *do* know him. So I don't have to explain—"

"That I'd better have all my T's crossed and my I's

dotted?" John kept typing as he spoke. "No, ma'am, you don't."

Granny Bob kept their sweet teas full and supplied some chocolate chip cookies as John Hunter worked with Lee on the estimate. A little later he had a rough number, broken down into various categories and wholesale supply costs. He saved it and emailed it to both Lee and her father.

"Thank you, John. This is amazing." She looked up from the estimate. "You too, Granny Bob."

"It's our pleasure," Granny Bob responded, giving Lee a hug. "Now, John Hunter, you go walk her home and make sure she's settled. I'll see you tomorrow sometime and then you make sure to come over for dinner. You call me if you have any questions. Night now!" She dismissed the two and disappeared into the kitchen.

"Night!" They both echoed after her retreating form.

CHAPTER EIGHT

Lee whistled to the snoozing Charlie who had settled himself next to Granny Bob's chair. "Time to go, buddy. You don't need to walk me home, John," she said as she clipped on Charlie's leash. "I'm a big girl and it's just down the street."

"Oh, that's okay." He shrugged and packed up his supplies. "It's on my way home."

"You live in this neighborhood?"

"Yep, just around the corner."

John opened the front door for Lee and Charlie and followed them out. "I told you I like old houses and this neighborhood was just too good for me to pass up. I kept waiting for a fixer-upper to come on the market and a couple a years ago, old Mr. Robinson's came up for sale. 'Member him?"

Lee nodded.

"The house was in pretty bad shape, but Wade helped me with some of it and the rest I just took my time with. She's getting closer and closer to being done. Don't want to rush it, though; I try to keep her original feelings in mind when I take on a new room."

Lee chuckled. He made it sound like the house was a

woman he loved. She pictured him walking through an old empty house, eyeing the eaves and the floorboards, gently caressing the walls. Trying to discover its secrets. For some reason the image made her shiver and she banished it from her mind.

"I live in a fixer-upper too."

"Do you now?" John opened the gate and let them out to the sidewalk in front of Granny Bob's house. "I had you figured for a fancy new apartment sorta girl."

"No, I love old houses too, although *old* in Durango is probably a bit misleading, compared to the South anyway. Mine was the first built in that area, an original farmhouse, and it's only about a hundred years old."

"What's it like?" His voice came from the warm darkness next to her. Lee described it as best she could. She didn't know a lot of the technical terms, but as she explained different features or repairs to him, John would nod or offer her words like *cornice, eave* or *bolster*.

"It sounds like you did a good job with it." They stopped before the front gate of Nana's house, but John made no move to open it. "Now you know I've gotta ask, how's it landscaped?"

Lee laughed. "Well, we have very different weather than here, but I think you'd recognize some of the plants. I've managed to keep most of them alive. I have to cover some of the more delicate things if it gets too cold. Last winter we had a blizzard that got the temperatures down to almost fifteen below with wind-chill."

She felt him pretend to shiver next to her. "Dang,

that's cold. Too cold for my blood anyway. Why do you wanna live in a place like that?" He gave her shoulder a gentle nudge.

"Oh, but John, it's so beautiful in the mountains! Everything's more extreme, but it's a savage sort of beauty. The kind that might kill you if you're not careful, but it gets inside you and you can't forget it."

John was silent beside her and Lee felt her cheeks grow warm with embarrassment. "Sorry, I just really love where I live. Sometimes, I get a little—"

"Hey, don't apologize." He shifted away. "If there's anyone who understands loving where you live, I do. When you describe it like that, it almost makes me want to come see it."

"Well, maybe you should."

"Maybe so," John said. "Even if it has been about 20 years since we last spoke."

"That long?" Lee tried to sound surprised.

They fell silent and she studied the sky above, the easy banter now gone like the last of the sun's fading rays.

John cleared his throat and reached over to open the gate. "Better get you on inside. Sounds like you have a big day tomorrow. Let me know as soon as you get the okay from your daddy and I'll start work on the yard—" He broke off when Lee gasped next to him.

"What? What is it?" He caught her hand.

"The fireflies!" Lee answered, her voice full of wonder. "I'd forgotten about them." She pulled away and walked toward the twinkling lights that sparkled through the darkness. Suddenly her voice was shaking with laughter. "Look! John, look at Charlie."

She'd let go of his leash when they walked through the gate. Chasing at the flashes of light, Charlie leapt into the air, snapping at the glowing insects around him. His shaggy paws and mask were dimly visible in the porch light.

"You've never seen these before, have you, buddy?" She ran after the dog. "Aren't they beautiful? Don't kill them." She stopped under an old magnolia tree and tried to grab one, but they were flying too high.

"John!" she called, "I can't catch them. See if you can get me one." She reached higher and higher, but it was no use. The bugs had been spooked by Charlie and were flying in the branches now.

"Here's one." John's voice was right behind her. Startled she turned around and crashed into him.

"Hey, careful, you don't want to crush the little guy." His cupped hands rested between their two bodies.

"Sorry," she gasped. The warmth of his breath on her forehead sent shivers down her back. She felt as if the fireflies were now zinging through her body, lighting their way throughout her entire being.

"Ready?" His voice was quiet. "Cup your hands and I'll try to slip him in. He can be your night-light tonight." She heard a smile in his voice and remembered how they had done the same thing when they were children. She saw the faint glow coming from the cracks between his fingers as he gently transferred the bug into her hands. It was dark for a moment and then a flicker came from within her cupped hands.

"I've got him!" Her voice jumped with excitement. "He's right here. Look!" She glanced up, searching the darkness.

"John?" No answer. "John, where did you go?"

"Right over here." His voice came from the sidewalk. "Wanted to make sure that gate was closed so Charlie didn't take off." She heard the latch click and saw John's form move on the other side of the fence.

"Give me a call when you hear from your daddy. Night now." She saw his dark shape hurry into the darkness.

"Night," she called as she leaned against the tree trunk. Forgotten, the firefly slipped between her loosely clasped fingers and retreated to the company of his friends.

I've always loved fireflies. In my later years, of course, I had a harder time chasing them, but creaky bones and arthritic joints don't stop me now. I guess that's one silver lining in this strange cloud.

While John Hunter and Lee try to capture them from the ground, I go on up my old magnolia tree and watch the flickering fireflies from the branches, just like when I was a girl. Then I look down and see those two with fireflies and late summer leaves dancing around them.

Suddenly comes an image so vivid, so intense, I can't tell if I've left Eden Grove or if I'm caught up in a memory.

Fireflies blend into papers and streamers and I'm back with my roommate Doris. She had dragged me to a ticker tape parade that snaked its way around Manhattan.

It was Victory in Europe Day, but I didn't want to go. All I wanted was to hole up in my room, smoke cigarettes and try to block out the noise, the excitement. But it was hard not to get swept up in the emotion of the moment. Children waved flags, young boys ran up and down the streets, businessmen in their black suits walked side by side with poor immigrants from the further reaches of the island.

And soldiers. Soldiers everywhere. They'd been trickling in from Europe for months since the Allies dealt Germany a death blow. In the past few weeks the trickle turned into a flood and today the streets crawled with them, ready to receive their hero's welcome.

I didn't begrudge them the cheers, even the hugs and the kisses. But all the time my heart was shrinking and breaking away while my loss became more real.

One soldier pulled me into his arms and without a by your leave, he kissed me. Something deep inside me broke. It would be so easy to pretend it was William's arms around me, his lips on mine. The floating bits of paper brushed my hair, my eyes, my cheeks.

"Why, what's the matter, sweetheart?" the soldier asked when he pulled away and noticed the tears streaming down my cheeks. "This isn't a day for tears!"

"Just so happy for you boys," I could barely choke out. "So glad you're finally all coming home."

But they didn't all come home. My William never came home.

CHAPTER NINE

The song of the cicadas grew louder as Lee watched John Hunter disappear down the street and around the corner.

"What was that about?" she asked the emptiness around her.

A howl of frustration competed with the cicadas and Lee turned to see Charlie leap against a scrubby, overgrown bush. The fireflies twinkled among the leaves, well out of reach of the dog's snapping jaws.

"Charlie, quiet." Lee grabbed his collar and gently pulled him toward the front door. She settled him in his crate in the laundry room for the night before returning to her Jeep to grab her suitcases. The stairs groaned as she walked up the narrow passageway. At the top Lee paused and scanned the length of the gloomy hallway to both her right and left. Empty rooms surrounded her on both sides.

Her first instinct was to go to the right, to the room she and Jenny used to share when they were little. It was a big room, with two twin brass beds and large gabled windows that overlooked the front yard. The beds were covered in patchwork quilts made by her great-grandma, with matching throw pillows. She cracked the door and peeked in, but decided she'd been sleeping in a queen-sized bed for too many years to downgrade to the tiny twin.

She shut the door and dragged her suitcase down the hall. The door to her left was the old guest room where her dad had always slept. Lee opened the door only to find that Nana had turned it into a storeroom. There were bags and boxes scattered all over the floor and on top of the bedspread. The thought of trying to organize that chaos before bedtime exhausted her.

Next she passed Nana's upstairs office and den. The only other door led to Nana's room, and Lee hesitated to open it. She knew Nana had passed away in her bed, and although Granny Bob assured her everything had been "taken care of," Lee still felt strange entering the room.

A wash of sweet memories and Nana's perfume greeted her when she finally pushed through the door and all her reluctance and fear fell away. When Lee was little, she, Mark and Jenny would sneak into this room, without waking her dad, and hop into bed with Nana. She had a TV in her room, an unimaginable luxury when Lee had been a child. Mark would watch cartoons while Lee and Jenny tried on Nana's heels, wrapped themselves in silk scarves and danced around the room pretending to be princesses. The final touch was to drape themselves in as many of Nana's jewels as possible. It was the one time Lee let go of her tomboy ways to embrace her feminine side.

Nana's graciousness with her belongings made Lee chuckle. She knew now that many of the designer heels, scarves and jewels were worth a small fortune. She walked over to Nana's *jewelry box*, a large chest of drawers stuffed full of every gem imaginable, none of which had been off limits when they were little girls. A large strand of uncut amethysts and matching earrings lay in a jumble on top, along with various pieces of silver and turquoise necklaces, earrings and hair ornaments Nana had used in her French twist.

"Jenny and I were probably wearing thousands of dollars when we played dress up and Nana never batted an eye." Lee picked up one of Nana's rings.

Her gaze traveled to Nana's bed. Freshly washed and folded linens sat atop the stripped mattress. As she made it up, Lee wondered if Granny Bob or Nana's cleaning service had set these out in preparation for whoever came after Nana's death.

Although the central air was pumped to full capacity, Lee cracked open one of Nana's large windows. The sound of the cicadas, before only a dull thrum, exploded into the room. Lee took one last deep breath of the warm, fragrant air, changed out of her clothes and settled herself onto Nana's massive oak spindle bed. Tired as she was, she couldn't seem to fall asleep. After an hour of tossing and turning she decided it was time for reinforcements.

Even though she knew Nana wouldn't have approved, Lee padded through the darkened house to Charlie's crate. A few minutes later, with Charlie curled up next to her, she grabbed her phone and texted Jenny.

Are you still awake?

Yep. Heartburn. I'm always awake. How are you doing?

Pretty sad.

Yeah?

The house doesn't feel right without Nana. Too empty. Too quiet.

I'm calling you.

The phone rang and Lee answered, "Hey, you didn't need to call. I don't want to keep you awake."

"I told you I have heartburn. I ache all over and have to pee every few seconds. I promise you're not the one keeping me awake." Jenny laughed, then sobered. "So it's pretty rough there, huh?"

"The house is so empty without Nana. I don't think I ever realized what a large presence she was. You know how she filled a place to the brim without even seeming to try?" Hot tears squeezed between Lee's eyelids and memories flitted through her mind like a slideshow on fast forward.

"Yeah." Jenny's voice broke with emotion and she was silent for a moment. "It's not right that someone who lived as large as Nana could slip away so quietly. I wonder if we lived closer, could we have known?"

"I don't know," Lee said. "You were planning to visit her after you had the baby, right?"

"I was."

"I'm glad you have that. You knew Nana was looking

forward to you coming. But me, the last time I saw her was a couple of Christmases ago when I dropped in for a long weekend. And I hadn't scheduled any time to see her for the next year. How selfish is that?"

"You've been busy with work."

"I'm always busy with work." She hesitated. "To be honest, I think was avoiding her."

"But why? Did you two have a fight?"

"No, I mean not an actual exchanging of words," Lee said. "But you know how it was between us. We always seemed to butt heads. She got along better with you, but I think my stubborn, pig-headed streak drove her crazy. I know I wasn't the sweet Southern lady she would have liked."

"That's not true! She loved you."

"I don't know." Lee's tears flowed in earnest now. "It feels like I always disappoint those I care about the most: you, Nana, Mark, Dad. Probably even mom if she had lived to see us grow up."

"Lee, stop it! You don't disappoint us, we—"

"No, it's true. I see the way you are with people. How you share yourself with others, the connections you make. They seem so effortless. But me? I've got acquaintances and business contacts but no one close. I wish I could be more like you. It's like you sprinkle joy wherever you go."

"Well, I don't think Spencer would agree with the sprinkly joy statement. I'm pretty cranky right now," Jenny said.

"Well, you're almost nine months pregnant. You have

a good excuse."

"I think you're just more of a loner than me. I've always been a social butterfly. That's not better, it's just different."

"That's no excuse," Lee said. "I should have done a better job of staying in touch with Nana. Even if we didn't always get along, I should have visited her more. It's something I've thought about a lot in the last couple of days. I think I'll regret it for the rest of my life."

"You're being too hard on yourself. Like always. Nana knew you loved her, and you came to see her every time she visited Spencer and me in Denver. Now promise me you won't worry about this anymore. You've got to be exhausted after your drive down there and you need some sleep."

Jenny continued to give helpful advice and Lee pretended to be comforted. When she finally got off the phone Lee lay back against the pillows and stared up at the dark ceiling.

"Nana, if you're up there somewhere, please know I'm sorry. I loved you so much. It's a small thing, but I promise to do my best with getting your home and belongings settled. Hopefully the way you'd like."

Just then Charlie sat up and pawed her knee. He let out a low noise, something between a growl and a whine. Lee rose on her elbows to shush him. "Lay back down, Charlie. I'm fine." Charlie balked, but then reluctantly complied.

Lee settled back into her pillow and felt a warmth

steal over her head and her shoulders. Despite her tears, a comfort enveloped her and she knew she'd be able to sleep now. She pulled up the soft, cool sheets and tucked her feet under Charlie.

Well, I do have to say I was hopping mad when she brought that great shaggy thing onto my bed. I mean, really, my duvet is made out of silk and down. How on earth are you going to clean that up if the dog has a mess on it? And now his ugly white fur is getting all over everything.

But then I stop worrying about the dog and look at Lee lying there, so sad and alone. When I listen to her phone call with Jenny, I can't help but cringe.

"I could have called you too!" I want to tell her, but of course she can't hear.

She's right about us butting heads; she was used to being a little mama to Mark and Jenny and didn't much like it when I tried to give my two cents. I can see now that I was threatened by her, this little adult in a child's form.

When Mr. Mardell, my late husband, died, I got used to having things my own way and I may have gotten the teeniest bit domineering and bossy. But for heaven's sake, I was the head of my department at the university. I was used to saying "jump" and hearing "how high?" Then Caralee would march into my home and there was no "how high?" from her, believe me.

The problem is the two of us are too much alike. She

and I, both straight shooters who've made our way in tough, male-dominated professions and aren't used to taking no for an answer.

Not to mention our other dirty little secret. We both let the busyness of life, the unrealistic goals we've set for ourselves, keep us from dealing with something neither of us is none too comfortable with: our hearts.

Oh, now I see it all so clearly, but even if I could materialize back among the living and explain away all the whys of our relationship, my words would be cold comfort. Words don't keep a person warm at night, can't keep loneliness away.

Without thinking I reach over to stroke her head and rub her shoulders, not that she feels it, but it makes me feel better anyway.

CHAPTER TEN

In the morning, Charlie's whine and scratch at Nana's door woke Lee. She rubbed her eyes and checked her phone.

"Nice, Charlie, 5:30." She stumbled out of bed and opened Nana's door. "For a big dog, you have a bladder the size of a walnut."

Pulling on one of the silk robes that hung on the back of the chaise lounge, Lee trailed Charlie's mad dash to the back door. She jerked the French doors open and watched as the dog catapulted toward the neighborhood squirrels. The creatures were used to sole domain of Nana's long-neglected yard and Charlie's arrival still seemed to shock them.

She filled his water and food bowls and set them on the deck. "Enjoy yourself. I'm going back to bed."

The crisp, cool sheets pulled her back into sleep almost immediately. Her early morning dreams traveled to the mountains of her home. Lee was just summiting a route at Turtle Lake that she'd never been able to conquer when a loud explosion pulled her from her moment of triumph. The dangling prisms on Nana's chandelier lights tinkled together as the walls vibrated.

Lee leapt out of bed, heart racing and limbs trembling. *That wasn't a dream, was it?*

First she thought of Charlie. Grabbing the crumpled silk robe from the floor, Lee ran to the back of the house. She quickly spied the dog sniffing around the foot of a bedraggled tree, so Lee went to the opposite side of the house and flung open the front door.

Just a few yards from Nana's property edge lay a confusion of broken glass, twisted metal and hundreds of...watermelons?

When her gaze traveled to the epicenter of the chaos, Lee gasped. A large industrial truck, the top of which was almost mangled beyond recognition, stood abandoned at the side of the road, its doors akimbo. Steam or smoke rose from its hood.

Disjointed scenarios and observations raced through Lee's mind, as she ran out front. She found the driver of the delivery truck sitting in the empty lot next to Nana's.

"Are you all right?"

He nodded, then laid back on the ground.

"Did you hit your head?" Lee's heart raced. "Let me grab my phone and I'll call 911."

"Already on it," came a voice from behind her. Lee turned a saw a young woman with a curly-headed toddler in tow. She held a phone to her ear.

"Hello, is this 911 emergency? Yes, this is Emma Stewart and I'm calling to let you know someone's crashed into the old railroad bridge again." The woman paused and listened for a moment. "Yes that's right, Eden Grove. No, he appears to be conscious, but there's watermelons just everywhere." She paused again. "I'll do that. Thank you very much. Bye now."

She pocketed her phone and crouched next to Lee, shaking her head. "I just can't believe this happened again. That's already two times this month."

"This month?" Lee studied the old railroad bridge a few hundred feet away. "But how? You said this happens *often*?"

The woman took off her sweater and propped it beneath the man's head. "Now, sir, speak to me. Are you all right? Can you hear me?"

"Yes, ma'am," he whispered. "Hit my head real hard against the windshield—I'm dizzy but I don't think the Good Lord's taking me home just yet."

"Well, of course not. The ambulance is coming and you're going to be just fine." The woman turned to Lee. "My name's Emma, by the way. This here is little Davey." She pointed to the small boy playing with a pile of sticks a few feet away. "You're Kathryn Mardell's granddaughter, aren't you?"

"Yes, I'm Lee Trenton. Nice to meet you. And Davey."

"Now, Lee, you don't mean to tell me you've never been around when that bridge got hit?"

"No," Lee said and Emma raised her eyebrows. "I think I would have remembered the noise. It sounded like a bomb went off."

"A bomb?" Emma's laughter rattled in Lee's groggy head. "Who'd want to bomb Eden Grove? It's just that old eyesore of a bridge. Everyone keeps asking the railroad to take it down. They don't even use those tracks anymore, but it's all controlled by the federal government." She rolled her eyes. "And we know how fast they get around to fixing things that are broken."

"Somebody hit the bridge again?" John Hunter's voice came from behind them. "Hey, Emma. Hey, little man." He gave Davey's curls a tousle. "He okay?" John nodded to the delivery man.

The man offered a weak smile. "I believe I'm all in one piece. You folks have been mighty kind."

"Good." John squatted down next to them. "Hey, Lee." He finally turned to greet her. His gaze skittered across her body and he quickly looked away.

Lee looked down and realized Nana's robe hung agape giving a clear view of her skimpy pajamas. She grabbed the fabric at the neck. "I was asleep when I heard the explosion. I ran out here as fast as I could—I thought a bomb went off."

"You mean you never heard someone crash into the bridge before? Even with all your visits here?" John crossed his arms. "I just can't believe that. Someone's hitting this bridge every couple of months." Emma nodded in agreement.

Lee felt a wave of annoyance wash over her. "Well, I haven't ever heard or seen something like this before, believe me. I'd have remembered it. Why are people always hitting it? Is it falling down?"

"No," John answered. "Just old. When this was built,

bridges didn't need such high clearance for trucks and cars. I think it's from the Model-T days."

"But I still don't understand, doesn't Eden Grove only have five or six main streets?"

"Eight," John answered, annoyance creeping into his voice as well.

"Then why do people keep hitting it? Surely they know it's there? It's not like this is downtown Chicago." Lee's sharp laugh died in her throat when she saw the look on John Hunter's and Emma's faces.

"Well, sometimes people just forget," Emma said after a moment of taut silence.

"'Course it could just be all the dumb, backward hillbillies we got down here, that what you mean, Caralee?" John's exaggerated accent made Lee's face go red with embarrassment.

"No, that's not what I meant. I only—"

"There's the sirens," John interrupted. He turned to the delivery man. "You okay to get up, sir?"

John helped him to his feet and helped shoulder him to the curb. An ambulance pulled up, squashing several watermelons before it came to a halt, and two EMTs jumped from the vehicle with a gurney. John Hunter helped lift the man onto it, waved at Davey and walked back in the direction of his home.

"I didn't mean to sound like I was ridiculing Eden Grove," Lee tried to explain, as Emma bent to retrieve her sweater. "I just meant...this, this doesn't happen where I live. I'm sorry."

"It's all right." Emma reached for Davey's chubby hand. "I'm from Atlanta myself, so I know what you're saying." Emma's gaze followed John Hunter's retreating form, "but nobody likes being thought the fool."

"But I didn't—"

"I'm sure it'll all turn out fine. Don't worry about it." Emma reached over and squeezed Lee's arm. "Now you'll know for next time."

"Next time a truck hits the bridge?" Lee laughed half-heartedly.

"Exactly. If you'll excuse me, Davey and I gotta get back to our breakfasts, don't we, Davey?" Davey nodded shyly and then raised his arms for his mother to lift him up. He peeked at Lee through dirty fingers.

"I think he likes you, Lee." Emma held him close. "You'll have to come over and have coffee and pie with the two of us sometime soon. Anytime you feel like it."

"Um..." Was Emma only being polite? Although she'd done it gently, the woman had just finished chiding Lee on her manners. Probably the invitation stemmed from nothing more than social convention.

"Come," Davey said from the safety of his mother's arms. "Come for yie-yie."

"That's how he says pie," Emma whispered.

Well, I can't tell him no, Lee thought as she studied Davey's soft blond curls and chubby cheeks. "I'd love to come over. Thanks for inviting me." She smiled at the little boy.

"We'll expect you real soon." Emma waved and

carried Davey back across the street.

"Bye," Lee called after them. The sickly sweet smell of a hundred cracked and crushed watermelons enveloped her and she wondered if she might still be sleeping. The last ten minutes seemed too surreal not to be a dream, but when John's sharp words played through her mind again, she spun around and walked back to Nana's house. Charlie, nose pressed against the glass storm door, wagged his tail when he saw her coming up the steps.

"Were you worried I left without you?" Inside the house, she sank to the floor and pulled him onto her lap. "You know I'd never do that." Charlie licked her cheek and she rubbed his ears while John Hunter's words kept repeating in her head.

It could just be all the dumb, backward hillbillies we have down here, that what you mean, Caralee?

"Why do I do that?" She bowed her head down to Charlie's and gazed into his clear blue eyes. "Whatever's going on up here," she pointed to her head, "pops out of here," she touched her lips, "with no editing in between."

Charlie licked her cheek. "I guess things have been awkward between John Hunter and me for years, so that's nothing new. But Emma..." Her stomach clenched with embarrassment. "I'm such an idiot."

Another scene flashed into her mind, and John's angry voice was replaced by her father's from a conversation they'd had only a few weeks ago. Lee had just informed him of her decision to turn down a large outdoor company's offer to buy Play Harder. They'd promised her a substantial amount of money, but Lee refused based primarily on the fact that they would let all her employees go and that she didn't agree with the company's policy on conservation. Or rather, lack of policy.

"You've turned into a bleeding heart liberal, just like all the other crazies you hang out with," her father informed her during a rare family dinner at Jenny's house.

"Dad, I think it's important to protect the mountains I rely on for my income. I also think it's my duty as a human being. If that makes me a liberal, then fine, call me whatever you want. But I'm not going to sell my business to a company that has absolutely no policies that protect the mountains I love and depend on."

Her father finished the meal in silence then quickly made his excuses and left.

Jenny sighed as she began to gather the dishes. "Lee, you know things like this make him crazy. It's just better to avoid the subject. In the interest of peace."

"But he asked me why I wouldn't sell. Was I supposed to lie to him?"

"Duh," Mark said from his place on the couch, without turning from the TV. "That's what the rest of us do. Who cares as long as it keeps him quiet?"

"I care!" Lee felt the helpless anger of her childhood threatening to consume her again. "I'm an adult. Why do I have to lie about a decision I've made? He can't walk around bullying people all the time. We *are* actually allowed to have different opinions than him, you know. This is America."

Jenny shook her head and chuckled. "Yeah, but you're the only one brave enough to tell him that."

Lee had left early the next morning, cutting her visit short, as she usually did. During the whole drive back from Denver to Durango, she felt sick to her stomach. *Why do I always ruin things? Why can't I keep my mouth shut? Why can't I be more like Mark, who just doesn't care or Jenny who finds it easy to keep peace? I don't mean to create conflict, but I can't seem to help it.*

Stopping at her home only long enough to drop off her bags and collect her climbing gear, Lee sped off to Hermosa Cliffs. Several hours later she stood atop a stark promontory, exhausted from the solo climb and the mental determination it took to reach the summit, but now completely at peace. The wind ruffled her hair and dried her perspiration. The cry of a solitary black hawk floating through the white clouds and the delicious coldness of her bottled water filled her senses. She sat down, leaned against a lichened rock and let the beauty of the moment cleanse all the broken places inside her heart.

A tear trickled down her cheek as she whispered to the lonely pine tree above her. "Why can't I just stay here. Forever?"

A loud magpie cry startled Lee out of her memories and she found herself in Nana's entry way again, her stomach tense with emotion. Leaping up, she pulled the robe tightly around her and tied it with a jerk. She whistled for Charlie to follow her into the kitchen.

"Time to work," she told him a few minutes later over

the soft rumble of the coffee maker. “We’ve got a lot to do before we can leave.”

The Colorado mountains in her memory still beckoned but she shook them off. There was no alpine escape for her here.

CHAPTER ELEVEN

A few hours later from her perch on the big porch swing, Lee watched Granny Bob come up the front sidewalk. Dressed again in khaki shorts and a sweet t-shirt that said "No. 1 Grandma," Granny Bob set a plate of cookies on the side table next to Lee along with a mason jar of what appeared to be more sweet tea.

"Thank you," Lee mouthed, computer on her lap and phone to her ear. She gestured for Granny Bob to sit next to her. The older woman pointed toward the house and returned a few seconds later with two large glasses filled with ice. She poured the tea and offered one to Lee as she finished her phone call.

"Thank you, Sarah Beth. Thank you so much. Tomorrow, a little after noon? Wonderful. I can't tell you how much I appreciate your getting someone here so quickly. You too. Good-bye."

Granny Bob looked up from her frosty glass. "Sarah Beth fixing to head over here and look at Nana's furniture?"

"Yes, she's coming tomorrow." Lee paused and took a large sip of the tea and closed her eyes. "Oh my, Granny Bob, that's good tea. I don't want to know how many calories are in it, but it's so hot out here I don't care."

"Most people would stay indoors next to the fan if they were hot," Granny Bob said, giving the swing a practiced push with her foot. "But I know you're the kind of girl who can't hardly stand being indoors."

Lee smiled and took another sip as she eyed the still gooey chocolate chunk cookies on the side table. After an all too brief battle, she gave in and grabbed one. "I'm going to have to do a major sugar detox after I leave here, but your food is just too good to turn down."

"So you don't eat sugar either? Why, honey, what on earth do you eat?"

"A lot of hummus and soy for protein. Beans and vegetables. Fruit. Grains." Lee licked at the melted chocolate chip on her finger.

"Sounds like horse food!" Granny Bob said, horrified. "No wonder you're so skinny. Now, where on earth do you get all that stuff?"

"In the grocery store," Lee laughed, "the same as you get your food."

"Really? Well bless your heart, I'm not sure we carry anything like that here." Granny Bob leaned back against the cushion.

"I'm pretty sure you carry fruit and vegetables. Maybe I could make dinner for you sometime. You could pretend you were going to a strange, exotic restaurant."

Granny Bob hesitated for only a second. "Why, that sounds real interesting. Not exactly my type of food, but I think John Hunter would be excited to try anything you made. He loves traveling and trying new things."

"Really? But I thought he—"

"Thought I what?" John Hunter appeared on the side of the porch, startling both Granny Bob and Lee.

While Lee tried to brush the spilled tea off her lap, memories of similar scares flooded her mind. "I forgot how much you love to do that. Sneaking up on people hasn't lost its charm yet, hmmm?"

"Wanted to be a spy when I was little. Guess old habits die hard." He vaulted over the porch railing with his long legs and grabbed a handful of cookies. "Hello, Granny."

"Hello yourself, and yes, you may have a cookie," Granny Bob said. "Would you like some sweet tea too?"

"Yes, ma'am. Please," he added after glancing at Granny Bob's face.

"I'll go grab you a glass." Lee tried to stand.

"No, honey, I'll get it. You just guard those cookies, else he'll have all of them shoved in his mouth before you can blink, and I made them special for you, not him." Granny Bob shook her finger at John Hunter before marching into the house.

"I guess she's got your number," Lee joked, but the scene of the watermelon disaster flitted through her mind.

"Always has," John responded, grabbing another cookie and flinging himself into the swing next to her. The chains groaned and the seat swung crazily.

Silence settled between them. *What is taking Granny Bob so long?* Lee wondered. She glanced over at John's face. Was he still angry about this morning? She felt anxiety knotting her stomach, but then forced herself to relax. Studying the familiar wave of his hair, the irritation ebbed. Maybe she had come off as snooty and belittling. She'd been half-asleep, after all.

"Sorry about earlier today. I didn't mean to sound like—"

"Why you always apologizing?" John interrupted her. He crossed his arms and gave the swing a shove.

"I'm not *always* apologizing!" Her momentary Zen-like peace evaporated. "You're just irritated no matter what I do."

"Irritated?" He looked genuinely confused and Lee felt the urge to smack him.

"Yeah, irritated, annoyed, ticked off—"

"I know what *irritated* means, Lee." He rolled his eyes. "But I don't understand what *you* mean by it."

"I mean, whenever I...Oh, just forget it." Her head began to throb and she closed her eyes. "This whole experience is such a nightmare." She jerked her knees up under her chin and the swing groaned in protest. John Hunter shifted next to her.

"I'm sorry, Lee." He spoke after a moment, his voice serious. "I keep forgetting you're not here for another summer vacation. You're here because Nana died and I know that's hard."

Lee frowned and nodded.

"You know me, I like to joke around and it's so easy going back to the way things were between us, you know?"

"Mmm."

"Don't you remember? Shoot, we always getting into trouble." He chuckled and leaned back with his arms behind his head.

Memories that she hadn't thought of in years danced at the edge of Lee's mind.

John turned to her again and touched a silver streak across the top of his slightly crooked nose. "This scar for instance. Don't tell me you don't remember giving me this."

A single memory leapt in front of the others.

"You were spending the night over at our house with Tammy, and Granny Bob had let us watch that scary movie," John said.

Lee closed her laptop. "One of those Friday night horror movies, I think."

"Yeah, and I could tell you girls were real scared, so I waited in my room, across the hall from y'all until I heard you stop whispering. Then I climbed through my window—"

"Wait," Lee grabbed his arm. "Weren't you dressed up like something?"

"Yeah, that's right. I put on my Halloween monster costume. Cape, mask, claws, the whole nine yards. I snuck around the house, over to Tammy's window, and started scratching at the screen."

"You scared us to death." Lee laughed.

"Wouldn't have ever known it, with you anyway."

John shook his head and chuckled. "You girls woke up about the same time. Tammy screamed like a tornado siren and pulled a pillow over her head, but you, heck, you seemed like it didn't even faze you."

Lee remembered how she'd been convinced something was about to kill her and Tammy. Without thinking, she grabbed Tammy's bedside lamp, ripped it from the wall and hurled it through the flimsy screen with all her might. It hit the startled John Hunter square in the face.

"Thank goodness you had a mask on."

"Yeah, but you still broke my nose! I remember seeing stars and falling flat on my back in Granny's hosta bed, blood spurting so bad I could hardly breathe. Do you remember what you said?"

"No, not really."

"You crawled through the window and said, 'I'm really sorry, John Hunter. I didn't know it was you. I thought you were a werewolf. I was trying to kill you.' Then you grabbed me by the hand and pulled me back in the house."

"You didn't get in too much trouble, did you?"

"Only because I looked like you'd knocked me across the face with a shovel. They would have tanned my hide, except for your good aim."

The two of them laughed and Lee suddenly felt a searing desire to go back to that simpler time.

"You were like my best friend, Lee. You know that, right?"

Lee turned to find him studying her again. "Was I?"

Something flitted through John's eyes and he sat up. "'Course you were, dummy. You think I would'a spent that much time with a girl otherwise? Rumor was, y'all had cooties." He leapt off the swing and grabbed another cookie. "Granny, where the heck did you run off to?" he called as he walked into the house.

The swing, in chaos from John's hasty exit, jolted back and forth at a crazy angle, almost hitting the porch railing. Lee gripped the arms and calmed its movement by dragging her feet on the smooth planks of the porch.

"Slow down," she muttered under her breath, and the swing eventually returned to its gentle glide. "Just...slow down."

She opened the laptop again and banished the images of young John Hunter and Caralee far from her mind.

Watching the two of them on my front porch swing, I can't help but notice what a nice couple Caralee and John Hunter make. Too bad their mule-headed personalities keep getting in the way of them discovering that. This morning, for example, I know she apologized but Caralee did sound uppity to my ears, going on and on about the railroad bridge.

What Caralee doesn't understand is that rickety piece of junk is a town mascot, really. It's just like Hardhide, the alligator in my cousin Arlene's hometown in Louisiana. Is Hardhide ridiculous? Of course he is! But do they still wheel him down Main Street in a little red wagon at every town parade? The locals would have a fit if they didn't.

That's the thing Yankees like Caralee can't seem to get. Just because something is old, silly or worn out doesn't mean you get rid of it. If you do, you destroy all the memories and dreams that have grown around it.

And now look at her: even though she's physically here sitting next to me on the porch swing, I can sense she's counting the moments until she returns home. Lee's talking, typing and organizing away the last threads of my life. As I glance at the porch around me and sway back and forth on this ancient swing next to her, I can't help but think it isn't time for things to end yet.

There's still new chapters to be written in the Abney family story. There's still kinks that need to be worked out in our family line. Things went terribly wrong between William and me, but the world was at war, for land's sake. What's Caralee's excuse? Why is she alone and miserable? I know her life hasn't always been easy, but every door in the world is open to her right now. How can she not take advantage of all her opportunities?

If that girl doesn't make some changes soon, it'll be too late for her too.

CHAPTER TWELVE

Granny Bob and John Hunter left a short while later and Lee forced herself upstairs. Although most of the furniture and decorations had the possibility of being too valuable to donate, Lee felt confident that she could at least sort through towels, sheets, old books and magazines without accidentally throwing away some priceless treasure.

Earlier this morning she'd called the local secondhand shop to ask about their hours and drop-off procedure. The manager, like so many other people she'd contacted, had known Nana, loved her and was happy to help Lee.

"Why, sweetie," the manager had said, "I know you probably don't remember me, but I met you when you were just a bitty thing. You and your family were up visiting for Christmas and Dr. Mardell brought you and your sister up to the campus to show you where she worked. I was a student there at the time. It was Christmas break, but I was working on a few last-minute things in the fashion department."

"I'm sorry. You're right, I don't remember you, although I do remember playing in Nana's office while she graded some papers."

"Well, I remember you because you looked so much like your grandma. You have the exact same eyes, you know. Tell you what I'll do, hon. You just box up all your donations and set them in the back alley. Then call me when you're ready and I'll have my driver come pick them up. It's the least I can do. For Dr. Mardell."

Lee considered the conversation as she taped up some of the boxes. She felt like a part of this community even though she hadn't been to Eden Grove in years. It made her wish she'd continued to visit her grandmother regularly, even after entering the commitments and struggles of adulthood.

When Lee came to the old board games in the corner of the room, she felt a little catch in her throat. She'd spent hours playing those games with Jenny, Mark and Nana, usually at the kitchen table with a mug of hot chocolate or glass of cold lemonade, depending on the season. The dilapidated cardboard cases had been touched by generations of young hands and even as Lee eyed her trash sack, she knew these particular belongings were destined to head home to Colorado with her.

"Guess I'll add these to my things," she said to Charlie when she passed his snoozing form in the hallway.

Her *things* in Nana's room, the mementos she wanted to take home, were growing at an alarming rate. First, it had only been some of the old family photographs. Lee knew Jenny would want them.

Then Lee found a piece of furniture that she'd fixated on when she was a little girl—a tiny Louis XVI boudoir chair. She'd loved the way it seemed just her size when she was growing up. The wood was painted gold and it was covered in shiny satin, much too ornate and gaudy to match anything in her home, but Lee couldn't bear the thought of never seeing it again. Maybe she'd use it as a desk chair so that most of its golden glory could remain hidden.

Next came an old hand-carved cradle and matching chest of drawers that looked as though they must have been in Nana's family for years. She remembered that Jenny and her husband Brad were still looking for nursery furniture. And how fitting to have a cradle that had held generations of Abneys.

Other various and sundry items, remembered favorites had made their way to the collection and Lee knew it was getting too large.

"There might be room in my Jeep for all this, but it'll be close." She spoke to Charlie who had followed her into Nana's room. "I've only sorted out the top floor of the house so far. Maybe I'll have to rent a trailer."

Several hours later, she carried boxes ready for the secondhand shop out to the alley. After that, Lee tugged down the old twin mattresses that had been on her and Jenny's beds. They looked nearly threadbare and even with her lack of taste, Lee knew the appraiser wouldn't consider them a priceless find. She decided not to tackle the box springs without help since she didn't want to scrape or dent Nana's walls.

Setting the last box on the curb, Lee stretched her

aching back in relief. Her cell phone rang and she checked the number. It was Jenny.

"Hey, Sis, how's it going today?" Jenny's voice chirped across the line. "Are you feeling better?"

"Yeah. I was just a little emotional last night. How's the baby?"

"Still not here," Jenny answered, her voice weary. "I can't even describe to you how swollen my legs are. I look like the elephant man."

"Bed rest isn't helping?" Lee walked back upstairs and began wiping dust off the now empty furniture.

"Not that I can tell, but at least I don't have to go into work looking like this. About all that fits me now are Brad's T-shirts and boxer shorts."

Lee smiled at the picture of her usually impeccable sister so attired.

"Speaking of Brad," Jenny said, "you know he says he can fly down and help you out if you need it."

"I know, but I think it's probably more important he be there for the birth of his first child. Babies are the ultimate trump card, you know."

"Well, in case you need anything just remember."

"Got it. Hey, you'll never guess who I ran into down here." Lee changed the subject, knowing she'd never let Brad leave Jenny during the last month of her pregnancy.

"Who?"

"Well, Granny Bob of course—"

"Oh, I love her," Jenny interrupted. "What about Tammy?"

"Nope, Granny Bob told me Tammy still lives down in Baton Rouge close to her mom. She's married with three kids now."

"That's too bad, but tell me who else?"

"John Hunter," Lee answered.

"Jon-Jon? Are you...happy about that? You haven't spoken in what, like fifteen years?"

"Twenty," Lee immediately corrected, then paused. "To be honest, it is a little strange. The way he went off after that last summer and never..."

"Never what?" Jenny asked.

"Nothing. I guess it's just like old times. He's still crazy old Jon-Jon from when we were growing up."

"What does that mean?"

"Like teasing, being sarcastic, you know how he is." Lee threw her dirty, dust-covered rag in the hallway and started with a clean one.

"Basically a big kid?"

"Well, he's grown up too," Lee said. "He's working on his doctorate from the University of Tennessee."

"Oh my gosh! I cannot picture that *at all*," Jenny squealed. "Dr. Fairchild. How dreamy!"

"Jenny!"

"Oh come on, Lee, every girl in that town had a crush on him. I had to join in too, you know, or stay an outsider."

"They did?"

"Of course they did," Jenny answered. "He has to be married, right?"

"Nope."

"Dating?"

"I don't know." Lee was starting to get annoyed. "He just got back into town right before I did. He actually owns a landscaping business now. I'm waiting to hear back from Dad if John Hunter can work on the yard. It's a complete shambles."

"Mmmm, wish he'd come work in my yard."

"Jenny! What's the matter with you?"

"Sorry, sorry, pregnancy hormones. They make you a little crazy."

Lee changed the subject to the cradle and chest of drawers that she'd set aside. Jenny couldn't wait to get them in her nursery. They chatted a bit more until Lee was done cleaning the room and then rang off.

She checked the time and saw she had time for a quick shower before she was expected at Granny Bob's. When she got out, her phone bleeped letting her know she had a message. It was from her dad.

"Lee, got your message. So John Hunter's back in Eden Grove? If you feel comfortable working with him, I'm fine with his firm doing the work on Nana's yard. I looked over the numbers he gave you and I think he's being extremely generous. If you decide to work with him, tell John thank you on behalf of the family. Gotta go. Love you. Bye."

Lee blinked at the phone in surprise. If she felt comfortable working with him? What did her dad mean by that? She shrugged and left the question alone. She'd stopped trying to puzzle out her father long ago.

"Too bad Jenny's not the one packing all this up," Lee

told Charlie as she clipped on his leash. “She seemed pretty excited by the idea of working with John Hunter.”

What about you? She could almost hear her sister badger her.

“Me?” She answered the imaginary Jenny. “It’s been too long since my last climb and pretty soon the aspen leaves will be changing. I can’t wait to get home.”

CHAPTER THIRTEEN

Later as she sat at Granny Bob's table, Lee was proud to report that she'd reached almost everyone on the list and set up appointments with them.

"And Mr. Etherby said he'd send somebody around in a few days to appraise all of Nana's jewelry and see if I'd be interested in selling any of it on consignment," Lee told Granny Bob and John Hunter as she helped herself to a second serving of hush puppies.

"That's wonderful." Granny Bob smiled and took a large bite of greens, but not before Lee heard a catch in her voice.

The older woman had been so supportive Lee knew she'd taken for granted that as Nana's best friend, Granny Bob must be struggling with intense grief of her own.

"I was wondering if you wouldn't mind looking over all of the jewelry before Blake comes by," Lee said. "I'd like you to help me decide which pieces to keep for my sister, but I'd also like you to take a few for yourself."

"Oh no, honey, I couldn't," Granny Bob said.

"I insist." Lee set her fork down, knowing she'd have to argue this one. "You were like Nana's sister. If she'd ever gotten around to telling us what to do with her things, I know she'd have wanted you to keep some of them."

Granny Bob shook her head but Lee continued. "What about something you helped her pick out? Wouldn't that be a special keepsake to remember her by?"

Granny Bob didn't respond. Lee looked toward John Hunter, her eyes pleading.

"C'mon, Granny," he coaxed, "if you don't do it, Lee and I will and who knows what you'll get then? Probably some worthless, gaudy piece of junk from the dollar store."

"Hey," Lee played along, "my taste isn't that bad."

"Hush up, girl." John poked her in the side. "Granny, please promise you'll pick out something."

"Oh, all right," she agreed, wearily, and Lee's heart broke for the older woman. Even with her and John's silly banter, she could see that Granny Bob was close to tears.

"Why don't you go put your feet up? You've been slaving over a hot stove all afternoon and you must be exhausted. Please let John Hunter and me clean up the dishes."

"I guess I will, honey, and thank you for the offer. I think I'll just go watch my show and relax a little." She squeezed John and Lee's shoulders on her way out of the kitchen.

"What's her show?" Lee asked as she and John stood to gather up the dishes.

"Pimp My Ride."

"What?" Lee almost collapsed on the counter in

laughter. "You can't be serious!"

"Yes, ma'am, I am serious," John answered. "You know how much she loves cars."

"But it's so gangster." Lee filled the sink with hot water.

"Well, what can I say, the heart wants what the heart wants." He continued to stack the dishes next to her. "So how come you don't want any of Nana's jewelry?"

"What?"

"How come you don't want any of Nana's jewelry?" John repeated. "You said you were getting some for your sister and you wanted Granny to have some, but you're gonna keep something too, right?"

"Oh, I don't know." She scrubbed at the casserole dish. "I'm not a big jewelry person. Plus Nana's style was a bit more ornate than mine."

John's eyes swept to the simple drop at her neck and the studs at her ears. "I guess that's true, but what about for remembering Nana, even if you don't wear it often?"

Lee spent several moments considering his question. "It's hard to explain John, but Nana and I weren't really that close."

"What in the Sam Hill are you talking about?" John paused in wiping off the counters. "Nana loved you, was so proud of you. She talked about you all the time. Said that you were like two peas in a pod."

"Did she?" Lee absently rubbed her sapphire drop. "I guess we just kind of grew apart after I stopped..." She froze, knowing the why of that decision stood right next her. "I mean she was just so *sassy*. It was always her way or the highway. I think we butted heads a few too many times."

"Sassy and her way or the highway." John chuckled. He moved next to her and dried the clean dishes she handed him. "Yep that just about describes the two of you to a T."

"Yeah." She shrugged. "What can I say? It's a high and lonely calling."

"What?" John paused in his drying. "What are you talking about?"

"Nothing," Lee answered, her cheeks growing pink. "Did you get all the dishes off the table?"

"A high and lonely calling? What's that supposed to mean?"

"It's nothing. Just something I joke about...with my therapist." She pulled a large soup pot into the sudsy water with a loud splash and began to scrub vigorously.

"Your therapist?"

"Yes, lots of people go to therapists, John. It's not a big deal," her voice echoed from inside the pot.

"Sugar, it is a big deal if you're sad about something."

She sensed his eyes boring into the top of her head, but refused to look up. "I shouldn't have said anything."

"Is it your daddy?" John Hunter said. "He could be pretty harsh on y'all when you were kids. Sometimes it seemed like nothing was ever good enough no matter how hard you and your brother and sister tried. Made me so angry, I wanted to punch him."

Silence.

"Lee, answer me. Come on, now, I mean it." He grabbed her hands from the now spotless pot and forced her away from the sink.

"It's my dad some," Lee finally admitted into the thick quiet of the kitchen, "but I think it's my mom too. She died when I was so young, I can't really remember much about her. All I do remember is Dad being stressed and needing help with Mark and Jenny.

"Really, it's just relationships in general." She studied the floor, but the gentle squeeze of his hands caused her to look up. The tenderness she saw there broke through her usual restraint.

"I have a hard time connecting with people, John. I tend to keep them at arm's length. It's just easier to play the distant card, you know? To keep people from getting too close." She flinched at the pity she saw creeping into his eyes. "But it's fine. I shouldn't have brought it up. I've made my peace with being a loner and I like it now."

The drip of the leaky faucet was the only sound in the kitchen. John let out a deep breath and shook his head. "I can see that. It's kinda like you created this perfect shell that makes you seem untouchable...to the average Joe anyway."

Lee stared at him, waiting for the other shoe to drop, for some teasing remark about how she took herself too seriously. "Are you for real?" she finally spluttered.

"Yeah, I am. Heck, you intimidate me and I remember you running around in diapers."

"I intimidate you? *Me*?"

"Yeah, you."

She continued to stare at him. "But you always tease so much, I thought..."

John returned to the wet dishes and Lee studied his back as he dried them.

"C'mon, Caralee." His voice was quiet now. "You're good at everything you do, and you've got a successful business, from what I gather. You're smart and you're sweet too. You're, well you've grown up to be..." He set down his dish and braced his hands against the counter. "You're beautiful. Who wouldn't be intimidated by all that?"

This didn't feel right. She couldn't remember him ever complimenting her before. "Are you—"

"John Hunter!" Granny Bob's voice came from the living room. "Your cell phone's ringing."

"Who is it?" John called over his shoulder.

"It says it's Kiki," Granny Bob's voice called back, followed by, "Why hello, Kiki, this is Bobby Fairchild, John Hunter's grandma."

John turned to Lee and shrugged. "Guess I'd better go take that."

"Oh, right." Lee forced a smile and returned to the sink as John brushed past her.

"Lee?"

She turned to see John paused at the edge of the kitchen. "Yes?"

"Don't you go doubting who you are. The Good Lord

broke the mold when he made you."

Before Lee could answer he turned and left. Then his voice floated from the front room. "Well, Kiki McGraw, how you been doing, girl?"

Lee finished cleaning up the kitchen before she joined Granny Bob and Charlie, who was dozing in the front room. John sat on the front porch now, but his muted conversation and laughter were still audible from behind the door. Lee tried to ignore it, but the barks of laughter grated at her nerves. Finally she turned to Granny Bob.

"Who's this Kiki person?"

"Wade's sister. They went to high school together before he moved down to Baton Rouge," Granny Bob responded without looking up from the TV. "Now what in tarnation are they doing with that car's suspension? It's a '64 Chevy for law's sake!"

"High school?" Lee's response came out louder than she intended and Granny Bob glanced her way. "Why is she looking him up after all these years?"

"I saw her in town today and mentioned that John was back from Ashville. The two of them seem to get back together whenever he's in town. She's been carrying her torch for years now."

"Well, great!" Lee's voice sounded brittle even to her own ears and suddenly she just wanted to be in bed, away from this minefield of emotional confusion. "I'm pretty wiped out too, so I think I'm going to head back to Nana's."

"You do that, honey, and I'll see you tomorrow night

for dinner?"

"Only if you let me bring something." Lee found Charlie's leash and clicked it onto the sleeping dog's collar. "I can't let you keep feeding me without pitching in."

"Well, if you must. Only don't bring any of that horse food, you hear?" Granny Bob's eyes twinkled.

"Oh, I'm going to bring my horse food." Lee leaned down to hug her. "And you're going to love it." She let herself out the front door and tried to rush past John Hunter, but Charlie seemed to feel a prolonged good-bye was in order.

"Come on, Charlie," she demanded, tugging at his leash, but he nosed his head under John Hunter's hand and settled in for a good scratch.

"Hey, boy," John whispered. He nestled the phone against his shoulder to give Charlie an exuberant roughing around his collar.

Traitor! Lee tugged at the leash again and Charlie inched away from John reluctantly. "Bye, John," she called over her shoulder and hurried down the street.

I follow Caralee back to my house from Bobby's and wish again that I could shake her.

She has a terrible memory, that's all I can say. What's all this nonsense about her not wearing jewelry? I could remind her of a time or two when she was little. Wasn't she the one that piled on my necklaces, bracelets, brooches back when she and Jenny used to play dress up? Why, sometimes she could barely stand from the weight of it! And for her not to remember how she used to love my little diamond elephant...she would beg me to let her wear it the whole time she visited. I treasured that silly little elephant, just because she loved it so.

I guess now she's going to give it all to Blake, and my jewelry's going to be pecked at by a pack of strangers. I can't hardly bear to think about it. But what cuts me to the quick is her memories of playing dress up with Jenny and me seem to be gone. Vanished. Like those good times never existed. I can't believe she forgot our mornings together, when the girls would dress up and Mark would watch cartoons. Those are some of the memories I hold closest to my heart.

I follow her as she puts the dog in his crate and then stops to sit at the kitchen table. My anger fizzles. The poor thing looks so alone. I settle down next to her and wish I could hold the hands that she spreads on the table in front of her. I'd sure ask her some questions if I could.

What's this hogwash about her having a hard time connecting with people? And a therapist? Sometimes I think this generation just makes up problems for the fun of talking about themselves. In my day, we didn't bother with therapists. We had friends, real friends. The kind that didn't bat an eye if you showed up on their doorstep crying and begging for a good talk to get your feelings in order.

When Lee fills a glass of water and heads up the stairs, I stay at the table, next to the stupid dog, and think some more about her conversation with John. Here's one more piece of advice I'd give her if she could hear me: "Sometimes you go past a crossroad and don't realize there's no turning back until it's too late. You don't get any do-overs! Life is too short to live pinned under your fears."

I study the dark, empty room around me and realize it's easy to preach now, but I sure do wish I heeded my own advice a little better. Maybe my life would have turned out different if I had. Maybe Lee would have had a house full of cousins and aunts and uncles to help her through this difficult time.

The regret doesn't last long. It's hard to feel too attached to what might have been in my current state. I'm more worried about where and, more importantly, when I'm going.

Speaking of worry, here's something Caralee should watch out for: Kiki McGraw.

I see storm clouds on the horizon.

CHAPTER FOURTEEN

Exhausted, Lee settled between the sheets with her cell phone. She needed to email Nick and Cassie and see how things were going back home. Although she tried to focus on the words she typed, her mind raced through the schedule of the following day. *Meet with the furniture assessor in the morning, go into town to talk to the Realtor, and—*

Then she remembered that she hadn't told John Hunter about her father's message. Lee exited out of the email and opened a new text. It was then she realized she didn't have his phone number. After debating with herself for a few minutes, Lee decided to drop off a note at his house. She was too tired for another conversation with John and hoped fervently that he was still on Granny Bob's front porch catching up with his oh-so-wonderful Kiki. She found a paper and pen and jotted him a note.

John Hunter,

My father agreed to your proposal and we'd really like to have you do the landscaping for Nana's house. Thank you again for the very generous offer and I would appreciate you starting as soon as possible. Please call me if you have any questions.

Lee

She included her phone number and then read it over. It was nice and professional. All she needed to do now was slide it under his door.

Walking down the street, Lee took in the delicious smell of the evening; a mixture of flowers and post rain shower, only without the rain. If only she could bottle that fragrance and take it home. It was the essence of her childhood. Even though she'd only spent a handful of her 33 summers in Eden Grove, its unique smell was both familiar and comforting.

The humidity clung to her as she tried to remember the way to John's home, or what she'd known as old Mr. Robinson's place. She turned the corner and spied it immediately three houses down on the right side of the street. It was twilight, but the front of the house glowed in the disappearing rays of summer sun.

Lee paused at the front gate, almost breathless at the beauty in front of her. A riot of flowers enveloped the yard, broken only by the pathway that led to John's front door. She opened the gate and felt as though she'd arrived in a fairy tale. Silky petals and leaves brushed her bare legs when she walked, filling the air with an even deeper fragrance. Golden-orange honeysuckle blossoms climbed the pillars surrounding the porch. Lee paused to take in their delicate, sweet fragrance, and John's words about the plant replayed in her mind. *Pay attention to your dreams tonight. You're gonna dream about your one true love—the one who'll never leave you.*

An old-fashioned screen door gave a dim view of the rooms inside the house and the sound of music floated through the air. She walked up the brick covered stairs and creaked across the wood-planked porch. The music was louder now and she heard John Hunter singing to its honky-tonk tune. The sound of his voice made Lee smile and she bent down to slip her note under his screen.

John Hunter had played the tough guy routine so well when they were growing up that Lee was surprised at the adult he'd become, the artist that time had revealed. She stood up and traced the woodworking detail along the door frame. Her gaze traveled to the cozy wicker loveseat next to her.

A meow interrupted her musings and Lee started at the sound. Turning, she saw a small, striped house cat perched on the edge of the porch.

"Well, hello there, pretty girl." Lee crooned and crouched down with her hand extended. It did the trick. The cat sidled up to her and rubbed its whiskers against her outstretched fingers. "Do you belong to Jon-Jon?" She scratched its back and the cat arched to meet her hand.

A sense of deep peace enveloped her and she suddenly wished she could crawl up on the cushioned wicker couch with this little tabby and drowse to the sound of John's voice meandering through the screen door.

The singing suddenly grew louder and the cat shied off

the porch and bounded into the neighboring yard. Lee froze, crouched next to the loveseat. The screen door squeaked open and John stepped onto the front porch.

Still humming to himself, he walked opposite Lee and dumped something from a large metal can over the railing.

Please don't see me, please don't see me, Lee begged, but in vain. As soon as John turned, he spotted her, jumped in surprise and dropped his can. It clattered and banged across the porch and into the yard.

"Lee, you scared the tar outta me! Why are you sneaking around on my porch?" His voice was sharp.

"I wasn't! I didn't mean to. The sneaking around part," she stammered. "I was petting your cat." She gestured vaguely in the direction where the animal had run.

"Cat? I don't have a cat. What are you talking about? Why are you here?" He looked around the porch in confusion. "Were you...were you spying on me through my window?"

"What?" Lee stood in outrage. "No, NO! Of course not. I'm not some creepy *Peeping Tom*."

"Then why were you hiding down there?" John took a step toward her.

"I told you I was petting your cat—a cat, your neighbor's cat!" she amended when John tried to interrupt her. "It ran off next door when you came out."

John studied her for a moment before offering her a half smile. "Hmm, I guess Mrs. Davison does have a cat, but I still think you were spying on me. See anything good?"

Lee gasped with embarrassment. "No, I told you. That's...yuck!"

"Oh, yuck? Thanks a lot, sweet thang," he laughed.

"No, not yuck, I'm—" Lee's head throbbed with embarrassment and she rubbed her temples. "I don't have your phone number and I thought it would be easiest to drop off a note."

John took a step back and looked around the porch. "Don't see any notes here."

"It's inside now. Or it should be. I promise!"

"You know, Lee," he shook his head, "after your high and mighty attitude when you attacked me in Nana's house, I'm a little surprised that you seem to have a problem of your own with breaking and entering. Next time you can just let yourself inside and get a ring-side seat. You'll have a much better view."

"Don't be an idiot, John!" she yelled, anger overtaking embarrassment.

John just raised his eyebrows. His goading transported her back to childhood, and he had always known how to push her buttons. Lee lunged at him, punching his chest with her fist.

He grabbed her forearms after a few seconds. "Hey, Bean Pole, you're a lot stronger than back in the day." He didn't let go as she tried to jerk away. "I think you may have even given me a bruise or two. You know, to add to your fireplace-poker special."

Lee stopped struggling. "Well, you deserved it," she said, the last crackles of anger still popping inside her.

"Well, maybe I did," John agreed, his voice soft. Lee, still pulled tight against his chest, looked up into his eyes and caught her breath. Time went backwards and she was in the sycamore tree again. Only this time she knew what was coming.

"Well, well, what's going on here, y'all?" A voice broke into the moment and Lee and John Hunter jumped away from each other. As she stumbled against the porch railing, John reached out to steady her but she brushed his arm away. A half smile twisted his lips before he shook his head and turned.

"Hey, Kiki, you made it," John said and walked down to meet the owner of the voice, a curvy blond in sky-high heels. "This is Lee Trenton, Kathryn Mardell's granddaughter. She's here settling up her grandma's things."

Kiki's eyes traveled between the two of them for a long moment. Then she smiled, wrapped herself around John and purred, "Looked like she was settling more than that, Johnny."

"Oh. Just a misunderstanding. Lee was—"

Kiki silenced John's excuses with a finger on his lips.

"I'm just teasing you, Johnny." She leaned up and gave him a lingering kiss. Lee cringed when John's arms, after a brief pause, wrapped around Kiki.

"John, calm down." Kiki laughed and pulled herself away. "We can save that for later." She turned to Lee and smiled. "Let's not be rude to your company."

Kiki reminded Lee of a snake as she undulated her way

up to the front porch. Stopping in front of Lee, Kiki gave her a once over and smirked. "What's your name again, honey?"

"Lee Trenton." She studied Kiki's massive mane of blond hair, glossy nails and slinky sundress. She was tiny; even in her heels she was a good few inches shorter than Lee. Everything about her made Lee feel big, awkward and messy, but she forced herself to make eye contact and smile. Even though it was all she could do not to bolt off the front porch, Lee knew she couldn't back down. She'd seen how this type of thing played out plenty of times at the dog park with Charlie.

"And your name is Kiki? That's certainly...cute."

"Why thank you. Aren't you just the sweetest thing?"

"Not always." Lee crossed her arms and smiled. "But I do try."

Kiki's eyes narrowed and she moved back to John. "Well, I hate to have to excuse ourselves, but Johnny and I made plans for a nightcap this evening. I'd invite you to tag along, but I'd hate for you to feel like a third wheel."

"Oh, I never tag along." Lee came down the porch and brushed past them on her way to the gate. "John, that note should be somewhere inside your front door. Look it over and let me know what you think."

"I'll do that, Lee." John's voice came from behind her. "Thanks for dropping it off."

"No problem," Lee called over her shoulder without turning around. She walked regally through the gate and down the street, but as soon as she turned the corner from John Hunter's street she broke into a run.

"That snotty little cow!" Lee exploded as her flip-flops slapped on the pavement. "Who does she think she is? She doesn't own him!" Lee stopped, softly panting in front of Nana's gate, as she replayed the whole incident over in her mind.

What had really happened in the last 20 minutes, she asked herself. All she'd wanted to do was drop off a note at John's house, but instead...

"Instead John Hunter thinks you pass the time by peeking in his windows at night and Kiki's convinced you're out to steal her boyfriend. Nice job, Trenton," she muttered. "Why make things easy for yourself?"

Lee shook her head and dragged herself up the stairs. "And what's with all the drama? Why do I care who John Hunter's with? I'll be out of here in two weeks' time and probably never see him again, just like before."

But as she peeled off her clothes and flung herself in bed, Lee couldn't help but wonder what John Hunter and Kiki were doing at that exact moment.

After watching the drama at John Hunter's house, I follow Caralee home.

I kept hoping with John Hunter going away to Ashville for his doctorate work that Kiki would give up and find somebody else to hitch her wagon to. Bobby and I both knew Kiki was wrong for John. She'd railroad all over his gentle personality until he was a shell of a human being. I told him so more than once toward the end. That's one of the nice things about growing old: you can boss people around all you want and usually folks are too respectful to disagree to your face.

When I'd tell him Kiki wasn't right for him, polite boy that he is, John Hunter nodded and smiled and thank-you-ma'amed me.

Then he went off and did exactly what he wanted. Just like a man.

But here's the truth of it: Kiki McGraw is meaner than a sack full of rattlesnakes when she wants to be. And now Caralee has gone and gotten herself stuck in Kiki's crosshairs.

I watch as Caralee flings herself into bed rubbing at her forehead the way she used to when she was little and a migraine was coming on.

"Oh, baby girl." I sit next to her. "That silly Kiki isn't worth all this. And neither is John if he thinks she is." I stroke her head, which I know is pointless, but like last time at least it makes me feel better.

Maybe I imagine it, but it seems to help Lee too. I notice her forehead, her shoulders relax and finally she falls asleep. I lean down to give her a kiss before I head downstairs. Then I get a flash, sort of like the old days when you were searching for a channel on the television and you'd get that brief picture before it turned back to black and white snow.

There's an image of Lee on the edge of a lake, the wind blowing something fierce. And then it's gone. I sit there and puzzle over what just happened. I reach over to brush her hair off her forehead and it happens again. Another image, only this time Lee's swimming in the lake, fighting huge waves, and a hand reaches out to save her.

Next, I see a man holding Lee in his arms and stroking her damp hair while she cries. Then the image disappears into a vague grayish fog. I wait a few minutes but nothing changes.

I sit there most of the night considering this interesting turn of events. Was that Lee's dream? If I can see into her dreams, could I see anyone else's? Or even talk to her through them? Maybe I'm not so useless after all.

CHAPTER FIFTEEN

Lee woke up the next morning with a start. She looked over at the clock; it was only 6:30. Sleeping in for three days had been a luxury, one her body had evidently decided she'd had enough of.

She studied the ceiling above her with a sleep muddled brain, and tried to understand the sick feeling that danced through her stomach. What was the matter? And then it came back like a shot: Kiki. John Hunter's front yard. Lee pulled a pillow over her head.

Again and again, she pictured John coming out of the house and finding her crouched on the ground. And then Kiki. The only way she could have been more obvious in her possession of John Hunter was if she had peed all around him.

And then, the most troubling part: why did she care so much?

Lee leapt out of bed and looked around for something to distract her. Her eyes landed on her half-unpacked suitcase on the floor. Running shoes peeked out from under a pair of jeans.

Running. No wonder her thoughts were in such a jumble. She hadn't worked out once since she'd arrived at

Nana's. Running, climbing, hiking, whatever; Lee knew the radio head in her mind only ever quieted when she was doing something physical. As if the shoes weren't temptation enough, a delicious soft breeze danced through the open window and she knew it was still cool enough to take Charlie with her.

Remembering the walking trails that crisscrossed the campus, Lee decided to head in the direction of the university. She looked toward John Hunter's house as she ran past, checking if Kiki's sports car was still parked out front. It wasn't.

A surge of adrenaline filled her. "Come on, Charlie, let's really run." The dog needed no urging and the two of them took off down the deserted street.

An hour and a half later, a Piggly Wiggly grocery bag slung over her shoulder, Lee and Charlie returned to find John Hunter sitting on Nana's front steps.

"Where've you been?" He stood.

"Running. Shopping for food." Lee opened the front door and John followed her in. Silently, he watched Lee put away her groceries and she felt her post-run high recede. "What are you doing here, John?"

"I got here at 7:30 to start work. I thought you and your daddy wanted me to start ASAP. At least that's what your note said."

"Oh, so the note *did* exist." Lee turned and leaned on the counter. "Guess that shoots down your Peeping Tom theory."

"Who's to say you didn't try to kill two birds with one

stone?"

"So I'm assuming no apology then?" She filled Charlie's water bowl and set it in front of the panting dog.

"You know me well." John smiled.

Lee studied him for a moment. "Seems like Kiki knows you pretty well too, or at least thinks she does."

"Well, we've been together off and on for a few years now." John crossed his arms. "She's very loyal."

Lee took a large gulp of water. "Loyal, huh?" That wasn't the word she would have used to describe Kiki. "How'd your date go?"

"Just fine," John said. "But enough about that. Why don't you let me show you what we'll be starting on today out in the yard?"

For the next half hour John Hunter slipped into his role of experienced landscaper and Lee felt relieved. The drama from last night had no place in her plans for today. There was too much that she needed to get done.

"Sounds good," Lee said when John had finished. "I'll leave you to it."

"And what is it that you're going to be doing today?" John pulled a rubber band over his papers. "Sorting through Nana's things?"

"Yeah, in a little bit. But I'm feeling a bit stir crazy after spending all that time in the car and Nana's house. I thought I might do a few outside projects myself before I start on the inside."

"I think my team and I have most of the outside stuff handled. What exactly were you thinking of?"

"Do you see all that debris up on the roof and in the gutters?" She pointed above them to the branch-strewn roof. "I thought I'd climb up there, just for fun, and see if I could knock most of it down. According to Granny Bob, Nana re-roofed the house in the last few years. I think it might be passable for potential buyers if we get it cleaned up."

"That's pretty dangerous, Lee," John said as he studied the steep pitch of Nana's roof. "Why don't you hire someone to do that for you. I'm sure it wouldn't cost more than a couple hundred dollars."

"Who would I hire to do that kind of thing?"

"Well, I don't know. Nana's handyman? Maybe you could pay the painters extra to do it? I could contact my contractor friend for a suggestion."

"The painters will have their hands full with their work. I'm sure they wouldn't appreciate me tacking on an odd job," Lee said. "And I would like to get that roof cleaned off before you and your team get the yard redone. I don't want to dump a bunch of old, rotten leaves all over your pretty flowers."

"How on earth are you even gonna get up there? Do you have any idea just how steep and slippery that roof is? Can you imagine what would happen if you fell?" John's voice grew tighter with each question.

"Gosh, I guess it could hurt real bad." Lee nodded. "Maybe you're right."

"Well, yes, I think so," John said, letting out a deep breath. "I know it's easy to look at a project like that and think you can do it yourself to save money, but sometimes it's best to leave it to the professionals. They know what they're doing."

"Right," Lee agreed. "Well, I'll let you get to your work and I'll start looking for that professional you mentioned."

"Great," John said. "See you in a bit."

"Yes, you will." Lee spoke after John had disappeared around the side of the house.

A short while later, amidst the whine and growl of the two Bobcats attacking Nana's jungle, Lee pulled out her climbing duffle she always kept in the back of her Jeep and carried it to the deck. She laid her supplies on Nana's large wrought iron table, organizing her gear as she would before a climb. After that, she walked away from the house so she could study the roof once more.

"This shouldn't be too hard," she said to Charlie as he pranced around her in circles. "I think I can go up one of those maples and secure myself to the brick chimney. I'll attach a push broom to a rope and pull it up when I get to the top. At least I could get most of the larger junk off the roof and out of the gutters."

Charlie gave an excited howl and Lee turned to him. "No mountain adventures for you today, mister." Charlie's tail froze in place and Lee's heart melted at the show of disappointment that followed. Charlie slunk away from her as if he'd been beaten, then flopped down in the shade of a holly bush with a moan.

"I know you miss our climbs, but there's no way you can follow me up the roof." Charlie turned away from her and crawled further under the bush.

"You go ahead and pout. I'll catch up with you later." Lee chuckled then went in search of a broom. She found one in the old garden shed and tied it to a length of rope attached to the side of her climbing belt. Although she'd scrambled up and down these trees barefoot as a child, Lee didn't think her feet were tough enough to handle that punishment now, so she pulled on her climbing shoes. Cleaning the roof barefoot didn't sound safe either.

Approaching the tree, she stretched out her arms and shoulders. A smile curved her lips as she gently brushed the tree trunk with her fingertips. For all her hours spent ascending cliffs and boulders, she couldn't remember the last time she'd climbed a simple tree.

Lee had been introduced to climbing at a summer camp when she was 14 and had fallen instantly in love. Taking her meager babysitting funds, she joined a climbing gym, which she visited with religious fervor. After that, she joined a climbing group and spent her weekends tackling the mountains around her childhood home. Soon the hobby became an addiction. Just a few years later, Lee enrolled in a professional climbing institute where she meticulously worked toward and passed various levels of certification.

She grabbed at a low branch above her and began to work her way steadily up the tree. When she was about halfway to the roof, Lee balanced on a toe hold and turned to take in Nana's yard below her. She saw John Hunter and his team gathered at the foot of the tree, surveying her progress with various degrees of alarm.

"Hey!" she called down. "Nice day for a climb, isn't it?"

"What in the Sam Hill are you doing?" John's voice bellowed up through the branches. "I thought we agreed this was too dangerous!"

"No, we agreed that I needed to get a professional." Lee turned and started climbing again.

"Well, why didn't you?" John's voice sounded panicky now.

"Maybe you've forgotten what it is I do?"

"Take people on hikes?"

"I'm a professional climbing guide," she hollered over her shoulder. "I've made over 400 ascents and I'm on my 35th Fourteener." Grabbing a branch above her head she made her way, tightrope fashion, across the large branch beneath her feet.

"I have no idea what you're saying," John called from directly below her. He mirrored her progress in the tree with jittery steps on the ground.

"I'm saying I know what I'm doing," she murmured as she gauged the distance to the roof. The shingles looked slick, so to be safe, she secured a rope through her harness to the branch above her. Then, hand over hand, she swung toward the roof. Lee tested the shingles with her foot before allowing the full weight of her body to rest on them. Crouched near the rain gutter, she pulled the rope back in, so she could tie it to the chimney.

Conversation from below floated toward her, and she

peeked over the edge. Most of the workers were heading back toward their equipment, but she spied John leaning against the side of the house.

"Hey, down there," she called to him while pulling up the broom. "Are you going to make it?"

John looked at her, his face unreadable in the glare of the sun. "I guess it does look like you know what you're doing but be real careful, you hear?"

When its handle came over the ridge of the gutter, Lee grabbed the broom and stood up straight. "I never take any unnecessary risks, John."

"Sugar, you already did. There's a painter's ladder in my truck. You coulda just climbed up that and saved me the heart attack."

"Now where would be the fun in that?" She winked at him and disappeared over the edge of the roof.

Later, Lee rappelled down the tree and packed up her gear on the deck where John Hunter sat with a bag of chips and a bottle of water.

"You sure got a lot of stuff there." John motioned to Lee's duffle. "You really like to climb, don't you?"

"I love it. I'd do it every day if I could."

"Sounds like you do it often enough with all those titles you were hollering at me from the tree."

"It's less than I'd like, though, with all the responsibilities of running the business. We get more clients every year." She sighed. "When I climb with them I have to teach them what to do, watch to make sure they're safe. It's not like I get to enjoy and focus on climbing for myself."

"And I guess you can't do it in the winter, right?"

"Depends how much snow we get, but if there's too much snow you can always go ice climbing. I love that too."

"Ice climbing? What the heck is that?"

"It's like rock climbing, but done on ice, and the gear's a bit more dangerous to handle. The courses where I live are usually man-made, but the idea is like a frozen waterfall or glacier. The ice climbing capital of the United States is just down the road from me in Ouray."

"No kidding?"

Lee grabbed a water bottle from the kitchen and settled into a chair next to John. "They hold competitions there every year and it's one of the most beautiful places I've ever been."

She continued on, rambling about the little mountain towns and the competitions she so loved. After a while, Lee glanced over and saw John observing her from half closed eyes.

"Sorry, I kind of turned into a Colorado Bureau of Tourism ad."

John continued to study her. "It must be killing you to be here."

"What do you mean?"

"I guess I didn't realize you had stayed such a free spirit, even as an adult. Sorting through boxes and jewelry and clothes, as much as you loved your Nana, is probably driving you crazy."

Lee studied the sky above her. "A little. All of this brings back some very sweet memories, but some of them break my heart." She felt tears prick her eyelids and tried to blink them away.

"It's hard for me too, Lee. Every time I have a new idea for Nana's yard, my first inclination is to find her and tell her." John shook his head. "But then I remember, she's gone and it rips me up inside all over again."

The two sat in a mournful silence.

"That's why I went up on the roof today," Lee admitted. "I climb when I'm stressed or sad, but I don't have a lot of access to that particular coping mechanism here."

John stood and squeezed her shoulder. "Well now, next time it gets hard, I've got a big old oak tree in my backyard. Now that I've seen you in action, you're welcome to come climb up on my roof any time." He gave her a smile before bending to scratch Charlie's ear. "I'll catch up with you two later. Back to work for me."

Lee nodded and watched until his long, lean form disappeared around the corner.

CHAPTER SIXTEEN

It gives me a strange feeling to watch two people I care about so deeply mourn my passing while I sit a gnat's breath from them. On the one hand, it's nice to be missed, but on the other, I feel so sad for the two of them that I wish I could holler, "I'm right here!"

When John goes back to work, I look over at my granddaughter and chuckle. She's such a little daredevil. If I hadn't had one already, the sight of her climbing around on my roof would have given me a heart attack.

And poor John Hunter, I swear that boy nearly fainted when he caught sight of that girl halfway up the tree. He looked almost ill when Lee was telling him some of her more daring climbing stories. But I can tell he admires her spunk.

Climbing. That reminds me...then suddenly, I'm sucked into another memory. Once again, it's so vivid, I can't tell if I'm actually reliving it or not.

It was around 11:00 at night and I knew I was in a heap of trouble. I shouldn't have stayed out late dancing, but I just felt so bad for the soldiers at the USO dance. It was their last night on leave and I could never shake the feeling that it might be their last dance ever before they were shipped off to face the Germans or the Japanese.

My friend Janette and I jitterbugged and Lindy Hopped until we could barely feel our feet and the soldiers had to get back to base.

"Look at the time, Kathryn," Janette said when we told the boys goodnight. I glanced at her watch and felt sick.

"Can I spend the night at your house again?" I asked. The YWCA where I lived locked its doors at 10:00 pm, no exceptions. If you were late, you'd best not bang on the door after curfew—that's how you got expelled.

"No, my mother'll kill me if you do," Janette told me. "You know she put her foot down the last time we stayed out late."

Janette walked me to the YWCA and then trotted off in the direction of her apartment on the lower East Side. I looked up to my corner room on the third floor. "Guess I'll just have to climb up."

I pulled off my shoes and stockings and shoved them into my purse. Then I yanked my skirt up from behind and tucked it into my waistband. The drainpipe along the edge of the building seemed sturdy enough when I yanked on it. There was a lot of little ledges along the side of the building I could balance on as I pulled myself up the pipe. It wasn't much different than climbing a tree, something I always excelled at.

I was halfway up to my room when my foot slipped on a bit of loose brick that tumbled to the ground with a loud clatter. As I grabbed wildly at the drainpipe, one of the straps of my purse came loose and my shoes and brand new silk stockings fell to the ground.

"Dadgum it!" I muttered under my breath. Stockings were nearly impossible to find then; I only got that pair because of Professor Conti at the university. He told us students he had connections it was best we didn't know about.

I scrambled up the last few feet to the ledge outside my window and pulled it open. After I flung one of my legs over the windowsill, I looked down toward the street, expecting to see my shoes and stockings scattered about on the sidewalk below.

Instead I saw, illuminated in the nearby street lamp, a tall, dark-haired man grinning up at my window.

"Hello there," he called softly. "I think you dropped a few things on your way up." He waved my stocking in the air.

"Stop it," I hissed down at him. "Those are just about priceless, you know."

"I'd say the legs they cover are what's priceless," he said, eyeing my bare leg hanging over the window ledge.

I whipped it inside the room and leaned back over the sill. "You should be ashamed of yourself. You leave my things alone!"

"Well, if they're as valuable as you say they are, I'd be a fool not to go try and sell them at the pawn shop."

"You'd better leave those shoes and stockings by the front door, or else I'll call the police."

"While I'm sure they'd enjoy that, I think I'd rather take my chances with you."

"What do you mean?"

"Let me take you out to dinner tomorrow night and I'll give you back the shoes and stockings undamaged and free of charge."

"Why thank you, kind sir, for extending me the courtesy of returning my own things free of charge."

"Take it or leave it."

"Fine," I said. "Meet me outside tomorrow at five. And those stockings better not have any runs."

"Scout's honor." He saluted me and sauntered down the street chuckling.

Oh Lordy, what have I gotten myself into this time?

CHAPTER SEVENTEEN

After Lee returned her climbing gear to the Jeep, she decided she had just enough time to hop into the shower and get cleaned up before the furniture assessor came by to look through Nana's things. She was just running a brush through her damp hair when she heard voices from downstairs.

"Lee," John Hunter's voice echoed from below, "Sarah Beth is here, so I brought her on inside. I have to get back to work."

"Thanks," Lee called. "I'll be down in a minute."

As Lee came down the stairs, she could see Sarah Beth in the living room running her hand over the back of Nana's couch. The older woman turned at the creak of Lee's footsteps, and ignoring her outstretched hand, pulled Lee into a tight bear hug.

"Bless your heart. It's so good to see you again, but I'm sorry it has to be under these circumstances." Sarah Beth stood back and studied Lee's face. "You're the spitting image of Kathryn when she was your age. I'm sure you don't remember me, but I met you once at church. I helped out in the Sunday school a few times when your family was visiting."

It was a strange feeling to have everyone remember her while Lee struggled to recognize anyone outside of Granny Bob. It was especially strange since Sarah Beth certainly didn't seem like the kind of person to fade into the background. Lee struggled to maintain eye contact as Sarah's almost fluorescent red hair and pink suit kept intruding into her peripheral vision. She wondered if Sarah's heels matched the rest of her ensemble. She hazarded a quick glance. Fuchsia.

Sarah Beth grabbed Lee's hand and tugged her into the living room. "Well, honey, I have to tell you that as a frequent attendee of your grandmother's parties, I've been eyeing most of this furniture since she bought it. Like this Chippendale sofa. It's a gorgeous piece and a real find. They haven't made these since the late 1800s.

"Nana's things are beautiful, but I wasn't sure if you'd be interested in them or if I should just take them to the secondhand shop."

"Oh my, no." Sarah shook her head violently. "You mustn't, honey. Most of Nana's things are much too valuable."

"I wasn't sure. So, for example, how much would this be worth, do you think?" Lee asked, her hands resting on the back of the blue silk couch."

"In its condition? Somewhere upwards of $15,000."

"Are you serious?" Lee thought of her IKEA and warehouse knockoffs. Nana's couch was probably worth more than all the furniture in Lee's entire home.

"Your grandmother certainly knew how to find

treasures." Sarah Beth moved over to the piano and knelt down to inspect the keys. "I was one of the first people she'd call up when she discovered something like this. No matter how hard I tried, I could never find the bargains and deals she did." Her voice cracked as she reached into her purse for a tissue. "Excuse me, honey. I just miss her dearly."

"I'll get you a glass of water," Lee said. "Or tea if you like."

"Tea would be wonderful, thank you," Sarah said as she excused herself to the bathroom.

For the next hour Sarah Beth moved from room to room, taking extensive notes and pictures, while Lee followed along in stunned silence. She knew Nana had loved quality, but it was beginning to dawn on her that Nana's attitude toward furniture was something Lee couldn't even imagine.

"I'll need to go do some research, but I can probably get back to you in the next few days about what we'd like to take," Sarah Beth told her as they walked to the front door. "Offhand let me say that I'd love to sell most of her furniture on consignment or offer them to my contacts at other antique stores in the area."

"Granny Bob said I could trust you, so I'll leave it in your hands. I couldn't begin to judge the value of all of Nana's things, so I appreciate that you can. They should go to people who recognize their value."

"Professionally, I agree," Sarah Beth said, "but, honey, it's going to be real hard to see your Nana's furniture leave this house. These things were a part of her. I'm not speaking as an antique dealer now; I'm speaking as Kathryn's friend. Are you sure you want to let all of this go?"

"I am keeping a few odds and ends. You saw my stash in Nana's room."

"Yes, I did, but I want you to promise me you'll think long and hard about the pieces I've told you I'd like to have. Once they're gone, they're gone for good." Sarah Beth squeezed Lee's hand before she fished a pair of cat-eye sunglasses out of her purse. "I couldn't hardly live with myself if I thought I'd caused Kathryn's granddaughter a moment's regret."

The two women said their good-byes and Lee pondered Sarah Beth's words as she watched the brightly clad woman click down the walk in her fuchsia heels. Pausing in front of the living room and dining room thresholds, Lee imagined this home empty of Nana's belongings. As she checked off another job from her list, Lee realized more and more bits of her grandmother's existence were vanishing.

The loud whine of a chainsaw and Charlie's yip of outrage jerked Lee out of her reverie. She walked into the kitchen and saw through the back window that John's crew was beginning to cut down some of the overgrown trees and saplings that had invaded the yard. Charlie, who had been relegated to his crate for safety's sake, gave an anxious howl.

Lee opened the door and let him out, but Charlie

huddled around her legs.

"I've got to go to the Realtor's now." Lee clasped his shaggy face between her two hands and stroked his nose. "It's not safe for you outside, but it looks like you're not too happy with all the noise even from in here. Let's swing by Granny Bob's and see if she can take care of you while I'm gone."

The older woman was home and more than happy to watch Charlie. Lee gave them both a hug and sped off to the Realtor's office while dialing her father's number.

"Lee, I was hoping to hear from you." Her father's voice answered after the second ring. "So what's the status on your grandma's house?"

"Um..." Lee pictured the yard as she had left it, looking like the muddy abode of several large and industrious gophers. "Well, like I said, the inside isn't too bad. The outside's pretty overgrown."

"Did you decide to hire John Hunter?"

"Yes, he's working on it now."

"Do you feel comfortable with that?"

Again, that word *comfortable*. What was her father getting at? Could he know? No, she'd never told a soul about that last night up in the tree house. Lee cleared her throat. "Both he and Granny Bob have been incredibly helpful. I would be lost without the two of them. They're even feeding me at night."

"Good. Granny Bob always was a saint. But I cannot picture that scrawny kid running a landscaping business. How old is John Hunter now?"

He's certainly not scrawny anymore. John's lean, tall form popped into her mind. She tried to force the image away. "He's three years older than me, so that would make him around 36, 37."

"Does he seem like he's grown up? Become a trustworthy man?" her father asked.

"I guess so. He's writing his doctoral dissertation right now. And he owns a house around the corner from Nana's."

"Huh," her father said. "Well, his dad was a miscreant, but I guess John had a sincere heart, when he was a kid anyway. I always hoped he wouldn't turn out like his father."

"Granny Bob wouldn't have let that happen." Lee smiled.

"Granny Bob," her father chuckled. "Tell her I said hello. She did an amazing job with Tammy and John."

"I thought he and his gang of boys annoyed you."

"Of course they annoyed me. They were loud and crazy. I was already stressed out visiting your Nana's house and then they'd come banging through her home like a herd of buffalo."

"Why'd Nana's house stress you out?" Lee asked, pulling into the parking lot of the Realtor's office.

Her question was met with silence and a cleared throat. Finally, "Never mind. I'm feeling a little out of the loop here. Make sure to keep me informed about your progress."

Annoyance prickled in Lee's stomach. "I've been

pretty busy since I got here, Dad. I haven't had a whole lot of time for long, newsy emails."

"I'm not asking for *long, newsy emails*, Lee. Just updates what you're doing."

Lee clenched the steering wheel in front of her. "Look, you're the one who sent me here alone to take care of all of this. Please don't micromanage me. I'll take care of the insignificant details and keep you in the loop with the bigger ones."

"Fine."

His annoyance radiated from the phone, but at least he wasn't yelling at her.

"I'm going to have to go. I'm at the Realtor's office and—"

"Don't sign anything until I've had a chance to see it. Email or fax me any documents you get."

"I will."

"Bye. Love you, Lee." The call ended.

"Love you too." Lee spoke into the silence of the parked car.

CHAPTER EIGHTEEN

Two hours later, Lee pulled back up in front of Granny Bob's house, but she made no move to leave the car. Massaging her pounding temples, Lee leaned her head back against her seat and let out a soft groan.

The time at the Realtor's office had been draining and depressing. LaTanya was nice enough, another acquaintance of Nana's who claimed to have met Lee in her childhood. The appointment, however, had only reinforced the nagging feeling that the more she dissolved Nana's estate, the more her grandmother was disappearing.

The Realtor talked about changes that could be made on the inside of Nana's to accommodate a sorority, having had the same thought as Granny Bob about the stately home. As she described how easy it would be to *smash out a wall here or add a few bedrooms there*, Lee's stomach filled with dread and an image of an outraged Nana flitted into her mind.

"Nana, I'm so sorry about all this. I mean, John Hunter fixing up the outside of your home is one thing, but all these other changes." Lee pictured Nana's furniture decamping to glamorous antique markets and the house filling with blond Greeks who would paint the walls disturbing shades of pink and purple.

"I don't know what else to do, though." Anxiety built in Lee's chest. "It's not as if I can move in myself and keep everything the same. I can't afford to live in your house or keep it like a shrine either."

She startled at the tap on her window and turned to see Granny Bob outside. Lee hurriedly wiped at her cheeks, grabbed her keys and exited the car.

"I saw you sitting out here and I wondered if everything was okay?" Granny Bob laced her arm around Lee's back and led her toward the front door.

"No I don't think it is. I just...I can't—" Lee's voice broke and Granny Bob pulled her into a tight hug.

"It's all right, sweetie, you just let go. You've been so brave since you got here, but those tears need to get on out." She rubbed Lee's back and shushed her in a way that only made Lee's tears come harder and faster. It had been a long time, longer than she could remember, since anyone had hugged or shushed her.

Granny Bob pulled Lee into the house and settled her on the couch. She kept her arm around Lee's shoulders until her tears finally slowed. Charlie wandered in from another room and rested his head on her knee.

"Now tell me what all this is about. Did something happen at the Realtor's?"

"No, not really," Lee answered wiping at her eyes, "but as I see everything changing, I'm only now realizing that Nana's really gone and that things are never going to be the same."

Granny Bob sighed. "You're right. Things aren't gonna be the same without Kathryn around. And that's something that bites me in the butt every morning when I wake up." Lee choked out a laugh and looked up into Granny Bob's sad, smiling eyes.

"The thing is, sugar, nothing ever stays the same. Life's always changing no matter how much we wish it could stay safe and familiar."

Lee sat silently and tried to absorb this truth. "You're right, of course. It's just Nana loved her beautiful home so much and I hate disturbing what took her years and years to collect. And it's probably stupid, but I worry that she'd be mad if she knew what I was doing. How I'm changing everything."

"Well, I won't argue with that. She'd probably have an opinion about all this. And it might not be one you'd want to hear." Granny Bob turned to Lee and tucked a strand of her dark hair behind her ear. "But at the end of the day, Kathryn used all her beautiful things as a substitute."

"What do you mean?" Lee asked. "A substitute for what?"

"Well, now, maybe I shouldn't have said anything."

"You have to tell me what you mean," Lee insisted.

Granny Bob stared at her hands for a moment before standing. "Honey, you know I'm a good Southern Baptist, right?"

"Of course I do," Lee answered without thinking. Granny Bob was always helping a needy soul, or taking dinner to a new mother down the street or knitting hats for the babies at the hospital or a hundred other little acts of love. Plus, Lee very clearly remembered from slumber parties at Granny Bob's that Sundays were for church and Sunday dinner and not a whole lot else.

"Well, this isn't something I'd want spread about, it just being three in the afternoon, but I'm in the mood for something a little stronger than sweet tea," Granny Bob said, then walked into the kitchen. "I'm gonna mix us up a pitcher of Southern Comfort slush."

"What on God's green earth is going on in here?"

Lee stopped dancing and looked up. "John Hunter! Did you know your grandma was the 1943 Saskwa County Charleston Champion? We've been having so much fun."

"I think you two ladies might be having a little *too* much fun. I could hear this music from halfway down the block." He picked up the pitcher on the coffee table and took a sip. "Southern Comfort slushes, Granny? Shame, shame, you two. It's a weekday." John walked over to turn down the blaring big band music and Lee and Granny Bob collapsed onto the couch in laughter.

"You've turned into such a spoilsport, John Hunter," Granny Bob said, wiping away tears of laughter. "I seem to remember you having some fun of your own on weekdays not too many years ago."

Granny Bob turned and whispered something in Lee's ear. The two burst again into giggles.

John rolled his eyes and walked into the kitchen. "I

think something's burning in here," he hollered.

"Uh-oh." Granny Bob's hand flew up to her face. "I forgot all about the—"

John sauntered back into the living room holding a black smoking mess between two oven mitts. "Anyone for pot roast?"

"Noooooo," Granny Bob wailed and leapt unsteadily off the couch. "I worked on that all morning!" She raced into the kitchen followed by John. Lee flinched at the sound of clattering pots and pans. Wails of disappointment soon followed.

"Well, I guess you're not getting your sit-down dinner tonight," John Hunter said when he returned, this time without the scorched pot roast. "But then, you can't complain because you got to sample one of Granny's other specialties. And usually she's pretty secretive about this one." He took another sip from the pitcher.

"I have prayer group tonight!" came the older woman's shout.

"Granny, why don't you just go on to bed," John called over his shoulder. "I'll clean up the kitchen and call your prayer group. I'll tell them you're feeling a bit poorly." He turned to Lee and winked.

"Thank you, John Hunter, I do appreciate that." Granny Bob appeared from the kitchen and stood next to John with concentrated dignity. "I think I might go ahead and retire for the evening. Sorry about dinner, Caralee."

"Please don't worry about it." Lee wobbled to her feet and gave Granny Bob a hug. "The Charleston lessons more than made up for it. Thanks."

Granny Bob smiled and disappeared down the hall.

"Guess I'd better hit the road," Lee observed and tried, unsuccessfully, to clip Charlie's leash onto his collar. "Come on, boy. Stop wiggling around so much!" The dog eyed her ruefully from his still, prone position on the floor.

"Why don't you let me drive you back to your house?" John Hunter asked after a few more attempts to leash Charlie.

"I'm fine, John. I'm a big girl. I can take care of myself!" Lee finally clipped the dog's collar.

"Yes, you've made that more than clear, but I...I forgot my pruning shears at Nana's. I need to run back and get them anyway."

"Well, if you're already headed that way." Lee closed her eyes in an attempt to stop the room from spinning. "Granny Bob's slush kicks in even stronger the longer you wait."

"Yes, ma'am. They're lethal. That's why I steer clear of them, myself."

"But I only had a little bit!" Lee protested while John led her to his truck.

"It doesn't matter. A little bit is all it takes."

Minutes later they pulled into Nana's carport, and Lee focused all her energy on walking steadily to Nana's back door. John trailed behind, which irritated her. She was only a little bit tipsy and didn't need him to hover.

"Do you have anything for dinner tonight?" John asked.

"I'll just order a pizza or something." Lee struggled to insert the key in the lock.

"I thought you didn't eat cheese. Or meat."

"Fine, food police," she snapped. "I'll order a cheeseless, meatless pizza." She finally engaged the key and opened the door.

"Sounds tasty." John followed her into the house and released Charlie from his leash. "Nice to see you're an angry drunk. I woulda been so disappointed if you'd been a silly one."

"I am *not* drunk." Lee turned too quickly and had to catch herself against the counter top. "I'm just a little tipsy. It'll pass soon."

"Well, whatever you are, let's get you into the den." John gently pulled her by the arm, and after a moment's hesitation Lee allowed herself to be led.

"What did you and Granny talk about?" he asked as Lee teetered and the two sank into the couch.

"I can't quite remember. Granny Bob wanted to tell me about the old days when she and Nana were girls. I think it was hard for her." The room continued to spin and Lee let her head drop to John's shoulder. "They were like sisters, you know?"

"Yes, I do," came John's voice, and Lee realized his arm was around her shoulder. And that it had tightened.

"She said something else about someone named William. That he and Nana had been close. Maybe even *engaged* close. I...can't quite remember. Have you ever heard of—" She turned to find John's face inches from her own, his dark eyes studying her. The words on her lips fell away.

Frozen in intimacy for a moment, Lee felt a warm radiance fill her being. “This is nice,” she whispered. “I think I’ve missed you, John Hunter.”

She caught her breath as John leaned toward her. The heat of his strong arm around her shoulder urged her to melt into him. He paused, then blinked. Something like pain shot through his eyes and he looked away.

“I should probably get those pruning shears.”

“Yes, of course,” Lee said, embarrassment searing away all the other warring feelings inside her. She struggled to stand, banging her shin against the coffee table.

“Are you okay?” John Hunter leapt up and tried to steady her.

Lee shook him off. “Those drinks were evil! How could someone as innocent as your grandmother all but roofy me?” She tried to laugh, but found she couldn’t. “You go now. I’m sure you’re exhausted from your long day. And of course, you have Kiki.”

“What are you—”

“Thanks again, John, for all your hard work!” She stumbled to grab his hand and pulled him to the door. He needed to leave now. “I’ll see you bright and early in the morning.” Lee jerked the door open and practically shoved him out. “Bye now!” She registered a look of...was it pain? pity? on his face before she slammed the door.

Humiliation and resentment snaked their way through

her stomach and she sank to the floor. She was exhausted from stumbling through this minefield of dismantling Nana's possessions. And why did John Hunter have to be here—his presence so alternately comforting and disturbing? It felt like a cosmic comedy of errors. She buried her head in her arms and shuddered.

"I've worked so hard to make my life simple," Lee whispered when Charlie sat down next to her and licked her cheek. She allowed herself until the count of 50 to revel in her misery and then smacked the floor with her palm. "I'm not letting Eden Grove destroy that."

Bobby and her Southern Comfort slushes! I cannot believe she served my poor granddaughter one of those hideous concoctions.

The thing about Bobby is she seems so sweet and innocent, an act she's been perfecting since she was a child, with her church group and her charity work. But the truth is, Bobby can raise more Cain than the rest of us put together. I cannot count the number of times she's made those blamed drinks for some poor, unsuspecting soul and gotten them drunker than a skunk.

I wonder if Caralee will remember what she said about William. I shared the important details with Bobby when I moved back to Eden Grove, probably under the influence of one of her slushes, but I sure as heck didn't tell her everything. Still, I know she pieced together more than she let on. She was my best friend after all.

Speaking of William, I find myself slipping more and more into this memory world to be with him, something I didn't allow myself to do much when I was living. Like right now. I only have to close my eyes and then I'm meeting him in front of the YWCA the day after he caught my shoes and stockings.

"You're here!" he said when he spied me by the front door.

"Of course I am," I snapped. "I want my things back and you weren't gentleman enough to leave them for me."

"I'd have hated for them to get damaged or stolen," he said and passed me a brown paper bag. Inside were my shoes and neatly folded stockings. When I glanced up, I found his twinkling green eyes on my face.

"Well, thank you," I said, slightly less snappish. His eyes were pretty nice. "I suppose you want that dinner now?"

"Certainly," he said and took my arm. "It isn't every day I come upon a gorgeous woman scurrying up the side of a building. I thought for a minute that I'd stumbled upon a superhero and discovered a real scoop."

"Scoop?" I chuckled. It was hard to stay angry at him.

"Yeah, I'm a reporter for the Associated Press. Imagine my readers' delight if I'd have found a real, live superhero."

"Well, as much as I'd love to be your scoop, I hate to break it to you. I'm just boring old Kathryn Abney, a nobody from Mississippi."

He pulled me up short in front of a little Chinese restaurant. "I have to say, I'm not sure the facts support that theory, Miss Abney. I don't think boring nobodies climb up buildings in a single bound in the middle of the night with their dresses tucked up around their legs."

I felt myself blushing. "I didn't know anyone was watching."

"I believe I'll have to do a little more research on you, Miss Abney," he said. "I want to get to the bottom of this story."

"If you like," I said, my heart caught for a second in my chest. "I certainly don't want to stand in the way of a good story."

CHAPTER NINETEEN

The next morning Lee woke up with a dry mouth and pounding headache.

"What did Granny Bob put into those horrible drinks?" she rasped to Charlie as she stumbled down the dark stairway. Blinded by sunlight when she entered the kitchen, Lee staggered against the wall.

Seemingly oblivious to Lee's pain, Charlie walked to the back door and scratched it twice. He looked over his shoulder, his eyes glowing in the early morning light.

"Of course, you wouldn't have drunk three Southern Comfort slushes in a row," she said, opening the door to let him out. "I know you think I have no one but myself to blame."

Lee fished two aspirins out of her purse and downed them with a tall glass of water. By the time she had filled Charlie's water and food bowl, washed up a few dishes and wiped down the counters she was starting to feel almost normal again.

While Lee nibbled on a piece of toast and the pain of her hangover dissipated, embarrassment quickly took its place. She vaguely remembered snatches of her conversation with John, but could almost feel the warmth of his arm around her once more. At one point he'd seemed on the verge of kissing her, but then again, maybe she'd imagined it.

The doorbell rang, interrupting her looped mental rewind. Pulling her robe tight, Lee tried to smooth her bed-tousled hair. Through the window she spied Emma with little Davey on her hip.

"Hello there," Emma said when Lee opened the door. "I'm sorry to come over so early, but I just pulled some cinnamon rolls from the oven. Davey and I were wondering if you'd like to come over for a late breakfast." Emma's eyes scanned Lee's robe. "And coffee."

Lee's stomach growled. *Traitor.* Nice vegan she was. She imagined Emma's cinnamon rolls were probably dripping in butter and cream cheese. Her stomach growled again.

"Thank you, Emma. And of course you, Davey." She reached out and grabbed the little boy's outstretched hand. "I'd love to. Let me just go get changed and I'll be right over." She noticed John Hunter's crew beginning to pull up and asked, "Would it be all right if I brought Charlie with me? He'll probably tear up the house if I leave him here alone with all the noise from the landscapers."

"Sure," Emma said. "We've got an old mutt of our own who always loves a visit from a new friend."

Lee scurried to get dressed and freshened up. Fifteen minutes later, she and Charlie were on Emma's doorstep.

Emma ushered them into the house where they were greeted by Davey and Tiger. Tiger and Charlie quickly established a nose-sniffing, tail-wagging friendship and scampered off to the backyard while Emma led Lee into a kitchen so fragrantly delicious that Lee's hunger turned ravenous.

"I know I mentioned pie yesterday, but Davey and I were in the mood for something with cinnamon, weren't we, little man?"

"Mmmm, yes!" Davey answered, holding up his arms to be lifted into his high chair. "Cinnon holes are yummy."

Emma placed Davey in his seat and brought a large plate of cinnamon rolls dripping in creamy frosting over to the table. She served each of them one and then turned to Lee. "Do you like cream in your coffee?"

There's no going back now, Lee thought, remembering her rice milk at home. "Absolutely. And thank you, these look incredible."

It was hard for Lee not to join Davey in his noisy lip smacking and demands for more *cinnon holes*. Emma's pastries and coffee tasted like something out of a gourmet bakery.

"How do you not weigh 300 pounds, little Davey man?" Lee asked when the boy paused for a drink from his sippy cup. "With a mom who makes yummies like this?"

Emma chuckled. "I do have to cut him off after a while. He's got quite the sweet tooth." She studied Lee over the rim of her coffee cup. "You know who else loves my cinnamon rolls?"

"Who?" Lee asked, licking the frosting from her fork.

"John Hunter."

"Oh?" Lee said, looking up from her plate. "Does he come over often?"

"About once a week."

Lee studied Emma's hand. No wedding ring. "Are you two...?" Did this poor woman need to be warned about Kiki? Was John really that much of a lady's man?

"Lord, no!" Emma laughed. "John Hunter's a sweetheart and the eye candy of this town, but he's just like a brother to me. I'm married to Tom Peterson, did you ever meet him?"

"Maybe. I can't remember."

"He flies helicopters for the oil rigs on the Gulf Coast so he's gone for weeks at a time. He'll be home in a few days and you can meet him then. John Hunter stops in and checks up on Davey and me a coupla times a week." Emma pointed to her finger. "I don't have my wedding ring on at the moment because my hands are all swollen from the new baby."

"New baby?" Lee asked before understanding caught up with her question. "You're pregnant?"

"Yes, ma'am." Emma patted her stomach proudly. "Just about done with the first trimester, thank heavens. But back to John Hunter. He sure loves cinnamon rolls, pies and cookies. You know how to bake, Lee?" She smiled as Lee's face colored.

"No, not really. I mean, maybe. But why do you ask?"

"Oh, no reason," Emma said, helping herself to another bite. "No reason at all. It's just I couldn't help but notice some sparks flying between the two of you when we were congregating in front of the watermelon disaster."

Lee looked into Emma's knowing eyes. "Hmmm, I feel like you're hinting at something which I won't pretend to understand, but perhaps you've also met a certain someone named Kiki?"

Emma threw her fork on her empty plate, and Lee and Davey jumped in surprise. "Kiki McGraw is the biggest fool east of the Mississippi. Probably west of it too."

Davey swallowed his bite of food and shouted, "Fool, mama! Fool!"

The women burst into laughter.

"I can't say I've had the best first impression of her," Lee said. "I mean she all but scratched my eyes out the other night when she found John Hunter and me together on his front porch."

"More holes? More holes!" Davey banged his spoon on the highchair tray.

"No sir, young man. We don't bang on the tray like that, even if Mama just had her own little tantrum." Emma whisked the spoon and sippy cup away. "Now you need to go pick up those trains all over the floor in your room and put them in their bin. You promised Mama you'd help pick up your toys today."

Davy gave Lee a truly pathetic look and she felt her heart melt. Did he really need to go clean up?

"Don't let him fool you with those innocent little eyes of his," Emma said, pulling the toddler from the high chair and covering him with kisses. "He only has to clean up his trains; I think there's four of them."

Emma led Davey down the hall but returned quickly. "Now tell me all about your run-in with Kiki," she instructed after she filled their coffees again.

Lee glanced out the window. Should she make her excuses and run? It had been a long, long time since she'd delved into something like this with anyone other than Charlie. And Charlie's insights were fairly open to interpretation.

"Now you know I'm not just being nosy," Emma said. "The reason I ask is that barracuda somehow sunk her teeth into John when he moved back here and has held on for dear life ever since then. As I said, John Hunter's like a brother to me and I'd sure hate to see him end up with someone like her. But it looks more and more like that's just where they're headed."

"Well, I don't know how you see me fitting into all that," Lee answered. "I'm only here for another week or so."

"What I know is, you and John Hunter used to be real close. I know he'd probably listen to what you had to say, even if he won't listen to his other friends. Lord knows Tom and I have tried to talk some sense into him."

"I doubt anything I have to say would change John Hunter's mind. I was just a childhood friend. Besides, he and Kiki looked pretty comfortable together if you ask me."

"Hmm, well tell me about your run-in with Kiki anyway and let me be the judge," Emma ordered, serving

Lee another cinnamon roll.

Lee blinked at her plate. It would be nice to unload the story and Emma seemed like a sympathetic ear. In between bites, haltingly at first, she replayed the whole ridiculous incident.

"Ooh, it just makes me so mad the way she acts like she owns John Hunter." Emma collected the plates off the table and clattered them into the sink. "Do you know she had the audacity to stop by my house once and warn me not to, in her words, 'get too cozy with *her* John' or else?"

"What did you say?" Lee asked as she wiped the crumbs off the table.

"I told her that next time she came round my front porch she could expect either a dirty diaper or a slap in the face, and I couldn't make any promises as to which she'd get."

Lee doubled over laughing. "How'd that go over?"

"Don't know. I slammed the door, but she sure cuts me a wide swath when we pass each other at the Piggly Wiggly." Emma joined in with Lee's laughter.

"But seriously, I cannot imagine John Hunter chained to a human being like Kiki." Emma shook her head. "The nerve of that woman all but calling me an adulterous hussy to my face, when my husband specifically asked John Hunter to check up on Davey and me. When I told Tom, he was livid too. He actually confronted John about it."

"What did John say?"

"He made excuses for her, said she was just really

insecure. Because the head cheerleader and prom queen has every right to be writhing with insecurity, right?"

"But why do you think she's so possessive of John Hunter?" Lee asked.

"Honey, I think there's two types of females out there. The ones like you and me who see other women as their allies. Then there's the other type who see every other female as competition. And that's the sad truth." Emma started loading the dishwasher.

Lee considered her words. She felt a surge of warmth at being lumped into Emma's *ally camp*, a sense of belonging that warmed a forgotten part of her heart. But what about John Hunter? Family, friends and community seemed to be such a huge part of his life. How could he be with a woman, maybe even married to one, who viewed everyone as a potential threat to her control?

The whine of a Bobcat engine stirred Lee's thoughts and she checked her phone. "I guess I'd better get back to work. The furniture appraiser will arrive in half an hour to let me know what she's interested in."

"It's been so nice having you over," Emma said and pulled Lee into a warm hug. "You come on back over here real soon. And when Tom gets back I'd love to have you over for dinner so you can meet him too."

"I'd like that," Lee said. She collected Charlie and then Emma walked the two of them to the door. Davey scampered out of his room and gave Charlie a kiss on his nose.

"Thanks again, Emma," Lee said. "For everything. You

too, Davey."

"My pleasure," Emma called from the top of the porch where she and Davey waved good-bye. "And don't you worry none about Kiki. You just send her over to my house if you lock horns with her again."

"All right." Lee laughed, vividly picturing another run-in between Emma and Kiki. She certainly wouldn't want to miss that.

I'm so glad Emma invited Caralee over to visit. I get the feeling my granddaughter doesn't have a whole lot of friends other than her sister, and her ridiculous dog, of course. I watch over her shoulder when she's doing things on that fancy phone of hers, and I only ever see her emailing Jenny or the people that are running her business.

Work friends are all well and good, but they're not the kind of people you can pour your heart out to. And Jenny, why Jenny's a sweetheart, but she's getting ready to embark on the most exhausting journey there is: motherhood. I don't know that she's going to have a whole lot of time for her sister in the next year, especially if she has a fussy, colicky baby like many of us Abneys seem to be blessed with.

I wonder if part of Caralee's problem is that she had to grow up before her time, what with my sweet Cecilia dying so young and all. I guess that's why she always got along so well with John Hunter and his gang, them being a few years older. Plus, John Hunter was a pretty serious kid himself, after the stunt his daddy pulled when he was only seven years old. That man was always no-account, but running off on his young family like that, that took a special breed of cowardice.

I think that's why the two of them were always like two peas in a pod. When you find someone who understands you, who understands where you come from, it's a real treasure. You don't have to pretend with them because they already feel like a little slice of home.

William was like that. Even though he was from Maine, he felt like home to me. He was the first Yankee I met who didn't rush through things. Why, he didn't even kiss me until we'd been together for two months to the day.

To celebrate this little anniversary, he found a Cajun restaurant "to remind me of home," he said. I didn't have the heart to tell him that Cajun was a bit further south than I lived, and a whole lot more French. Still the gumbo was delicious and the band was hopping. We danced until the wee hours of the night. Then, exhausted, we bid the chef and his wife bonsoir.

I can still see us leaving the restaurant like it happened yesterday. My feet were so blistered from dancing that I took off my shoes and stockings as William and I walked the three blocks home to my apartment. Then the rain came, a warm spring rain. It fell in sheets, soaking our already sweat-dampened clothes.

William pulled me into an alcove, the entrance to a little bakery, covered by a tiny green and white striped awning. There was barely room for the two of us. He took off his coat and wrapped it around my shoulders, then pulled me close, enfolding us into a warm, dark cocoon that smelled of his aftershave.

I felt his muscles ripple beneath his thin damp shirt and knew he could feel me, the shuddery breaths I took as his closeness shattered the flirtatious wall I had so carefully kept between us.

"You're making my promise a little hard to keep, Kathryn," he whispered into my ear, nuzzling my cheek with his.

"Promise?" I gasped, barely able to speak.

"Yeah, I promised myself I wouldn't lose my head over you." He chuckled softly and tilted my chin with smooth fingers. "Too late for that now," he whispered as his lips met mine and the world around us melted into the gentle shimmer of rain.

If only things could have stayed that way forever, I think, as I follow Caralee back to my house. I want the memories to stop now, frozen forever in this first act of my story with William. But I know it's a foolish wish. They come hard and fast. Unlike my living years, I now have no way to control or stop them. Evidently, they must be relived.

CHAPTER TWENTY

"Any chance you could head over to my house for a bit?" John asked later that night after Lee had finished helping Granny Bob clean up her kitchen.

"Why?" Lee asked, annoyed at the way her heart raced. All day long her mind had involuntarily returned to the Southern Comfort debacle, trying to discern what did or didn't happen until Lee wished there was an off button she could push.

"I need you to look over a couple different options for Nana's yard. Normally, I wouldn't ask at this time of night, but I'm trying to get all this done as fast as I can. I don't want to waste any time tomorrow asking you questions about details."

Lee hesitated. She had no desire for another awkward, confusing night with John Hunter. All she wanted at this point was her bed and a good book.

"I meant to bring my plans here, but I worked so late I forgot."

"You must be exhausted," Granny Bob said, giving her grandson a hug. "You're burning your candle at both ends, aren't you?"

Guilt washed through Lee. John and his crew had

worked at Nana's all day and into the evening despite the sweltering heat. "No need to worry about the plans tonight, John. We can just talk about them tomorrow."

"Now, Bean Pole, it's no trouble. I'm gonna be up for hours longer anyway. I need to put in some time on my dissertation."

Granny Bob turned to Lee. "If he's determined, you might as well go with him."

Lee nodded and after hugging Granny Bob goodnight, followed John out the door.

"I can't believe you can work like that all day and then go write all night. How do you have the energy for that?"

"Lotsa coffee."

"Well, that's not good for you," Lee said as they walked down the street, cicadas beginning to take up their nightly chorus.

"Here comes the crazy, hippie propaganda. What should I be drinking? Some weird tofu and hemp oil smoothie?"

"No!" Lee laughed, and shoved his shoulder. It was too hard to keep a reserved distance from John. "That sounds disgusting!"

"Glad we agree on that." John gave her a gentle shove back. "I don't have to drink that much coffee, truth be told. I like my topic so much I get all riled up when I'm writing about it. Makes it hard to fall asleep, actually."

When they arrived, Lee paused in front of John Hunter's house. Her confrontation with Kiki battled against the wonder she felt once again as she gazed over the riot of flowers and shrubs that filled John's front yard.

"Everything all right?" John asked.

"Yes, your garden's just so lovely." Lee took a deep breath and followed John slowly up the path. Charlie had found too many good smells to move at anything faster than a crawl. Patience finally gone, she tugged the dog behind her and after a moment of balking he trotted along obediently.

When John Hunter opened the front door and flicked on the lights, Lee gasped in surprise.

"It's beautiful in here too!" she said.

John chuckled. "I appreciate the shock."

Lee gazed around the room in admiration. To her immediate left stood an antique dining room table strewn with papers, books, blueprints, a printer and laptop computer. Behind the table was a neat galley kitchen with beautiful knotty pine cabinets. To her right sprawled a cozy living room outfitted in comfortable-looking mission furniture that accented the exposed woodwork of the bungalow. The pale yellow walls made the room feel like it was suffused with warmth and light. On the walls were framed prints of old horticultural drawings and diagrams.

"Just give me a minute here to pull up the information on my computer. You and Charlie make yourself at home."

Charlie needed no second invitation. As soon as Lee let him off his leash, he trotted over to the rug under the coffee table and threw himself on the floor.

Lee nodded and walked over to the massive dining room table and studied the clutter on top of it. A few of the blueprints were, she could tell, of Nana's garden, but most of them were landscapes unfamiliar to her. Various textbooks on plants were stacked on top of each other, along with notebooks that looked to be filled with John Hunter's handwriting. She glanced over to John and did a double take. Bent over his computer, he'd put on a pair of wire frame glasses. Her heart did a strange little dance as she realized anew that the boy she'd grown up with was gone forever.

John, sensing her gaze, looked up. "What?"

"Oh, just your glasses." Lee averted her eyes. "Not used to seeing you in those."

"Yeah, I've had them for a coupla years now." He touched the frame. "Time waits for no man and the eyes are the first to go."

"You already look the part of the distinguished professor."

"Now I just need the diploma to match." John brushed his hair back and returned to the computer. The tick-tock of the grandfather clock in his living room and the clatter of computer keys were the only sound. "Just be another sec," John said as he clicked away at his computer.

"Take your time." Lee sat and, looking for something to occupy her hands, pulled the notebook in front of her close enough to read.

In Ozark culture, the rose was seen as both a benevolent and malevolent aid. Roses were given by young men to young single women as a sign of affection.

However, stray rose petals were considered bad luck, possibly because of the association with funeral rites for the deceased. Traditionally petals were sprinkled on and around the place where the deceased expired—e.g. bedroom, etc. Colors of affection: red, pink; colors of friendship: yellow; colors of death: white.

"I'm ready now, Lee, if you want to take a look."

"Thanks. This is fascinating. The part about the rose petals and the colors, where did you find this stuff?"

"Oh, from Miss Bess." John moved the laptop in front of Lee and sat down next to her. "She's this sweet old lady who still lives up in the Great Smoky Mountains in her family's original homestead. She knows more about plants and stories and traditions than most people will ever forget."

"How did you meet her?"

"Earlier this summer when I was hiking through the forests researching plants of the Smokies and the Appalachians, I found her homestead while exploring. She invited me in to sit a spell and served me some of her homebrewed rosehip tea. We got to talking and I realized I'd stumbled across a gold mine, so to speak."

"She sounds amazing."

"She is. She let me camp in my tent on her property for most of last month, while I picked her brain for facts about every plant I could find."

"For a month! What an experience. I'd love to do something like that." She traced one of John's drawings with her fingertips.

"Correct me if I'm wrong, but don't you *live* in the mountains? Why don't you?"

"It's like I told you with my climbing. These last few years I seem to spend most of my time running the business and tours. When I finish up, I'm usually ready to stumble back to the comforts of home. Still, I'd love to take a month off and get away from everything. In the middle of nowhere in my tent."

"It does sound like heaven," agreed John.

Lee glanced up and found his dark eyes studying her.

"Being away from civilization like that, it makes you realize what's really important." John spoke softly as his gaze traced the planes of her face. "It makes you take stock of your choices, where you're going. With life."

A rush of questions poured into her mind. She was working up the courage to ask one when John's phone beeped. He pulled it from his back pocket and frowned. Lee could see Kiki's name on the screen.

John stood then gestured to the computer. "Why don't you look through these plans? This program'll show you the different options and a breakdown of the cost. Read through those and tell me which one strikes your fancy. While you do that I need to make a quick phone call. You'll excuse me for a sec?"

John retreated onto the front porch and Lee studied the plans in front of her trying to decide if she liked the brick or paver pathways better. After a few minutes she became aware of John's rising voice. She tried not to hear his words, but the screen door opposite her made this impossible.

"Honey...honey. No, I know. I know. Yes, I know I said that and I'm sorry. But I'm meeting with a client right now, so I can't come over.

"Yes it is." He paused and then continued, his voice angry. "You're being ridiculous. No. She's a client."

"Well, that's your choice. I'm sorry you feel that way." Silence and then a soft groan.

Lee bit her lip and wondered if she should try to make a quick getaway. The screen door opened on protesting hinges and she turned her attention back to the computer.

"About done there?" John leaned down next to her.

"Um, if you need to go, I'll finish reading and write you a note with my answers. I can close up your house."

"No, no. I got nowhere to be but here. Now, do you have any questions?"

Lee studied his face. "Are you sure? That phone call?"

"I'm sure," he said, his voice almost sharp. "Now what do you think of those bricks?" He settled into the chair next to her again and pulled the computer between them. "I've worked with them before. At that big old two-story home next to the university? You know, the old president's mansion?"

"John, I'm not going to pretend I have any clue about what would look best," she said. "I think all your options are beautiful. But you're the expert here. Would you please just do what you like the most? I trust your opinion."

"Mmmm," John rubbed his stubbled chin. He took off his glasses and leaned back in his chair. "Not sure I feel comfortable with that."

"Why not?"

"What if something I choose is a little bit more expensive than another option? I could see that getting messy."

"No, John, that's not an issue. I said I trusted you."

"What about your daddy?" John asked after a pause. "Is he gonna understand? I don't want to get you in trouble with him. You might trust me, but that doesn't mean he does."

"I talked to him on the phone just yesterday and he was impressed by your proposal. And I vouched for you, so we should be good."

"Thanks." John chuckled. "I guess it's settled then, but I'm still running my ideas by you. And you feel free to say if you hate something, you hear?"

Lee nodded and glanced at the clock. It was only 8:45, but she'd promised herself a quiet, uncomplicated night with a good book. She studied the wave of John's hair as he saved the changes on his computer and knew it would probably be best to head home as quickly as possible.

"It's not too late. Charlie and I will take off so you can get back to your...to whatever you had going on tonight." Her cheeks began to burn as Kiki, the elephant in the room, all but trumpeted her presence. "Writing or, you know, meeting with someone."

"I rescheduled."

Lee looked up to where John was organizing his papers on the far side of the table. His dark eyes met hers for a moment and he gave her a half smile. Lee glanced at the clock once more and considered what to do.

CHAPTER TWENTY-ONE

"I should probably head out," Lee said, rising from the table. "Even if your...appointment canceled, I know you wanted to get some work done on your dissertation."

"Don't worry about it. I'm thinking I might just take the night off. Start the weekend off early, it being Thursday and all."

"Is it Thursday night?" Lee asked. "I hadn't realized. Without work, it's like the days all blur into one."

"Yeah, you've been here almost a week, working like crazy the whole time. Why don't you take a break and we can watch a movie?" John said. "Charlie looks comfortable." Both their gazes traveled to the dog sound asleep on the floor. "Fact is, he looks like he was shot."

"You don't mind?"

"Nah, it's gotta get lonely at that big house all by yourself. Besides, I bought a new movie and would appreciate the company while I watch it."

"What is it?" Lee asked even as a part of her still wondered if she should hurry up and leave. Her schedule for tomorrow was booked and she'd need a good eight hours of sleep to cope with the hectic day.

"Well, you're in luck." John walked over to the DVD

player of his large flatscreen TV. "It's a romantic comedy."

"Really?"

"'Course not, girl!" He handed her the case of a big-budget action movie. "I've been waiting for this one ever since it left the theater."

Lee laughed and plopped down on the couch. Ignoring all the *shoulds* that nagged at her mind, she propped her feet on the coffee table. "That sounds more like the John Hunter I grew up with."

"Yes, ma'am. Now I'm going to go grab me a beer. You want one? It's not a fancy pants microbrew like I'm sure you're used to, but—"

"That sounds great."

John returned right as the previews were finishing up with a bowl of popcorn and two frosty beers.

"Great minds think alike," Lee said as she took her beer. "Drinks, popcorn, and movie equal my and Charlie's night off." The dog, who, at the smell of popcorn had bolted up from his comatose position under the coffee table, placed a paw on her knee. Lee tossed him a handful, which Charlie snapped up in the blink of an eye.

"Sounds hot," John commented. "You must lead the party scene in Durango."

Lee threw a piece of popcorn at him, but a pang of agreement shot through her. Charlie really was her standing Friday night date.

As the martial arts action intensified and the beer kicked in, Lee lost what little interest she had in the movie. She glanced over at John Hunter and allowed herself to face the thought that had been dancing at the edges of her mind since she arrived. Right here, in this moment, she felt the simple contentment she'd always experienced when the two of them were together as children. Even though she'd blanched at his declaration on Nana's porch swing, she realized the same held true for her. John Hunter really had been her best friend and she'd missed him.

What if he lived in Durango instead of here? she wondered and her heart beat with excitement. Lee pictured showing him how to climb, the two of them hiking on her favorite trails or even going to the local festivals together. Then came the image of her house surrounded by several feet of snow with the two of them on the couch in front of a cozy fire, John's arm wrapped around her, and her head rested on his shoulder.

What are you thinking? she chided herself. *John Hunter's a grown man. He can't put his life or his career on hold to come play with you in the mountains.*

Then, the scene in the sycamore tree flashed into her mind and she tensed with the memory. The hurt and confusion were still there, along with the pain of betrayal, and that was something she couldn't forget. It still ached in her heart even with the numbing distance of time.

The innocent friendship they'd shared as children was a fairy tale, one she'd let herself be sucked back into this week, but no more. Thirty-something was pathetically old to believe in fairy tales. Any thought or wish that competed with this cold, hard fact needed to be silenced.

Weary with missing Nana and disappointed at silly dreams, she let her eyes close and fell asleep.

I may not be able to read minds, but I know what Caralee was thinking all the same. I saw her watching John Hunter instead of the movie and I'd have to be an idiot not to know what was going through her head. Which I'm not.

These two chickenhearts are letting something fragile slip through their fingers without even realizing it! Don't they understand that the chances don't keep coming? That to live a happily ever after you have to want and work at it something fierce?

This feels like a nightmare that I'm doomed to keep dreaming. I know the horrible ending that's coming but I have no power to stop it. How is it that Caralee seems to be repeating all the mistakes I made with William? Yes, we spent time together when she visited, but it's not as though she knew my story.

It reminds me of something I always used to hear at those big tent revival meetings my Granny used to take me to: the sins of the fathers will be passed on to their children. I never understood what that meant, but now I've got an inkling. Can't we learn from our ancestors' mistakes? Why must we replay them? Is it written in our DNA or the stars?

Oh, how I wish I could tell her my story now, or else I wish that Bobby would have gotten more of the details right!

But the devil is in those details and I can't forgive myself for that.

CHAPTER TWENTY-TWO

The movie finished in a culmination of martial arts grandeur that brought Lee back to a half-wakeful state. She felt something shift beneath her. Gradually, she realized that she was curled into a tight ball against John Hunter's side and that her head had dropped onto his chest. She felt his fingers gently moving through her loose hair and heard the steady thump of his heartbeat. The minutes ticked by on the old grandfather clock and John Hunter let out a deep sigh.

Finally, he moved again, brushing her shoulder with his warm, callus-roughened hand.

"Hey, sleepyhead." He softly shook her. "I think you might have missed that last fight scene. Want me to rewind it?"

"No thanks, I need to get going," Lee answered in a voice raspy with sleep. She felt John's arm briefly tighten then release her. Turning to thank him, her voice caught in her throat. She could read a question in his eyes, but it was one she didn't want to materialize.

Stumbling as she jumped to standing, Lee grabbed Charlie's leash. "I have an appointment first thing in the morning. Can't remember who, but I know there is one.

C'mon, boy," she ordered. "Time to get going."

"I'll walk you to your gate," John said with his back to her while he gathered their glasses and popcorn bowl. He moved toward the kitchen.

"No, John. I'm fine. You and Granny Bob don't seem to realize that I walk around on my own all the time in Durango."

"This isn't Durango, and I'm not in the habit of letting a young lady walk home at night by herself." He turned off the TV and held out his arm in an exaggerated gesture, the seriousness of the moment before gone like a puff of smoke.

"I said I'm fine." She gave Charlie another tug.

"I can either walk next to you or behind like a stalker." He flicked off the living room lights and made his way to the front door. "It's your choice."

"All right." Lee couldn't help but smile as she walked past him. "I say you follow me like a stalker."

"Stalker it is," John said, pausing on the porch steps. "Now you go on ahead about ten steps and I'll follow you."

"Would you just get up here?"

"Well, make up your mind." He jogged next to Lee at the front gate and grabbed her arm. Charlie frisked around them in excitement.

John continued his banter until they turned the corner. Both of them froze at the same instant.

"Another bridge collision?" Lee ventured after the space of a few seconds. Before them was a crumpled truck, bits of twisted metal and shattered glass and what appeared to be broken crates of canned vegetables strewn about the road. An ambulance and a police car's flashing lights illuminated the street. While an officer sat on the curb talking to the apparently uninjured driver, a small crowd of onlookers huddled around the edges.

"Looks like it," John said.

"But why didn't we hear it?"

"I think my surround sound was on so loud, it probably drowned out the crash."

"But I don't understand," Lee said. "How can there be *another* accident?"

"Don't you start with that again," John answered in a tight voice.

She grabbed at his shoulders. "Look at me. I am not being snobby about Eden Grove, but honestly don't you think it's *peculiar* that trucks keep running into this bridge?"

John just glared at her.

"How long has it been here?"

"Don't know. Maybe a hundred years."

Lee dropped her hands. "You have to admit it's a little...odd that people run into it with this much frequency," she almost pleaded.

John searched her eyes and a grudging smile broke onto his face. "Well, maybe it is a little funny."

"Thank you." Lee let out a deep breath.

"Funny to a pretentious Yankee."

"John Hunter!" she shrieked and punched him in the shoulder. Dissolving into laughter, John Hunter and Lee stopped when they noticed the emergency workers and onlookers glaring at them.

"Now you've gotten me in trouble with the authorities!" Lee leaned close to John as she tried to stifle her giggles.

"Well, I'm sure it's nothing you haven't dealt with before," John whispered into her ear. He wrapped his arm around her shoulder and gave her a quick squeeze. "Guess you'll be safe to make it home from here?"

"Yes."

"Better get on home and get some shut-eye."

She could feel the heat of his breath on her ear and closed her eyes.

"Night now." His voice trailed away from her. "See you in the morning."

Then he was gone.

"See you," she whispered after him before she turned and pulled Charlie down the can-littered street.

CHAPTER TWENTY-THREE

Instead of following Caralee home tonight, I decide to stay with John Hunter. He looks so lonesome and sad walking home after he dropped off Caralee and I can't bear for him to be alone. I know just how he feels and figure an invisible friend is better than no friend at all.

I follow him around his sweet little house as he turns off the lights and shuts the windows, sit on his bed while he undresses. Goodness me, I haven't seen me a chest like that in a month'a Sundays. Of course I look away real quick. Just wanted a peek to see what Caralee was missing.

When he lies down, I put my hand on his head, like I did on all mine and Bobby's children and grandchildren whenever they weren't feeling well. I wish I could stroke away the pain a little bit.

Then I realize I can see what he is thinking just like I could with Caralee, and he isn't even asleep. But then, John Hunter's always been a more open person than my granddaughter.

I see flashes of him when he was a boy and realize John Hunter's going down memory lane from back when Caralee and he were young. I shake my head over how crazy they were together. Bobby used to call me either laughing or crying about what those two got up to.

But when John starts remembering that last time Caralee came to visit, his heart beats with so much pain and regret that I almost pull away.

I remember that summer, the last that Caralee had one of her nice, long visits and the last before John moved away with his mother and sister to Baton Rouge. I knew something must have happened between the two of them, but Caralee never shared the details. Just closed it up in her vault, like always.

It seemed like she and John Hunter couldn't pick up where they'd left off. He was around 16 years old at the time and had turned surly and snappish. Poor tomboy Caralee was still a child at 13. She tried to tag along with John but it just wasn't the same. I heard him taunting her once on the porch, saying he "didn't have time for all her silly games" and "wasn't her babysitter."

I could tell it broke Caralee's heart. I admit wondering if Bobby and I should step in, try to help reconcile the two, but I always seemed too busy keeping Mark and Jenny out of trouble.

As I study the thoughts flitting through John's mind, the emotion I keep sensing is shame. Shame that his ugly words caused such pain for his good friend. Shame that he'd begun to notice Caralee's body and the soft curves that had developed on her once scrawny frame. Shame that suddenly his body was hollering at him to do things that he didn't even understand.

It all seems to lead down a dark tunnel of sadness to

one memory. A wound that he continues to replay, wishing that he could change how it ended.

We all have those memories.

From his bed, he lets out a deep sigh, and then I'm transported with him back to his 16-year-old self, hiding in a canopy of leaves in the lookout of the beautiful old sycamore in Bobby's backyard.

"John Hunter," Caralee's voice calls up from the bottom of the ladder. "Can I come say good-bye? We're leaving tomorrow."

I feel his heart sink with dread. He wishes he'd found a way to make up with her before she left, but now it's too late. She's leaving the next morning. Probably another 365 days until he sees her again. Caralee's visits are his favorite time of the whole year and he's ruined it.

There's a creak beneath him as she climbs the ladder. Desperation floods through him. He doesn't want to see that pleading look in her eyes, but a quick sweep of his surroundings shows him there's no chance for escape in his treetop perch.

"Hey." She crawls through the trapdoor and sits cross-legged in front of him. "We're leaving really early, so Dad said to say our good-byes tonight."

"Yeah." He studies the bits of broken twigs he's crushed between his fingers.

"I'm sad we didn't get to play together very much," she says with a catch in her voice. "Hopefully I act grown-up enough for you next time I come."

He grunts in response not wanting a next time in the

future, but wishing they could go backwards instead. Backwards to other visits that seemed as effortless as a summer breeze.

"Well, can I give you a good-bye hug?" she says, hesitantly.

"Guess so." His heart begins to race.

She stands and flings her arms around him with childish abandon, but John Hunter's response is the opposite. Her silky arms send explosions through his mind, his body. Overwhelmed by the unselfishness of her love, by the gentle, clean scent of her hair, his arms tighten around her.

"Oh, John, I'm so sorry whatever I did to make you mad."

"Hush up," he orders, embarrassed. Pulling back, he sees tears in her eyes and a look on her face that reminds him of how she looks when her daddy yells at her. Except this time, the tears are his fault. He reaches to wipe them away with clumsy thumbs and then, without even meaning to, he leans down and finds her lips with his.

Caralee gasps in shock, but the steely bands of John's control have given way and it's like the raging waters that surge through a collapsed dam. He crushes her body against his and kisses her with the wild impatience and roughness of an excited young man. His body and hands move freely, driven by passion, without thought of anyone other than himself. The headiness of his first kiss masks Caralee's fear and horror until it's too late.

"What are you doing?" She flings herself away from

him to the opposite side of the lookout.

"I don't know, I'm sorry!" he cries, wishing she were still in his arms. "I....you hugged me. I felt bad I made you cry. It just happened." Heart racing with confusion, fear and desire, he can't find the right words.

"Why did you have to do that?" Her voice breaks into sobs. "I can't believe you did that! I thought you were my friend!"

John Hunter moves across the lookout, wanting to comfort her. He grabs her hand, praying this is all a bad dream, that he'll wake up and everything will be the way it was.

"I'm sorry, Caralee. Please, it didn't mean anything. Just forget it."

"Forget it?" Her voice shakes with anger now. "How can I forget it? You're disgusting, John Hunter. I never want to see you again!" she shouts, then scrambles down the ladder.

And that's it, *I feel John think as he tosses the sheets off his bed and sits up.* That's the last time I saw or heard from Caralee in 20 years. A long time to carry the torch for someone. *He buries his head in his hands and groans with fresh shame.*

I whisper to John that it's not too late, that Caralee's not a scared, confused child anymore. "Right now, I just know she's lying in bed, same as you, wishing and dreaming. She's got her heart set on you too."

But I sent her those letters, *he rages against my suggestion.* For over a year I poured out my heart to her, apologizing, explaining, and she never once responded. *John Hunter jerks away from me then, pulls on his jeans and storms downstairs to his computer and his work. I drift down after him, my heart a mess of sadness.*

John types at his computer like a creature possessed. The words on the screen seem to suck him in and help him forget his sad rememberings.

I don't forget them. In fact, I add a few of my own to the mix and I wonder how much more sorrow I can handle.

CHAPTER TWENTY-FOUR

When Lee and Charlie exited the house the next morning for a sunrise jog, she was surprised to see that almost all the debris from the night before had been cleaned up.

"I guess they've gotten pretty good at their emergency response with smashed truck wreckage," Lee said to Charlie after they ran down the street.

The day was already warm, much hotter at this early hour than it had been yesterday, and Charlie's tongue hung almost to the ground before they reached the university. He began to lag behind and Lee stopped to check him.

"How are you feeling?" She knelt and gently pulled open his lips to check his gums. "I think you might be a little dehydrated." She stroked the fur of his muzzle. "Let's stop in one of these stores and get you some water."

Lee walked up the street and paused in front of the one business that didn't have a glowing *closed* sign in its front window.

"*Bridal Bliss and Buzz*?" she muttered to the heavily panting Charlie. Although she suspected it wouldn't be open at this early hour, Lee tried the handle anyway. To her surprise the door opened so she pulled Charlie into the cool, dark interior.

"Hello?" Lee called. She studied the racks of crinolined and be-jeweled wedding dresses that seemed to explode off the crowded racks before calling again.

Silence. Many of the overhead lights weren't even on and Lee suddenly felt like an intruder. She backed up pulling Charlie with her. They were just a block from the Piggly Wiggly. She'd go there instead.

As she turned to leave, a voice broke the silence. "Look what the cat dragged in. Or dog, I guess I should say."

She recognized the all too familiar drawl and for a split-second considered bolting out of the door without responding. But the steely part of her rebelled against the coward's way out, so instead she turned and tried to smooth any emotion from her face.

"Good morning, Kiki. I'm sorry to come in here so early. I was looking for a water fountain or sink."

Kiki moved from the back of the store to the counter and smirked as she eyed Lee's ponytail and workout clothes. "Looks like it would take more than a water fountain to freshen you up."

"It's for my—"

"I really couldn't care less, and technically you shouldn't even be in here. *No dogs allowed* and the store's not open yet. Can't you read?"

"Yes, for quite a long time now, actually," Lee answered, trying to keep her voice even. "Is this your shop?"

"Don't you get snippy with me." Kiki's voice took on a more menacing tone. "You're the one breaking into my store."

"Breaking into your store?" Lee laughed in disbelief. "No, I'm just looking for some water for my dog."

"So you say, but I'm not so sure I can trust you. How do I know you didn't sneak in here to steal something?" Kiki walked around the counter and stopped just short of Lee. "Seems like you get some kinda sick thrill out of trying to take what doesn't belong to you."

"You're right. I needed a wedding dress ASAP and decided I'd do whatever it took to get one."

"Excuse me? I wasn't talking about wedding dresses, honey. I was talking about the man you were hoping to use one with."

"I stopped playing *getting married* a long time ago. That's a little girl's game."

Kiki leaned forward. "Pathetic, that's what you are. John Hunter's mine and you just can't stand that. He'd never be interested in a mess like you."

Lee felt rage boil up within her. "I don't know what your problem is, *Barbie*, but I'll be out of here in a week and you can go back to your little chess game of controlling everyone around you. And I've never had to steal a boyfriend in my life, by the way. John Hunter's not even on my radar."

Kiki studied Lee for a moment before she returned to the counter. A smile curved her full, pouty lips and she picked up the phone. "Hello, officer? I'd like to report a breaking and entering at Bridal Bliss and Buzz."

"This is ridiculous," Lee sputtered. "Your door was unlocked!"

Kiki covered the mouthpiece of her phone. "And just who do you think the police are gonna believe? Kiki McGraw, town sweetheart, member of the junior league and country club? Or some outsider who swooped in to pillage her grandmother's home now that she's dead?"

Lee gasped in pain. "You heartless little—"

"Yes, officer, she's still here, standing right in front of me, bold as brass. You'd think a criminal would have the brains to leave the scene of the crime, but this one doesn't seem real bright." Kiki winked at Lee.

Lee's rage disappeared into dread. This was the last thing she needed to deal with right now. "If this is how you're going to be, I'm heading over to the Piggly Wiggly with Charlie. He needs some water." Lee called over her shoulder as she jerked open the door. "You can tell the police I'll be waiting over there."

"I'll be sure to tell them," Kiki called before returning to the phone conversation. "Not real bright, like I said. She just told me where you can find her."

"Can you believe her? She's seriously unhinged. Crazy!" Charlie trotted next to Lee as she stormed down the sidewalk. "Of all the shops to walk into, and now the police are on their way?" Charlie nosed her hand, but Lee was too upset to notice.

She found a water spigot outside the Piggly Wiggly

and cupped her hands for Charlie to get a drink. It took a while, but after he got his fill, she walked over to a shady spot in front of the store and sat on the curb, the first fire of her emotions burned out.

"I was really starting to love this place, Charlie," Lee said, and the dog curled into a contented ball next to her. "Now everyone's going to think I'm some kind money digging, boyfriend stealing psycho. I know word travels fast in small towns and with the police getting involved..." She let out a deep breath. "What if no one will work with me because I upset Kiki? Then Dad will have to come down here to finish the job himself. He'll probably unload all of Nana's things at the closest dump."

At that moment, she saw a squad car turn the corner and creep toward her, stopping in front of where she and Charlie sat. Lee stood, dusted off her shorts, and took a deep breath. The car door opened.

"Good morning, officer." Lee piled on the charm, hoping it might make a difference.

"Good morning, ma'am. Name's Officer Tucker. Heard you got into a bit of an altercation down at Kiki's wedding shop?" The officer, looking bored and sleepy, leaned against the hood of the squad car.

"I'm sure that's Kiki's side of it."

"Well, why don't you tell me your side of it Miss..." He flipped through his notebook.

"Lee Trenton."

"Lee? Caralee Trenton?" The officer closed the notebook and looked at her with interest.

"Yes, I used to go by Caralee. Sorry, do I—"

"Caralee, it's me. Grant Tucker!" He pulled off his hat and grabbed her into a crushing hug. "You remember me, don't you?"

"Of course I do." Lee laughed, struggling to extricate herself from his arms. "How are you doing? I didn't recognize you in uniform. You're a policeman?"

Grant nodded.

"Didn't you get into the most trouble of any of us?" Her mind dredged up instance after instance where Grant had led John Hunter's gang into its most thoughtless and errant adventures.

"Yeah, sure did, but I guess I spent so much time down at the police station, I got to liking it. Especially the Chief, Dusty Reynolds. You remember him?"

"I do," Lee said. "I think I may have been down at the police station a time or two myself."

"Sure you were, girl! You were in as much trouble as the rest of us, a lot of the time." Grant shook his head, chuckling. "Well, Chief Reynolds took a liking to me, I guess, and next thing I knew he had me doing odd jobs 'round the office. Before long, he had me working toward becoming an officer myself, and I'm much obliged he did."

"Well, you look great in a uniform." Lee offered him her most dimpled smile. This was going so much better than she could have imagined.

"Aw, thanks, Caralee. You don't look so bad yourself. Now what's this I hear 'bout you causing trouble down at Bridzillas and Buzzing, or whatever Kiki calls her shop?"

Grant adjusted his hat and flipped open his notebook. He still had a smile on his face, but Lee could tell he meant business.

"To be honest I'm confused over what happened, Grant. Kiki has some crazy idea that I've got it in for her."

"Now why'd she think something like that?"

"Well, you know her better than I do. But from what I've seen of her, my guess is she operates on the *dramatic* side, right?"

"Yeah, she does." Grant smiled. "You sure got her pegged."

"I'm here in town settling my Nana's estate—"

"Real sorry to hear about her passing." Grant nodded. "She was a mighty interesting lady."

"Thanks. Anyway, it seems that Kiki has developed this crazy idea that I'm back here in Eden Grove to steal John Hunter away from her."

Grant chuckled, slapping his notebook against his knee.

"I know, right?" Lee laughed with him. "I've barely been to Eden Grove a handful of times in the last few years and suddenly I decide to come *steal* John Hunter away? I didn't even know he'd moved back here."

"But what were you doing in her shop?" Grant asked as he studied his notebook.

"I was looking for somewhere with a water fountain. Charlie's not used to this heat. We'd gone for a jog and he seemed to be really hot and I was worried he'd become overheated. It's really easy for a husky to do that in hot weather."

"Well, he sure is a pretty dog," Grant said, reaching out to let Charlie smell his hand. Charlie sniffed and retreated behind Lee's legs, where he turned his back on the two of them.

"Sorry," Lee apologized, silently willing Charlie to put on the same show for the officer that she was. "He's a bit shy of strangers."

"That's all right." Grant chuckled. "Not so fond of them myself."

"This whole thing with Kiki is just a big misunderstanding." Lee shrugged her shoulders and gave Grant her best wide-eyed look of confusion. "I came over here to wait for you so Kiki wouldn't upset herself even more."

"Very wise of you, considering...well, considering the way she can be sometimes." Grant flipped his notebook closed, not having written a single word on it.

"Oh, thank you," Lee said, shaking her head. "I hated for there to be such a scene, especially over something as harmless as a drink of water."

"I think we've about got this cleared up." Grant tucked the notebook in his back pocket. "I'll head back to Kiki's and try to smooth things over with her." He rolled his eyes and winked at Lee, who giggled obligingly.

"I appreciate that so much, Grant." This at least was true. "I couldn't bear something else on top of everything. All this has been pretty exhausting." She felt herself drooping with the truth of the statement.

"Now, honey, you don't worry about a thing. I told you I'll get this all cleared up," Grant said and he walked back around his squad car. "How much longer you in town for?"

"Maybe another week. Why?"

"I wondered if you'd like some company?" His smile was hopeful. "There's the county fair all next week and a big Cajun band's coming to play at it. Maybe you'd like to go with me and see them? They put on one heck of a show."

"Maybe," Lee answered. "I'll have to see how far along I am."

"Why don't you give me your number?" Grant asked and Lee gave it to him. "I'll be in touch. And you call me if there's anything you need, you hear?"

Lee nodded, forcing another large smile.

"I'll see you later," Grant promised and then took off in his car in the direction he'd come.

Lee turned to Charlie and rolled her eyes. "Grant Tucker? I cannot believe he's a policeman. That kid was the worst hellion in this whole town! How does he become a police officer? And a pretty schmoozy one at that."

She started back toward Nana's house steering well clear of Bridal Bliss and Buzz. Charlie trotted alongside, seeming to radiate his disapproval. "Well, whatever I think of him, thank goodness he's the one that took Kiki's complaint, otherwise I might have been in trouble."

She crossed John Hunter's street and looked toward his bungalow. Maybe he was already at Nana's house working. Or else he'd rushed off to Kiki's damsel-in-distress call. He might even be waiting angrily at her front door. Oh joy.

"This is all getting a little too high school deja vu for me," she grumbled to Charlie when they approached Nana's front gate. She heard the whir of machinery and saw John Hunter and his crew already hard at work chipper shredding the brush they had cut down in the days before. John Hunter, sensing her gaze, looked up. He gave her a military salute, but quickly returned to his work.

Lee let out the breath she hadn't realized she was holding. "Maybe Kiki didn't call him after all," she whispered to Charlie. Another embarrassing encounter was the last thing she wanted. Maybe she could finish up with Nana's house without having any more scenes with the witch of Eden Grove.

The relief at not seeing Kiki again, however, disappeared at the thought of being done, of not seeing Granny Bob, John Hunter, Emma, Davey and even the sweet clerk at the Piggly Wiggly again. The realization surprised her. It wasn't as if she'd ever felt lonely or dissatisfied with her life before, but she wondered if that would still be true when she returned home.

No time for this now, she chided herself. "Come on, Charlie." She led the dog through the front door. "The Realtor is coming in a little over an hour and I need to get the kitchen and bedroom whipped into shape."

CHAPTER TWENTY-FIVE

So I had me a long think after sitting with John Hunter and seeing his dreams and lost hopes. I've decided I'm not going to let this go without a fight. Now maybe there's too much water under the bridge for Caralee and John Hunter, but then again maybe they just need a chance to see what could be. I owe them that chance and I owe it to William too.

So when I trailed Caralee this morning, I may have fiddled with the lock on Kiki's door until it unbolted. Then, I may have coaxed that big hairy dog to tug Lee into that store like he was desperate for water. I also might have buzzed and hummed in Kiki's ears while she was working in the back of the store to rile her up some.

I figured Kiki's such a big mouth that she'd get something moving even if it's a fight between Caralee and John Hunter. A blowup is better than those two coasting along wrapped in protective shells. Don't they see they're running out of time? No, of course they don't. They think they have all the time in the world. Just like I did.

The last month of my spring semester everything between William and me came to a head. The two of us had gotten serious so fast. But how could we not have?

When you find the other half of your soul, it's hard not to jump in with both feet.

The problem was, things were really starting to come together for me in the university fashion department at the same time. I'd been peddling my designs around to every fashion house, every designer, every shop in Manhattan without much luck, but that last semester Dr. LeBlanc took me under his wing and doors started opening.

He was the one who suggested I change my design name to Collin Abney instead of Kathryn Abney. He made sure I got invited to the right cocktail parties, fashion shows and business meetings. He suggested I work for him as a personal assistant after I graduated and said he could pull strings to get my designs seen.

I knew he had connections in New York, Paris and Milan and if I stuck with him at least I'd have my chance. Me, a nobody from Mississippi in the thick of the fashion world!

I also knew that these perks came with unspoken kickbacks, the kind women were expected to know and put up with in those days. Not that Dr. LeBlanc was a philandering monster, like some of them were, but he did expect to be lord of my life—that all my commitments and relationships would fall by the wayside to make room for his rather demanding schedule and desire for a pretty assistant at his beck and call. My William knew it too, and I can tell you that he hated Dr. LeBlanc even though I'd agreed to nothing at that point.

I think he could see the direction I was beginning to

lean toward, feel our chance to be together slipping away. So he held on tight, too tight for me, a free spirit just like Caralee.

"That man's taking over your life, Kathryn," I can still hear him lecturing me as we walked through Central Park. I'd had to cancel yet another of our evening dates because of Dr. LeBlanc's schedule. "This man doesn't want an assistant, he wants a slave."

"If it's the price I have to pay for getting my chance, then I'm willing to pay it," I snapped, fed up with William's double standard. He'd sacrificed and worked hard for his career. Couldn't I do the same for mine?

"He's squeezing me out, can't you see that? You barely have time for me anymore. And if you become his assistant, we'll never—" He grabbed my shoulders and pulled me close. "Haven't these last few months meant anything to you?"

I could see the pain in his eyes as I leaned up and kissed him. "Of course they have, you idiot. They've been the best days I've ever lived. You've got to know that!"

William led me to a bench in the shadow of the budding oak trees. "Then explain to me, please. How can you, for one moment, take that gargoyle's offer seriously?" He squeezed my hands. "I thought we'd dreamed, Kathryn, about a life together. I thought we'd decided that life is too short to waste even a moment of it apart."

We had dreamed together. First of a life in Washington, DC. He'd been offered a permanent position in the Washington office as a junior editor. We could get married and stay in DC until the war was over, he promised me. Then we would move anywhere we wanted. He might open a photography studio and work from home or get a job at a local newspaper. The two of us could raise our children together, maybe close to his family's farm in Maine, or back home where my family lived.

When he talked about it, I could see myself living that life, a happy, quiet version. One I knew that I'd be more than content with. But a little flicker of annoyance always popped into my mind too. What about my career? What about my chance to show that Kathryn Abney could take the fashion world by storm?

You see, there were two futures that tugged at me, and I thought if I put off the decision long enough, I wouldn't have to make one at all. What a silly fool I was.

So I nodded and kissed him. Said something non-committal; something I knew would soothe him. But I kept right on living my dual realities, like an ostrich with my head in the sand, hoping, somehow, to avoid the inevitable collision.

CHAPTER TWENTY-SIX

"Well, Miss Trenton, it certainly is a beautiful house," LaTanya Renault, the Realtor, complimented as they made their way down the grand front staircase. "Of course, I came to all of Nana's holiday extravaganzas so I had some idea as to the value of her home, but on closer inspection, I see it's truly one of a kind."

"I'm so glad you think so," Lee answered, leading LaTanya to the dining room and offering her a drink. "I guess it reflects its owner that way."

"Well, you're certainly right about that," LaTanya said, flicking her fingers through her smooth black hair. "Your Nana was one of the most fascinating people I ever met. The whole town will miss her."

"She was the kind of person you assumed would be around forever," Lee said, feeling guilty once more. "She was so full of life."

"That's just the right way to say it." LaTanya leaned over and patted Lee on the knee. "Full of life. We could all take a page from Nana's book."

Lee swallowed, knowing she was perilously close to bursting into tears. "So what else do I need to do before putting it on the market?"

"With a good clean on the inside and a fresh coat of paint on the outside, the house should be fine. The only other concern I have is the grounds. I see you are attempting to fix them up." She looked out the window. "Who is it you've hired?"

"John Hunter. He seems like he knows what he's doing—"

"Oh, John Hunter!" LaTanya clapped her hands. "Wonderful. Then that's no problem at all. He's the best, the absolute best. With what he'll do on the outside and what you've got here on the inside, I'll revise my numbers. I think we might be able to increase on the asking price I quoted to you the last time we met. If you'll give me just a moment?"

"Of course," Lee said.

LaTanya typed on her calculator and made notes on the paper.

"I'm just going to get a breath of fresh air," Lee said. LaTanya nodded and Lee wandered back toward the kitchen.

"It's real now, Nana." Lee whispered. She clenched the sink and leaned over it. "We're really going to put your lovely old home on the market and I'll never see it or you again. But I don't want to sell it. I want to see you here in the kitchen mixing margaritas and warming up your never-ending hors d'oeuvres. I want to dance the jitterbug with you at midnight and play dress up with your Hermes scarves."

A sob escaped and, not wanting LaTanya to hear, Lee

jerked open the back door and collapsed onto the loveseat on the patio. She covered her eyes and let the tears come.

"Hey there, Lee," came a voice from across the lawn, "hear you been downtown making a menace of yourself at Bridal Bliss and Buzz." John Hunter's voice trailed off.

"Honey, what's wrong?" he demanded. Lee felt his weight on the seat and sighed as his arms enveloped her.

"I just miss Nana so much. The Realtor is here figuring out an asking price and suddenly it's all so...real. She's gone, John. She's gone forever and I never said good-bye." Her voice was coming in gasps now and she felt the warm breath of his lips on top of her bent head. "Things always hit me too late, John. I never get it right. I always miss the moment. What's wrong with me?"

"Now you just hush up. Nothing's wrong with you."

"How can you say that? I always let my work come first and barely visited Nana, especially these last few years. My dad and I can barely stand being in the same room together. Jenny's getting ready to have a baby, and won't have time for me anymore. Mark is...an idiot. I haven't been on a date since I can remember. My strongest bond in life is with a *dog*! It's like I'm toxic to other human beings!"

"I'm sure that's not true," John said and grabbed her flailing hands.

"But it *is* true!"

"Look, you've always marched to the beat of your own drum, Lee. Even now it seems like you walk a different path than most people." His hands tightened on hers and he drew Lee closer toward him. “But that doesn’t make you toxic. Fact is, I—”

“Sorry, I do hope I’m not interrupting?” LaTanya’s voice came through the French doors. Lee jerked away from John Hunter and wiped at her eyes.

“Sorry, LaTanya, I guess all this is just a bit emotional for me.” Lee rose and walked back into the house. “Are you ready to talk numbers?”

She glanced over her shoulder before closing the door. John was still on the loveseat, face grim as he studied his now empty hands.

She thought about going back to him or at least voicing her appreciation, but John didn’t look up, and the moment passed. Lee turned sadly and followed the echo of LaTanya’s voice.

CHAPTER TWENTY-SEVEN

After silencing her frayed emotions, Lee finished hammering out the details of the contract with LaTanya, her father listening in through speakerphone. After LaTanya left, Lee hesitated. A part of her wanted to go back out onto the patio, to finish her conversation with John. *But how would you do that?* she argued with herself. *Fling yourself back on the loveseat in a sniveling heap?*

Instead, she made a quick retreat to the upstairs and consulted the list she'd created with Granny Bob on her first day in Eden Grove. There were already a good number of check marks on it.

She had collected most of Nana's belongings that held no sentimental value and left them on the curb. True to her word, the owner of the secondhand shop sent her driver by several times in the last few days to pick up Lee's donations.

The main things left in the house now were Nana's furniture, clothes and jewelry. Sarah Beth, the antique dealer, had scheduled to come the following day and load up the various pieces, decorations and china she wanted to sell. The jeweler was coming around the same time and, Lee checked the time on her phone, someone from the university was coming in a few hours to sort through Nana's clothes. After speaking to the head of the university fashion department, Lee had agreed to let several volunteers come look through Nana's clothing and tag anything they thought they could use in their archives.

After trying to sort through some of Nana's closet on her own, Lee felt relieved when the doorbell rang. She opened the door to three bright-eyed students pulling wheeled wardrobes behind them and ushered them upstairs to the bedroom.

She left them to their giggling commentary, punctuated with frequent oohs and aahs over some designer piece, and walked down the hall into the old den to sort through Nana's old bills and bookkeeping. Lee settled at the desk, shredding anything that seemed important, before throwing it into the box, which she'd later drop off at the recycle center.

As she fell into a rhythm with the repetitious task, the scene with John Hunter came back, and Lee cringed as she realized how much she'd revealed about her loneliness. And why did LaTanya have to interrupt them when she did? What had John been getting ready to say?

A few minutes later her phone rang. It was Jenny.

"Thank goodness it's you." She sighed into the phone. "A familiar voice is just what I needed to hear."

"I could feel you sending out the vibe," Jenny teased. "What's up?"

"Well, the fashion department is here sorting through Nana's clothes to see what they'd like to keep. The department head said I have to look through their selections when they're done, to make sure they haven't taken anything too valuable, but honestly, I'd have no idea if they did. You know how I am about clothes."

"In that as long as you are comfortable and not naked, you really couldn't care less."

"Exactly. How would I know if something's too valuable to give away?" Lee started on the next drawer of the desk. A packet of tattered letters tied with a dirty blue ribbon joined her discard pile. "Clothes remind me of a math word problem. Everything starts to blur together after a while."

"Only you would compare fashion to math, Lee. When they're done, why don't you call and describe each of the pieces they picked. If it sounds interesting, you can text me a picture and I'll let you know what I think. Call me back when they leave."

"Thank you," Lee said, relieved. "I'll call you the moment they're done."

Lee spent the next several hours finishing up the desk and sorting through other odd drawers, nooks and crannies around the house. After loading the bags of trash and recycling into her Jeep, while carefully avoiding any more contact with John Hunter, she made a trip to the dump and recycle center. When she returned, the fashion students were ready to leave.

"We have a little over two racks of clothes that we think the department would be interested in, ma'am," one girl with huge cat-eye glasses told Lee as she walked them to the front door. "Would you be able to look through them tonight so we could come pick them up tomorrow?"

"No problem," Lee said. "And what about the clothes left on the bed?"

"That's all just junk," the other girl said. "You can get rid of them. Drop them off at the secondhand shop."

"Lisa, that's rude," the glasses girl whispered, elbowing her in the side.

"Sorry, ma'am, I just mean, they're normal clothes. Not the kind of thing the department would want. And I don't have anything against charity shops. Why, this skirt's from one!" She gestured to the hot pink and purple tulle skirt that she sported over a pair of leopard skin tights.

"Wow, what a find," Lee said, mentally ranking it in her top 10 of hideous clothing. "Thank you girls so much. If you want to head over any time after noon tomorrow, I'll be done by then."

She ushered them out the door and looked at the time. It was a little after five and the last thing she felt like doing was making awkward conversation with Granny Bob and John Hunter.

As she dialed Granny Bob's number, Lee practiced her excuse: she had to finish up on the clothes before tomorrow, so she'd probably just grab something quick when she was finished and call it an early night.

"Ya sure, sugar?" Granny Bob sounded concerned when Lee gave her regrets. "I could have John Hunter run some food by your place on his way home."

"No thanks," Lee said, biting her lip. "I've got a bit of a

headache and an early night sounds like heaven."

"I'm sure you're right, sweetie, but you call me if you need anything, you hear?"

"I promise. Oh and remember you're stopping by tomorrow to help me go through Nana's jewelry, right?"

"Yes I am," Granny Bob agreed. "One o'clock sound all right?"

"Perfect." Lee hung up and collapsed into a chair. Charlie came and leaned against her. "Just you and me tonight, buddy." She spoke as she scratched his ear. "And that's the way we like it, right?"

Lee didn't realize it, but as she was sorting through my papers, she threw out some mighty special things. I guess if Jenny'd been the one to go through them, she might have been a little more careful. Family photographs, letters and cards. Oh, it felt like a part of me died all over again when I saw Lee tossing them in the trash.

I am *glad she missed my letters from William. I don't know if I could have stood her looking through something so personal. Keeping a record of my greatest regret is stupid, I grant you. The thing is, even after all these years, I couldn't bear destroying something William had touched. Sentimental, I know, but I have so little of him left.*

He wrote me those letters when he was down in Washington, DC doing a freelance story and checking out the lay of the land before he started up his new job as junior editor. They're the sweetest, most beautiful love letters a girl could read. My William had a gift of speaking out the music of the heart without a single note sounding silly or trite.

I think it was easier for him to pretend everything was still perfect between us in those few weeks he was away, even though a part of him must have known the two of us were headed toward disaster.

He wrote about a little apartment he'd found us, right up the street from where he worked, about the cafés that he couldn't wait to take me to, and the park we'd visit on Saturday mornings after breakfast in bed. I hated myself for it, but I didn't write him back much. I was too involved in my senior project, my own line of evening gowns and the parties and social whirl that I was becoming enmeshed in.

I could tell by William's last letter that he was getting ready, ready to make a final stand for us when he returned home in three days' time. I also knew that Dr. LeBlanc needed my answer within the week. I kept pushing it from my mind, though. Surely a magic resolution to both problems was right around the corner.

I guess I thought all this would be less painful now that I'm gone, but if anything I feel worse about my William than I have in a long, long time. These sad memories seem like all I have left.

CHAPTER TWENTY-EIGHT

After her grumbling stomach finally catapulted Lee from cleaning out the bathroom cabinets, she gave herself a few hours of downtime before calling Jenny.

Jenny answered after the first ring and the two sisters got down to business, painstakingly discussing every outfit that the fashion department had marked as one they wanted for their archives.

Most of the clothes ended up staying on the wheeled racks. Jenny and Lee had no use or interest in many of Nana's very formal three-piece suits, dresses and ball gowns, but there were a few things they kept mainly for sentimental reasons. Like Nana's fox fur coat.

"Do you remember when Nana wore it to church that one Christmas she came to visit?" Jenny laughed.

"Yes," Lee said, "and how angry Dad got because he thought she was trying to show off for everyone."

"Which she probably was a little bit."

"Yeah, and kill two birds with one stone by driving Dad crazy too," Lee said, running her fingers through the silky soft fur. "I always wondered if she tried to rebel a bit on our behalf when she came to visit."

"I think so," Jenny said, her voice soft with emotion.

They also kept out the skirt and jacket Nana wore to Jenny's wedding. Nana had taken a beautiful silk sari bought on an India trip and tailored it into a gorgeous dress suit. Its shimmering folds and patterns were so beautiful that the dress nearly stole the show at the wedding.

"Did that make you angry at all?" Lee asked Jenny. "How she wanted the spotlight on her, even at your wedding?"

"Nah, that was just Nana. I mean if she had shoved me out of the way and tried to marry Brad, I might have gotten upset."

"Brad too."

After they made their way through almost the entire rack of clothes, Lee found a drapey, white A-line dress, complete with a matching fur-trimmed cape. The fabric was so silky, she had the childish urge to rub it against her cheek.

"This is cute," she observed and decided to photograph it. As it was sending she said, "The dress is a bit more simple than Nana's usual fare but really nice."

"What's the label?" Jenny asked.

Lee searched for a few minutes. "I can't seem to find one. Maybe it fell off?"

"Go to the seams," Jenny said. "Do they look like they were made with a machine or by hand?"

"I wouldn't know the difference if I saw it."

"Machine stitching is perfect. Every single stitch is the exact same size and length. They're tiny," Jenny said.

"Hand stitching will have some irregularities every once and a while. The stitches might be uneven. The seam allowance might be slightly longer on one side. There's little clues all over."

Lee turned the dress inside out and began to examine it more closely. "I think I see what you mean. There's a few places where the stitches aren't perfect where the top part changes into the skirt."

"That's pretty normal."

"So what does that mean?" Lee asked.

"It means that you've found an original dress." Jenny's voice quickened with excitement. "Nana was always telling me about the designer originals she got from fashion shows during those summers she worked in New York."

"So that means this might be valuable?"

"Very valuable, especially if it's from a well-known designer's early collection. It could be priceless," Jenny said. "If I were you, I'd take that dress up to the head of the fashion department, first thing tomorrow morning and see what they have to say. If Nana had a really valuable piece, knowing her, she probably would have bragged to someone about it."

"What if they ask to keep it?"

"No, I think bring the dress back here, no matter what they say," Jenny advised, "but maybe they'll be able to shed some light on the LWD."

"LWD?" Lee asked.

"You know, like LBD? Little Black Dress? But LWD for Little White Dress? How can you be related to Nana and know so little about fashion?" Jenny chuckled.

Lee looked around at the wonderland of garments that surrounded her. "Wish you could be here so much, sis. This would be like your Shangri-La."

"There's a reason you're there," Jenny said. "Maybe you needed to say your good-byes. You know I visited Nana about six months ago, so I got to say mine."

"Maybe."

"Or maybe you have some unfinished business with someone there? An old childhood friend, perhaps?"

"Subtle, Jenny," Lee said and took a large gulp of wine. "I can't imagine what childhood friend you're referencing, but I have had several run-ins with someone named Kiki McGraw. Did you ever meet her?"

"Kiki?" Jenny said. "No, I don't think so. I'm pretty sure I'd recognize a ridiculous name like that."

"I know!" Lee exploded. "Everything about her's ridiculous!"

"Whoa, what did she do to you?"

"Nothing."

"Well, she had to do something," Jenny pointed out, "otherwise you wouldn't sound like you want to kill her."

Lee remained silent.

"Spill it, Lee."

"We've just had a few run-ins regarding..."

"Regarding?"

"John Hunter," Lee said after a pause.

"Ah, and now we come to the unfinished business with the childhood friend."

Lee could almost picture her sister rubbing her hands with glee. "Jenny, I really don't want to talk about this right now."

"And why not? Come on, sweetie, you're already under enough pressure trying to handle all of Nana's stuff. If something's bothering you, unload it on me and my elephant-sized ankles. Baby and I can handle it."

"Fine, fine." Lee was smiling now. Jenny always knew how to get her way. "So, I've been working pretty closely with John Hunter on Nana's grounds."

"Yeah, you mentioned that last time I called."

"Well, there's been this...tension between us since I got here and I thought it was just because."

"Because?" Jenny prompted.

"Well, this weird thing that happened between us the last summer we were here together."

"Weird how?"

"I don't want to go into it," Lee said firmly. Jenny didn't get to call all the shots. "The short of it is he did something that betrayed our friendship. I told him I never wanted to see him again. He moved away shortly after that, so I never did."

"But now that you have seen him? Are you still angry?"

Lee considered Jenny's question. Was she still angry? "No, I'm just confused." Could John have forgotten? Or maybe it hadn't been that big of a deal to him? In retrospect, she realized he was probably just a confused teenager, but it wasn't even the physical act that had hurt her as much as the vanished friendship that followed. Like it had meant nothing to him and wasn't worth the bother of trying to make amends.

"Is it horribly awkward between the two of you?"

"It's strange but a lot of the time, no. Actually it feels like how things were between us when we were kids," Lee said.

"You mean how he acted like your honorary big brother? Always teasing you and joking around?"

"Yeah, exactly," Lee said. "It's been really nice. I guess I realized how much I've missed him."

"So what's the problem?"

"I don't know. It seemed to change a day or two ago, and now I'm not sure." Lee took another sip of wine, stalling as she tried to understand the myriad unexplored emotions churning around inside of her.

"Is it possible that you're attracted to each other?" Jenny asked, after a moment of silence.

"NO! He was only ever my friend." My *best* friend, at least for a while.

"Sweetie," Lee heard the smile on her sister's face. "That was then, and this is now. Things change. Has he said anything that makes you think he's interested in you?"

"Maybe, but you know what a sweet-talker he is." Lee began to hang the clothes back on the rack. "I don't really take anything he says seriously."

"What?"

"Well, he's always saying *honey* and *sugar* and

darling." She imitated his drawl. "That's just his way, don't you think? Him being Southern and a charmer and all that?" She trailed off uncertainly.

"Well, I wouldn't blow off everything he says just because he's charming," Jenny answered, almost angrily. "I mean, I know you'd rather sit alone at your house every night with Charlie—"

"Hey!"

"Oh come on, Lee, you barely have a social life. When is the last time you went on a date?"

"Not too long ago." *Except it wasn't a date,* her mind sided with Jenny. *It was a business meeting with a 50-year-old grandfather.*

"I don't believe you."

"Fine. Don't."

"All I'm saying is, if a nice guy like John Hunter is whispering sweet nothings into your ear, maybe you shouldn't be quite so quick to dismiss it. I mean what if he actually cares about you?"

"Even if all that were true," Lee said, jerking the clothes onto their hangers now, "he lives here and I live in Durango. How stupid would it be to start something up when there's 2,000 miles between us?"

"Well, you could visit each other and maybe one of you could move."

"I don't think so, we're both very committed to our careers. Listen, I don't want to talk about this anymore," Lee said, her voice taut with unspoken emotion. "I'm more confused than I was before, and I just want to finish what

I'm trying to do here."

"All right, all right, don't shoot the messenger," Jenny grumbled. "You know I'm a hormonal mess right now, so don't snap at me or I'll start weeping."

"I'm sorry, Jenny," Lee said, softer now. "I can't keep wrestling through all this. I feel like I've been fighting a migraine all day."

"Got it, got it," Jenny said. "Just promise me, you'll keep an open mind?"

"I promise," Lee answered. "Now I have about five more dresses to go through with you."

After ringing off with her sister, Lee glanced at the clock. It was almost 10:00 and she was ready for bed. She quickly finished hanging the clothes that Jenny had okayed for the university, and carefully transported the clothing racks to the bottom floor, parking them in the foyer.

Charlie was waiting for her at the back door and she let him in. He trotted past her and straight up the stairs. As she locked the front door, Lee noticed a note taped on the window. She opened the door and pulled it off.

Hey Lee,

Davey and I would love to have you over for breakfast tomorrow morning. French toast, eggs and bacon? We're celebrating because Tom just got back today and I would love for the two of you to meet. Pop over around 8:30 if it works with your schedule.

Emma

Lee read through the note several times. She turned to the stairs, ignoring the feeling of disappointment that tried to worm its way into her heart. Tomorrow's breakfast was going to be delicious, she knew, and it was silly to be sad that the note was from Emma. Why on earth would it be from anyone else?

CHAPTER TWENTY-NINE

The next morning Lee and Charlie stood on Emma's doorstep at 8:30 sharp, Lee holding a bowl of fruit salad she quickly whipped together after her morning jog with Charlie. It wouldn't compare to anything Emma made, but Lee felt she couldn't go to anymore meals without contributing at least something.

Emma pulled open the door, her face alight with smiles and Lee could hear Davey's shrieks of joy in the background.

"Welcome, Lee, I'm so glad you could make it."

"Thanks for the invite." Davey's shrieking grew louder and the little boy ran past the two women with all the grace his chubby legs allowed. A tall, sandy haired man followed him and Emma grabbed his arm before he could race by.

"Tom, honey, I'd like to introduce you to Lee, Kathryn's granddaughter."

"Pleased to meet you, Lee," Tom said and shook her hand. "You certainly made an impression on Davey. As soon as I got back in last night he was telling me 'Lee this' and 'Lee that.' Couldn't understand a whole lot of the rest of his jabber but I'd say he's got his first crush."

Lee laughed and followed Tom and Emma into the kitchen. "Well, he's stolen my heart too," Lee said and reached out to grab Davey's upheld hand.

"I hope you're hungry," Emma said as they sat down. "This is Tom's favorite breakfast, so I made tons."

"Yes, you did," Lee said studying the full table in front of her. The smells wafting from it made her mouth water and she quickly overturned the vow she'd made to herself that she wouldn't overindulge. "It looks amazing, Emma."

As Emma cut up and served Davey small bites of the meal on his high chair tray, Tom passed Lee waffles, scrambled eggs, bacon and grits. The conversation turned to Lee's progress on Nana's house.

"Sounds like you've gotten a whole lot done," Tom said. "I'm real impressed. Nana's place is huge and I'm sure it's a lot for one person to tackle alone."

"Thanks," Lee said, "and now that I've listed it off, it makes me realize that I've actually accomplished quite a bit in the week I've been here." She took another bite of her chili cheese eggs and forced herself not to gobble up the rest with Charlie's table manners. "But it certainly hasn't been alone. Granny Bob connected me with all the right people and everyone's been incredibly helpful. I feel like I've been adopted by the town of Eden Grove."

"By everyone, that is, except nasty-pants McGraw," Emma said and took a sip of coffee. "Kiki seems to have developed quite an aversion to poor Lee."

"Poor you is right." Tom shook his head. "The bad side of Kiki McGraw ain't a great place to be, but the two of us have survived it so far. Maybe there's hope for you too."

"So far," Emma giggled, "but who knows? The town might not be big enough for the two of y'all. I feel a showdown coming."

Lee almost choked on the large bite of waffle. "Well, yesterday morning we did have another run-in."

"Surprise, surprise. What happened this time?"

Lee told them of her incident at Bridal Bliss and Buzz. Thanks to Tom and Emma's sympathetic comments, she felt a complete sense of validation by the time she was done with her story.

"Yep, that sounds just like her," Tom said. "That woman is meaner than chicken—" Tom paused and looked at Davey. "Well, you know. She's always looking for something to be angry about. You want me to go talk to her for you?"

"Oh, I—" Lee faltered. She had faced the dragons of her daily life solo for so long, she wasn't sure how to respond. "I think I'll be able to handle it for now, Tom, but that's very kind of you to offer."

"Well, you let me know if you change your mind," Tom said, and the conversation turned to lighter things: Lee's thoughts about Eden Grove, the unusually mild summer they'd had and Tom's work on the oil rigs.

Davey, now full, began to bang on his high chair with his spoon and squirm in his chair. Emma rolled her eyes, but smiled at the wiggly toddler. "Guess that's my cue for a diaper change and letting this little one run free for a bit."

Davey glowered at her beneath a furrowed brow, "No." He pointed to his mother with a chubby finger. "No, Mama. Dada play!"

They all burst into laughter.

"Guess he wants a little more daddy time and I certainly don't mind letting you handle the diaper, honey." Emma handed the squirming Davey to his father.

"Dada!" Davey's squeal of joy floated down the hall.

"Let me help you get this cleaned up." Lee stood and began to gather the dishes.

"Oh no, Lee. You let me do the clearing up. You're our guest and I know you've got a lot to do at Nana's. Leave this for me and you can get back to whatever's on your schedule for today."

Lee tried to insist but Emma wouldn't hear of her helping, so Lee gave Davey a hug and made her good-byes. Tom and Emma followed her to the door.

"Can I have one more quick word, Lee?" Tom stopped her before she left. "Davey's busy with his book at the moment and I—"

Tom glanced at Emma. His wife gave him a small nod.

"Emma and I are real worried about John Hunter." The words burst out of Tom and Lee could tell he'd been rehearsing them. "Worried about him and Kiki, to be honest. The two of them seem like they're getting more and more serious."

"Really?" Lee said, the delicious meal feeling like a lead weight at Emma's affirmative nod.

"I think so," Tom said and put his arm around his wife.

"We know you've been friends with John since you were little ones, so we wanted to ask you, do you think he's happy?"

Was John Hunter happy? Lee wondered. She'd been so consumed with her own grief and confusion, she hadn't given a second thought as to how John Hunter was doing.

"He seems happy enough when he's talking about his research, his plants," Lee said after considering. "I think he's found his calling. Sounds like he has some pretty great plans for the future."

"We know that," Emma said. "But do you think he's happy with Kiki?"

"I can't really say," Lee answered. "He's not talked about her to me. Because of the run-ins we've had, she's sort of an uncomfortable topic."

Tom rubbed his chin and kicked at a leaf on the porch. "Personally, I think she's a harpy."

"We just can't see John happy with the likes of her," Emma added. Tom and I are worried he's making a huge mistake, but every time Tom tries to reason with him, he just clams up."

Tom nodded. "I think Kiki's the one driving the relationship. From the second he moved back, she's been all over him like white on rice. What I don't understand, and he won't explain it to me, is why he's with someone who acts so ugly and hateful?"

Emma's eyes brimmed with tears. "John Hunter's had a hard life. I feel like this thing with Kiki...well, it's like watching a train wreck about to happen and knowing you can't do a darn thing about it. That's why I wondered, we wondered, do you think that you might be able to say something to him about it?"

Lee ran her fingers through the loop of Charlie's leash. *As if there wasn't enough tension between John Hunter and me already*, she thought. *I'm sure he'd appreciate my critique on his choice of girlfriend. And one who hates me at that.*

"Look, if you don't feel comfortable, don't do it. But we'd never ask something like this if Emma and I hadn't already tried ourselves," Tom said. "I probably shouldn't be saying this, but he let slip something about a ring before I left for the oil rigs. I went back home and told Emma and the both of us about cried. John's like a brother to me and..." Tom trailed off, shaking his head.

"Well, I see your point," Lee answered after a moment of awkward silence. "I'll try to say something to him if I can. But I can't promise anything. I'm not sure I have a whole lot of influence in John Hunter's life."

"Of course you do," Tom said. "He brings you up all the time. Tells me crazy stories about the messes you two got into. You were a real important part of his life, Lee. He talks about you like you were family."

"All right, Tom. I said I'd try."

"Thanks," Emma said and surprised Lee by engulfing her in a hug. "I'll let you get to your work now. Thank you for listening to us. Sorry if we made you uncomfortable."

Lee waved and walked across the street with Charlie. She felt alternating emotions of annoyance at Tom and

Emma's question and admiration for their concern over a friend. Did she have any friends that she'd voice such an awkward request for? Probably not. Her gaze fell on Charlie who nosed his way through the crumbly dirt of a newly dug flower bed.

CHAPTER THIRTY

Lee settled Charlie into his crate with a new bone and checked the time. She had less than an hour before Granny Bob was coming over to look through Nana's jewelry and Lee needed to move all of it down to the dining room table. A few hours later Blake Etherby, the jeweler who'd agreed to look through and sell Nana's more valuable pieces, would be coming by to pick up what he wanted.

One at a time, she unloaded the drawers of Nana's jewelry into a few large cardboard boxes. When she finished the last drawer, Lee shook her head at the enormous collection of necklaces, earrings, bracelets and baubles. Only now as an adult did she have any idea of their value. As a child she'd thought most of them equivalent to the plastic pearl necklaces she always bought at the dollar store.

The doorbell rang just as Lee finished setting out all the items on the dining room table. Still in go mode, she ran to the door and flung it open. Granny Bob and John Hunter stood before her in the midst of what appeared to be an intense conversation. They froze mid-sentence.

"Hey, you two, come in," Lee said and forced herself

to take a deep breath. She'd finished the job in time and now Granny Bob would help her with the rest.

"Honey, are you all right?" The older woman reached toward her with concern and squeezed Lee's arm. "I don't have to look at the jewelry right now, if it's not a good time."

"No, no. Just a little frazzled," Lee said and led the two of them to the table.

She looked over her shoulder at John. "Did you want to stay too? And would either of you like me to get you a glass of sweet tea?" Lee thought guiltily of the sugar-laden gallon she'd bought from Piggly Wiggly the day before.

"No, just wanted to let you know we're making some real progress in the backyard. Why don't you come and take a look at it after you and Granny go through the jewelry?"

"Sounds good," Lee said, wondering where she could fit that into her already packed schedule. "I'll see you in a bit." Her phone beeped and she saw she had a new email from the Realtor.

"Granny Bob, I just need to check this revision to the listing agreement on the house, so we can finalize the last few details. Why don't you start looking through the jewelry? It's all in the dining room."

"You go on ahead, honey. Take your time."

Lee ran upstairs and quickly read through the agreement before noting two small changes in her email to the Realtor with a copy to her father.

Pausing at the top of the stairs, Lee took a deep

breath. She remembered Granny Bob's hesitation at going through Nana's things and knew this would be an emotional time for both of them. She steeled herself for the grief soon to come.

The dining room table seated fourteen comfortably, sixteen in a pinch, and yet Lee had used the entire table top and even some of the side boards for everything. She'd tried to organize the pieces in similar groups: plain gold, plain silver, gemstones, and Nana's late life obsession—Southwestern jewelry. Lee had also tried to put all the sets together, at least the ones she could recognize.

As she entered the room, Lee looked around, expecting to find Granny Bob by the table, inspecting one of Nana's many jaw-dropping pieces. Instead, Lee spied the older woman slumped in a dining room chair next to the window, a tissue clutched in her hand.

"Are you all right?"

Granny Bob startled. "I'll be all right, sugar. You know, I just got a little overwhelmed looking at all this jewelry. It brought back so many memories."

Lee nodded. "Did you see anything you recognized? Anything special?"

"As to recognizing it, of course I do. You remember how Nana would always start out her conversations describing what she was wearing? Clothes, jewelry, shoes, the works. Why I felt like I got a little taste of her fashion classes every time she came over to my house for coffee. Sometimes it got downright irritating, truth be told." She chuckled and dabbed her eyes.

"So what would you like to remember her by? I've already taken out the few things Jenny asked for."

"Well, honey, I don't know if I can." Granny Bob shifted in her seat. "Almost feels like stealing."

"Listen," Lee pulled out another chair and dragged it next to Granny Bob, "if Nana had made a will with details about her things, I know you would have been the first one in it. This is all going to the consignment jeweler if you don't take anything."

Granny Bob shrugged her shoulders.

"Please, would you do it for me? I'd hate it if you didn't take something of Nana's and I'd like you to take something as a symbol of my appreciation too. You've been so wonderful since I got here—the people whose names you gave me, your suggestions, John Hunter and his crew, feeding me every night. Please?"

"If you put it that way, I can't hardly refuse." Granny Bob took a deep breath and stood up. She walked around the table for a few minutes, considering, picking up a piece, studying it and then setting it back down. Finally she paused in front a necklace and matching earrings of uncut amethyst.

"I was with your grandma when she bought these," she spoke softly. Her voice cracked and she pulled out the tissue again. "We had just been to Acapulco for a week. Your grandma took me there for my birthday. It was my first time to ever leave the country, let alone the South. But you know what a world traveler Nana was. She demanded I come with her because she wanted to get my 'sorry butt out of Eden Grove for once in my life,' I think were her exact words."

Lee grinned. "That does sound like her."

"We were coming back from this amazing trip. Lord only knows how much it cost her, but when we walked into the duty-free shop, she homed right in on that necklace like a duck on a June bug. I could see it was true love in her eyes." Granny Bob chuckled. "The shop lady didn't seem very impressed; we were still dressed in our beach clothes and probably looked like two old hussies. But Kathryn didn't even blink, just said she'd take them.

"The shop lady turned to her, laughed and said, 'Ma'am, I don't think you realize how expensive these are.'

"Well, your Nana turned to her and said, 'Oh believe me, honey, I can afford it. You just wrap it up and bring it over to the counter.' Then she marched over to cash register sassy as a cat with her tail in the air."

"How much was it?" Lee asked, studying the massive loops of amethysts.

"I followed her, but as we were walking I said, 'Kathryn, you have any idea how much those are?'

"'I'd guess between $8,000 and $10,000,' she said real casual, like it weren't anything at all.

'You can't afford that!' I said and tried to grab her arm. 'Now come on, you proved your point to the shop girl. Let's just get outta here. She'll never know the difference.'

"'Now, Bobby, you know I can't do that. Plus I just got

this new platinum credit card in the mail. If that's not worth a little splurge, I don't know what is.'

"That shop girl rang us up, her face looking like she'd sucked on a lemon." Granny Bob laughed and slapped her knee. "Soon as she handed Nana the package, she ripped the tissue paper off of it, put the necklace and earrings on and handed the tissue paper back to the girl. 'Honey, would you mind throwing this away for me. I do believe I'm gonna wear these home.'"

"Did you ever find out how much it cost?" Lee asked.

"Well, she never did tell me and I thought it would be rude to look over her shoulder when she was signing the receipt," Granny Bob said. "But it musta been a lot. For a long time afterwards if she wanted to get something new or go out to eat or what have you, she'd tell me. 'Oh now, I forgot Bobby, I can't do that. I'm still paying off my airport necklace.'"

Lee laughed as she studied the glinting amethysts. "Airport necklace! But I guess she paid it off eventually."

"Eventually, but it sure took a while."

Lee scooped up the necklace and the earrings in her hand. "Here, you have to take it. That story's priceless and no one but you could appreciate what these are really worth."

"I'm not gonna take that necklace, honey," Granny Bob protested. "It looks heavy enough to hang an ox's head to the ground. But I will take the earrings to remember your Nana by."

"But you can't break up the set," Lee protested.

"Please take the necklace."

"No, I won't, darling, but I'll take this instead." Granny Bob picked up a 14-inch gold link chain. "It's what your Nana always wore for bridge night."

Lee tried to cajole her into taking the necklace for a bit longer, but Granny Bob was adamant.

"Now for you, young lady," Granny Bob said, gazing sternly at Lee. "Did you pick out anything for yourself?"

"No, I didn't, but you know I told you earlier, I'm not much of a jewelry person myself."

"Now that don't make a hoot'a difference. Maybe your daughter will be a jewelry wearer and you're gonna want to pass something of your Nana's down to her."

"My daughter?"

"Well, you know, someday. I do remember your Nana mentioning some pieces she wanted you girls to have. Let's see if I can find them."

Granny Bob spent the next few minutes sorting through the pile, pulling out baubles, many of which were old fashioned or out of style, but ones she insisted Nana would have wanted Lee and Jenny to have. She was even able to point out ones that had been in the Abney family for several generations.

Lee thought they were finished when she heard Granny Bob gasp in surprise. "Oh, honey, you gotta take this. I can't believe you almost gave it away!" In her palsied hand she held out a little blue box to Lee.

"What is it?" Lee asked. "I don't think I looked in it."

"It's her ring from poor William, of course!" Granny

Bob almost shouted, then covered her mouth in shock.

"William?" Lee felt a sudden jolt of deja vu. "Didn't you mention him the night of the Southern Comfort slushes? Who was he again?"

"Why her one true love, honey. She met him while she was going to college." She shook her head sadly. "I thought I explained all that."

"I don't think so," Lee murmured, struggling to remember something that seemed just beyond the edge of her memory.

Granny Bob let out a deep sigh. "Well, forgive me, Kathryn," she spoke to the air about her, "but I think it's about time we let the cat out of the bag." She turned to Lee with a determined glint in her eye. "William was special, Lee. He was Kathryn's *grand-ee a-mor-a* as she used to say."

"She never mentioned him to me. I only knew about Papa Mardell." Lee opened the jewelry box and gasped at the beauty that sparkled from within its velvety folds.

"Kathryn met William that year she was working on her master's in New York." With a trembling finger, Granny Bob traced the simple square cut sapphire set in a gold band. "The two of them fell madly in love. He bought her this ring before...before some misunderstanding the two of them had. Your grandma never really explained to me what it was about.

"I think he was a soldier or maybe a reporter." Granny Bob shook her head unable to remember the long buried details. "Then, after the misunderstanding, he shipped over to England. Or was it France? I can't remember. Anyway, shortly after, he died in a bomb attack."

"Poor Nana. Was she all right? Did she ever get over him?"

"I don't know as she ever did, sweetie," Granny Bob said. "I think there was a little place in her heart that she always saved for him. 'Course she loved your Papa Mardell, but not in the same way she loved William. She used to tell me that she'd 'squandered her chance at true love.'"

"So was this an engagement ring?"

"Well, she never would tell me straight, but I got the feeling it was," Granny Bob answered. "She always told me she wanted it to go to you, since you got the Abney blue eyes." She hesitated, withdrawing her hand from Lee's. "And because she worried..."

"Yes?" Lee prompted when Granny Bob faltered.

"She worried that you were too much alike. That you both tended to put your personal life on hold, and let it be trampled by everything else."

Lee closed the jewelry box with a loud snap. "Well, it certainly is beautiful. It matches the drop she gave me for my sixteenth birthday. I can't understand how I never saw this before. Jenny and I used to play with all her jewelry. I'm glad you caught it before I gave it to the jeweler...

"Can I get you something to drink before you leave?" she asked, trying to change the subject and get away from Granny Bob's gaze.

"You know, honey, I think I'll head on home now. I'm

pretty worn out from all this. Makes me miss Kathryn an awful lot."

"Let me grab you a bag to carry your things."

"No need. I'll pop them in my purse," Granny Bob said, walking toward the front door. "Now you make sure and come to dinner tonight, hear? We aren't gonna have you around for too much longer and I want to make sure I fix you my Yam Yummies before you leave."

"It's a date. I'll see you around six," Lee said and opened the front door.

After she watched Granny Bob walk slowly down the street, Lee pulled the jewelry box out of her pocket and opened the lid once more. She slipped the ring out of its fold and held it up to the light. It sparkled and glinted with blue fire. Lee hesitated for a second and then slipped it onto the ring finger of her left hand. It fit perfectly.

"Oh, Nana, you must have been brokenhearted," she whispered to the air around her. "How did you bear it? How did you keep living?" Lee's eyes smarted. She quickly yanked the ring off her finger and placed it back inside the box.

It felt like a desecration to wear it. Love still seemed to pulsate off the cold, smooth metal and she couldn't bear the feeling of it on her finger.

The ring. Well, I guess I'd rather Lee have it than a stranger, but it still hurts to look at after all these years. I had it hidden away in the back of my jewelry chest but I never forgot for one second that it was there.

When William came back from Washington, I knew it was only a matter of time until he popped the question. Most women would have allowed themselves to be swept up in dreaming of the happy event, but fool that I was, all I could feel was dread.

I spent hours and hours walking up and down the streets of Manhattan trying to come up with a solution that let me have it both ways. A marriage with William and a life in fashion design, but no matter how I played the scenarios in my head, there was never one that let me have my cake and eat it too.

I talked to Dr. LeBlanc about it, but he let me know there were many others who would jump at the chance he was offering me, even if I would not. I talked to my roommate Doris about it, when we lay in our tiny cramped beds in the YWCA at night, and she laughed at me. How could anyone say no to handsome, sweet William, she asked? Men like him didn't come along often, she said. And she knew because she'd spent a lot of time looking.

The night finally came, a beautiful night with dinner and dancing, champagne and stardust. Afterwards, William walked me home through Central Park. Halfway through, he tugged me to a bench, bent down on one knee, and asked me to marry him.

I remember it like it was yesterday.

"It's a sapphire, Kathryn, to match those beautiful blue eyes of yours. I want to grow old with these eyes," he said and kissed the closed lids. "I want to look into them the

first time we make love and when we hold our first baby in our arms." His lips moved to mine and I felt myself begin to melt into acceptance.

"No, William, I can't." I gasped and jerked away suddenly like I'd been burned. I hadn't known until that moment what my answer would be. "You're going to Washington and I can't...can't come. I have to see what I can make of myself here. I'd be a fool to give up this chance." A fool, that's what Dr. LeBlanc had said when I told him I wasn't sure if I'd stay.

"Kathryn, please don't throw this away," he begged and pulled me up, his arms still around me. "We'll find a way to make it all work out. I promise. I don't want you to give up anything for me. I know we can find a solution, but we've got to figure it out together."

"No," I said as I disentangled myself from him. "You're going off to Washington and I'm staying here. They're not that far apart." I tried to sound hopeful. "And then maybe...after the war?"

"After the war?" His sharp laughter cut through me like a knife. "You're so sure things can stay the same? The world's gone mad, Kathryn, and if we don't hold onto each other now, we're never going to get another chance."

"That's a ridiculous ultimatum, William. Yes, the world's gone mad, but let's not go mad with it." I reached for his arm, but he pulled away. "Let's just take this a bit slower," I pleaded. "Why don't we try a long-distance relationship for a while and see what happens? I'm sure it'll work out if it's meant to be. You know I love you,

William."

"As a matter of fact, I don't. But you keep that ring, along with your delusions."

He reached out and gave my cheek a gentle stroke. "Maybe it'll all work out in the end." He lifted my hand and gave it a gentle kiss, right on the ring. Then he turned and disappeared into the darkness.

It was the last time I ever saw him.

CHAPTER THIRTY-ONE

A loud knock at the door broke the silence. Lee shoved the ring back into its box and then inside her pocket before she opened the door. John Hunter stood before her, looking sweaty and exhausted.

"Hey, just saw Granny leave and I wondered if I could show you what my team and I got done so far in the backyard."

"Of course, but you look worn out. Would you like something to drink?"

"Nah, I'm okay." John's gaze fell to the floor. "I got a water cooler out here and I don't wanna get Nana's house all dirty."

Lee checked her phone. She had a little bit of time before the jeweler arrived. "I can come for a few minutes," she said, knowing this would probably be her only free moment during the whole day. She shoved her bare feet in a pair of flip flops and followed him.

"I think you're going to be surprised." John paused at the side of the yard. "I got the sod in while you and Bobby were meeting. It changes everything."

"I'll close my eyes and you lead me. That way I can get the full effect." She reached out her hands.

John hesitated at her outstretched fingers and wiped his grimy hands on his jeans.

"It's fine, John. I'm a rock climber. I'm used to dirt."

"All right," he agreed and gently tugged her toward the backyard.

"You can open your eyes now."

Blinking, Lee gasped at the change before her. If she hadn't known better, she'd have thought she was in the wrong backyard. Where there had been a jungle of overgrown trees, bushes and kudzu before, now there was a yard of manicured beauty that was reminiscent of a European garden.

Lavender clumps lined the gracefully curving flagstone walkway that ran from the house to the back of the lot. Clustered red rose bushes were placed in intervals along the path, which meandered between two stately magnolias John Hunter had left as sentinels near the middle of the space. The trees were surrounded by lush flower beds of hostas, ferns and bleeding hearts. Filling the space between the clusters of flowers and symmetrical beds, there now lay a fresh, bright carpet of grass.

The path ended next to two large urns near a tinkling fountain under a pergola. The urns were filled with ferns and trailing sweet potato vines. A flower bed surrounded the secluded enclave and daisies, more lavender, periwinkle and foxglove peeped in and out of the short wrought iron fence that surrounded it.

"John, it's, it's completely...I can't even find the words. You're an artist. This is more than beautiful, it's breathtaking."

"Glad you like it."

"Like it? The change is miraculous! It doesn't even look like the same place. Your landscaping makes the house look like it's a historic home and not an old, rundown place in need of some major help."

"Well, that was the plan."

She grabbed his arm, almost jumping up and down in excitement. "You have a gift. You know that, don't you? I was picturing something like your yard, which looks perfect with your little house, but that wouldn't have worked here, would it?"

John shook his head, smiling.

"You read this house. You knew how to make the landscaping reflect the beauty of the home. It's just like the inside of Nana's house now." She turned back toward the yard to drink in its beauty again. "Am I right?"

"Yes, ma'am, you are," John said. "See, the way I landscaped my house would have been all wrong here. I wanted my house to look like it sorta *grew* out of a wildflower field. But Nana's house—this is a place that wants you to stand up straight, slick back your hair and make sure your shirt's tucked in. I wanted the yard to look just like that, but not fussy. It's a house you gotta respect, but it's got a graceful beauty that needs to shine through."

"Sort of like Nana," Lee said, tears catching in her throat.

"Just like Nana." John's voice came softly from over her shoulder and he squeezed her arm in understanding.

Without thinking, Lee leaned back against him, her head coming to rest against his chest. After a moment, his arms wrapped around her waist. Lee sighed, feeling as if the weight of her grief had been temporarily shared, and cradled her arms on top of his.

A shout broke the silence and Lee spied a man peering around the side of the house. She tried to pull away from John, but he held her tight.

"Hey, boss! The truck with the mulch for the flower beds is here. Where do you want him to dump it?"

"Out front. Next to my truck!" John hollered over Lee's head, then she felt his breath against her ear as he spoke to her. "Guess it's time to finish up here and work some of this same magic in the front yard."

"I can't wait to see it," Lee managed to gasp, heat surging through her body where his arms encircled her. She was torn between wanting to jerk away and bolt back to the house or turn around to look into his eyes. Jenny's words ran through her mind: *that was then, this is now.* But did she want a now? Did John *deserve* a now? She stiffened.

"All right, then," John Hunter said, releasing her.

"All right," Lee echoed, her heart hammering in her chest.

"Boss! The mulch guy says you gotta come pay up now!" The worker's voice came again and Lee felt John move away. She took a deep breath and turned to him.

"I said I'm coming!" John yelled, his eyes never leaving Lee's face.

"See you tonight at Granny's?"

"Yes, I'll be there." Lee's voice was so faint, she wondered if he'd heard her.

John finally took a few more steps away and the spell was broken.

"Now don't you let your dog run riot back here and destroy all the work we've done," he said before turning away and jogging to the front yard.

"Yes," Lee looked around her, shaking her head to clear away the dream-like quality of the last few minutes. Her eyes returned to John's retreating form. "This would be all too easy to destroy."

CHAPTER THIRTY-TWO

The rest of Lee's afternoon spun away in a whirlwind of activity. Blake Etherby, the jewelry collector, stopped by and, after picking his jaw up off the floor, began to photograph, annotate and pack away Nana's extensive jewelry collection in several locking briefcases. He had to call his assistant to bring him several more.

While he was still in the middle of sorting, Sarah Beth from the furniture consignment shop arrived with two burly helpers. They loaded up a moving truck with most of Nana's furniture, artwork, china, silverware and decorations, except for the things Lee asked them to leave behind.

Lee spent the afternoon running back and forth between Sarah Beth and Blake, answering questions and helping where she could. The Realtor sent her another email in the middle of everything, which Lee had to read through before sending off the final draft to her father for approval.

She glanced at the clock as Sarah Beth's movers pulled away with their final load and realized it was only about twenty minutes until she was supposed to be at Bobby's house for dinner and that she'd never had any lunch. Her stomach growled. Lee sprinted upstairs and took a quick shower before feeding Charlie and heading down the street.

Later Lee felt almost dazed with exhaustion while she sat at Granny Bob's table and ate the pork chop Creole. Granny Bob moved to refill her plate.

"Thank you, but please don't feed me another bite. I think you might kill me."

"Well, I'm glad you enjoyed it, honey," Granny Bob replied as she put one more spoonful of yams and a slice of praline apple cake on Lee's plate.

"Enjoyed it? I don't think I've eaten like this since Thanksgiving, and your cooking is so much better." Lee turned to John Hunter. "Do you feast like this all the time?"

John chuckled and shrugged.

"How come you're not the size of this house?"

"Well, because he works his tail off all day, or hadn't you noticed?" Granny Bob laughed.

"Yes, he does," Lee sat up in her seat and gave a glowing report of his work.

"Your grandson's a real artist," Lee said when she'd finished her description. "I can't remember ever seeing such beautiful yards as yours, his and Nana's."

John Hunter just smiled.

"Well, after all the work you two have done today, I insist that you let me do the dishes tonight," Granny Bob said, rising from the table. "No, no, I insist," she interrupted their protests. "Why don't y'all take your sweet tea out in the backyard and relax. I'll join you when I'm finished."

The two agreed without too much protest. Lee called Charlie to join them, but he was firmly planted at the foot of the table where he waited for a chance to steal more scraps while Granny Bob cleared up.

John stretched and yawned as they walked onto the back patio. "You must be exhausted," Lee said. She spied a hammock in the corner of the yard and turned to him. "Why don't you go lay down. I'll drag a chair over by you."

John hesitated for only a moment. "That does sound nice right about now. Guess I'm worn pretty thin from these last couple days. Stayed up until three the other night working on my paper." He picked up a chair for Lee and set it next to the hammock.

"What section are you on with your dissertation?" Lee asked after she sat down and John lay on the lazily swinging hammock. She tried to listen, but with her stomach full of food and the soft drawl of John's voice, Lee felt herself relaxing to a state of near stupor. A giant yawn almost split her head in two. John Hunter cocked his head at the sound.

"Why don't you come over here and lay down too?" he suggested from the lengthening shadows. "Remember this thing is made for more than one person. I think a couple a times we had Tammy, me, you, your brother and sister all crammed here like a barrel full of monkeys."

"No, that's okay," Lee protested half-heartedly.

"Aw, come on, Caralee, don't be such a baby." John

imitated the imperious tone of his youth. "Get over here, before I make you!"

Lee laughed and stood up. "Oh, all right, but only if you don't hog all the room. I always fell through the end, thanks to you."

"I promise." John scooted to one side and Lee sat down on the other. She twisted and flipped her legs up, instantly rolling to the middle of the hammock where John Hunter's greater weight pulled her. She landed on the left side of his body, her head on his shoulder and her arm and leg flung across him.

"Sorry," she said and tried to push herself away to a less intimate distance. "I guess our weights were a little closer when we were kids." She kept struggling, without success, to get to the edge of the hammock.

"Just lie still," John said after a few more seconds of her thrashing. "You're gonna knock this whole thing over and I'm already bruised enough as it is, thanks to you."

"Oh, sorry." Lee went still. She'd hit him pretty hard with that fireplace poker.

Her body slid back towards John Hunter's and she held it rigid, away from his warm presence.

"Just calm down." His voice was softer now. "Lay still and close your eyes. I promise I won't bite. You won't even know I'm here."

She let out a tense breath and then relaxed as John slipped his arm under her head. This wasn't right. There were questions she needed to ask. Explanations she should demand. History that needed to be dredged. A few moments passed.

"See, isn't this nice?" John murmured softly, his lips next to her temple.

"Umm." Lee felt her eyes closing at the gentle *thump, thump, thump* of his heart. Maybe the questions could wait.

"You're so intense, sugar." His voice sounded sleepy now too. "Sometimes you just gotta let things go and relax, at least for a little bit."

"I'll try," she mumbled, before sleep overtook them both.

She woke to the gentle tinkle of dog tags. In the twilight shadows from where her head rested on John Hunter's shoulder, she could barely make out Charlie's white mask and paws as he nosed around Granny Bob's garden.

The soft cadence of John's sleeping breath held her still. She didn't want him to awaken yet, so she allowed herself to close her eyes again and pretend.

Every bit of her body felt completely at rest, almost as if she'd been drugged. The wind fluttered through the tree leaves above and the soft smell of honeysuckle and other flowers danced through the humidity. Nighttime sounds, the cicadas warming up to their evening serenade, a screen creaking and slamming shut next door, and a mother calling her children in for the night, filled the air.

It was one of those moments, Lee realized, that would be imprinted into the fabric of her memory for the rest of her life. A moment of supreme peace, similar to how she felt at the end of a long, hard climb, but a gentler version.

What if she didn't leave Eden Grove? The wild thought leapt into her mind. What if she stayed here with Granny Bob, Emma, Tom and all the other people she'd met in the last week? She pictured herself helping Granny Bob weed her vegetable garden and babysitting little Davey while drinking vast quantities of sweet tea.

And what about John Hunter? What could evolve with him if she gave it a chance? Unbidden, an image of them dancing on his front porch popped into Lee's mind. Her forehead rested against his cheek. His arms entwined around her back as the two swayed to the notes of a soft, slow song. Lee's bare feet absorbed the warmth from the wooden floorboards beneath them and her fingers wove through the dark waves of John's hair.

But then the reality of her world came barging into the lovely dream. She didn't live here, couldn't live here. Her business, her home, everything she knew was back in Durango. What kind of career could she make for herself here? Lee pictured the verdant green fields that surrounded Eden Grove. No chance for rock climbing or skiing; the image of her in John Hunter's arms faded away.

And of course there was Kiki. Now it was Kiki in John's embrace, her arms snaked possessively around the man she thought she all but owned. Lee knew she couldn't compete with a hometown girl. And from what Emma and Tom had said, it was too late to find out anyway.

Besides, there was too much history between John and her, on Lee's side anyway. Every time she thought of

John's kiss in the tree house it grieved her that he thought so little of it, so little of her. Either he'd forgotten the entire incident or felt it was so insignificant that it didn't matter. But he had been her best friend; it had been her first kiss, a milestone she was not yet prepared for. His stolen intimacy and then desertion broke her heart and she didn't think it ever truly healed.

She tensed with the realization and felt the confused, helpless rage of her childhood flood through her once more.

"You awake?" John's voice rumbled against her ear.

"Mm-hm."

"Guess we both sorta dozed off." John rubbed at his eyes with his free hand before returning it to Lee's waist.

"Guess so," she said, wishing for the sweet oblivion of sleep again.

She felt his lips brush her forehead again.

"Do you ever wonder, Lee," John murmured, "how things would have been if—"

"So what's the deal with you and this Kiki woman?" She forced out the question, her voice rough.

"What?"

Lee pulled away from him.

"I just...I had breakfast with Emma and Tom this morning and they told me you two were pretty serious." Lee hated the hurt in John's voice, but she barged on. "There was even talk of a ring?"

John Hunter untangled himself from Lee, flung his legs over the edge of the hammock and stood. "So y'all were talking about me, were you?" He spoke with an exaggerated drawl and Lee caught the glint of his eyes in the porch light.

She wrestled herself out of the hammock and faced him with arms crossed. "Yes, they're worried about you, John Hunter. And after meeting Kiki, I'd have to agree. She doesn't seem like a good fit. But then, who could ever know what's really going on in your heart? It seems to do whatever it feels like, regardless of who gets hurt."

"That's the pot calling the kettle black," John muttered.

"What?"

"Tell you what, Caralee, I'll thank you to mind your own business and I'll mind mine." John's voice was icy cold. "I think it's best you probably head on home now." He turned and stalked toward Granny Bob's house.

Lee watched him jerk open the door and slam it closed. A sob attempted to rip its way through her chest.

"No," she whispered brokenly to the reproving silence around her. "It would have been stupid to pretend."

"Come on, Charlie." She whistled and the dog trotted to her side, tail wagging.

Burning at her cowardice, Lee took off her belt and looped it through Charlie's collar rather than venture back into Granny Bob's house for his leash. She let herself through the side gate and ran all the way back to Nana's house, the sound of her shoes hitting the street like loud slaps echoed between the houses.

CHAPTER THIRTY-THREE

Watching those two on the hammock about breaks my heart.

Just like all those pretty flowers John's been planting in my yard, there is something beautiful growing up between the two of them. All they have to do is reach out and grab it. One kiss seemed to change everything back when they were kids. One kiss could redeem all the misunderstandings.

But they're both such cowards. Why won't they just be honest for once?

I follow Caralee back to my house, hopping mad, but when I see her fall down on my bed and cry her poor little heart out, I calm down.

Well, I've been in the exact same place. Didn't I cry my heart out after I turned William down? I tried to contact him a few weeks after his proposal to tell him I'd made a mistake, but by then it was too late. The editor at his old paper told me William had accepted a job with the International Press Service and gone to London. Only three days after he got there, his office was bombed. I told the newsman I didn't believe him, so he gave me the telegram to prove it.

International Press Service regrets to inform you London HQ bombed. No survivors. All staff presumed dead.

Remembering that terrible day I decide I can give my baby girl grace for making the same mistake as me. I sit down next to Caralee, all balled up in a knot of pain on the bed, and wish I could sing her to sleep like I used to.

Caralee always had a hard time falling asleep, especially when she was young. Her daddy would fill up her mind with watch out for this, *and* be careful of that, *and* you'd better watch your brother and sister, or I'm holding you responsible for anything that happens to them.

By the time she got here, she was wound up tighter than a top and the poor little thing could barely sleep for worrying at night. Usually around ten o'clock, I'd hear my door creak and her little feet pattering across the floor.

"Nana," she'd say, "could I just close my eyes with you for a few minutes? I'm having a hard time falling asleep."

I'd curl up around her back, "to keep away the bedbugs and bad dreams," I'd always say, and it never failed. Caralee would be asleep in a matter a minutes.

So tonight I do the same thing; I begin singing the song I'd always whisper in her ear on those nights from long ago.

Hush a bye, don't you cry,
Go to sleep my pretty baby.
When you wake, you shall have

All the pretty little horses.
Blacks and bays, dapples and grays,
All the pretty little horses.
Hush a bye, don't you cry,
Go to sleep my little baby.

I can sense her body relaxing, so I start talking. I finally tell her about William and my terrible mistake. Then I tell her what an amazing man John Hunter is. That she'd regret it the rest of her life if she doesn't give that boy a chance to earn her forgiveness and win her heart.

To my surprise she pulls me into her dreams and starts arguing with me.

"But Nana, life isn't a fairy tale. There's no such thing as the type of love you're talking about!"

"Well, there is and there isn't, darling," I say. "When you first fall in love, that person seems like a Prince Charming straight out of those fairy tales. But life marches on and you start to face the valleys and mountains together and fairy-tale love won't get you through that. So you'd better have something a little stronger up your sleeve."

"Exactly! So why even try? Why get your hopes up?"

"Why, don't you hear what I'm saying to you? Friendship, respect and loyalty are what get you through the valleys. Passion floats along and hits you like the lottery every once in a while. But you, Caralee, are a truly blessed woman. You've got love and friendship and passion and all sorts of beautiful things between you and John

Hunter. I've seen it."

She just shakes her head at me. "I don't know what I have with him."

"Honey, do you know how rare this is?" I plead with her. "Please don't throw it away! Most people would die to have a chance at what you could have with John Hunter."

"But what if it all falls apart again? We messed it up once, I'm sure it'll happen again." I can feel her little heart pounding when she tells me this. "It's better not to get your hopes up."

"I've seen the way John Hunter looks at you, and I've felt the way he dreams about you. You aren't getting your hopes up, I promise. But you're going to have to be brave, Caralee. I know you've been hurt, but think of the man you've worked with these last few days and the boy you knew growing up. You'll regret it if you don't give him a chance to prove himself. Trust him with your hopes."

"I'll have to think about it," she says.

It's about all I can do to keep my temper with her, but I keep reminding myself, this might be the last conversation we ever have, even if she doesn't remember it.

"You just let your heart dream about that boy a bit. See where it takes you. It's going to tell you what you really want."

I get up then and let her dream her dreams. It's her decision now, so I give my baby girl a squeeze and a kiss on the forehead. I spend the rest of the night in the wingback chair by the window, watching over her and that stupid dog.

In the morning Lee woke up with a sour taste in her mouth. The tension in her chest radiated through her whole body and she wondered how she'd been able to sleep at all. Not that she'd had much rest, she realized as the dreams of the night before began to come back to her.

She dreamed she was a little girl, sitting in the gazebo with Nana. Nana was scolding her for something stupid she'd done, but then soothed her when she started to cry.

She dreamed she was 13 again, and climbing up in John Hunter's lookout, but when she got to the top, she was an adult. And this time when he reached out to kiss her, there was no confusion, no shock at the way he held her. She kissed him back.

Last, she dreamed about her home in Durango, that she was asleep in her big queen bed, with Charlie at her feet, but when she turned over, it was John Hunter who lay next to her, his muscular arm thrown across her waist.

Then all of them began to fade away, the way dreams do, and soon the only thing she could remember was the anger in John's voice last night.

CHAPTER THIRTY-FOUR

After Lee forced herself out of bed she decided to go on an early morning jog with Charlie. She made a quick escape from the house, hoping she wouldn't run into anyone, but the street was deserted.

Had John Hunter been so angry last night that he'd decided to give up on Nana's yard? Her mind rejected this possibility almost as soon as it formed the thought. No matter how mad he'd been, John Hunter took his job way too seriously to let his personal life keep him from finishing a contract.

As she ran down the tree-lined streets, she noticed that most of the other houses, yards and sidewalks were deserted too. *Where is everyone?*

A police car pulled to a stop at the sleepy intersection ahead of her. The window rolled down after a moment and Grant Tucker leaned over the window sill.

"I wondered if I might find you running around with your dog instead of sitting in church like a good Southerner."

"Church?" Lee slowed to a walk and came alongside the squad car. Charlie jerked at the leash impatiently.

"Yeah, Caralee, it's Sunday. Doesn't anyone go to

church anymore where you're from?" He raised his eyebrow.

"Well, why aren't *you* in church, then? You being one of the good guys and all." She didn't feel like she could handle a lecture this morning.

"'Cuz the lawbreakers don't take Sunday off, which means I can't either," Grant drawled, letting his gaze travel over Lee's body.

Irritated, she craned her head to look down the two peaceful streets that branched from the intersection. "Yeah, I can see how it would turn into the LA riots if you weren't here, Grant. Thank goodness the law never sleeps." She tacked on a smile to her sarcasm, remembering he had done her a favor earlier in the week.

"Ain't you a little firecracker?" Grant chuckled. The radio attached to his belt blared to life. "Fender bender on the corner of 1st and Myrtle. Officer to the scene."

"Officer Tucker on 8th and Strachen. I'm on it," Grant spoke into the radio. "There, you see. Even if this isn't New York City, we still got our share of mayhem in Eden Grove too. Always fender benders after church on Sunday. Some of the old folks don't remember how to drive so well and this is about the only time they get out."

"Oh, right," Lee answered, regretting her harsh words. Couldn't he just leave her alone to run?

"Hey, before I go, wanted to check if you'd still like to go to the fair with me?"

"Fair?" Lee dredged her brain and their conversation in front of Piggly Wiggly came back. "Remind me of the details again."

"There's a big Cajun band coming to play on the first night of the county fair. I thought you might like to go with me?"

"I've about wrapped up with Nana's house," Lee said. The last thing she felt like doing was dancing the night away. "I'm not sure if I'll still be here."

"It's tomorrow night. You're not leaving before tomorrow, are you?"

Lee shook her head. The painters were coming tomorrow and she also needed to pick up her U-Haul sometime on Monday too. Then she'd have to spend the day loading it. She couldn't be out of Eden Grove until Tuesday morning at the very earliest.

"We could just stop by for a few minutes," Grant urged. "Wouldn't have to stay long. I just figure this'll be the last time you'll probably even be in Eden Grove. Might be nice for you to have one night on the town."

"You're right," Lee agreed. It would be her last time, she was certain of that. And she'd been so busy on Nana's house, she hadn't really stopped to enjoy the town she so loved as a child. "Thanks for inviting me. It would be a nice way to say good-bye."

"Great. I'll be by to pick you up about six o'clock? They'll be having barbecue before the dance."

"Yes, I'll be ready."

"See you then." Grant waved and rolled up the window.

As he pulled away, Lee glanced down at Charlie, who

seemed to stare at her with barely concealed disgust.

"All right, I know he's a little...but it's just for the evening. And hopefully we'll be leaving the next day. Now come on, let's run."

A little while later, Lee, whose mind had been absorbed with endless replays of last night's drama on the hammock, found herself at the outskirts of Lake Montikata. She blinked, surprised at how far she'd run, and registered Charlie's panting. His tongue hung far from his mouth, so she trotted to the lake and released him from his leash. The dog leapt into the water and began to gulp as if it might disappear.

"Take it easy, boy," she said from the shore. "You'll give yourself a stomach ache." Charlie turned to her with a happy, panting smile, then the movement of a catfish swimming under the dock caught his eye and he took off like a shot.

"Watch out for alligators!" she called after him.

Lee turned and studied the beach around her. The old resort that she'd loved as a child looked much the same, with only a few updates. The little beach shack where they could order a greasy burger or the largest ice cream cone they'd ever seen was where it had always been, only with a closed sign on its window this early Sunday morning.

During her childhood summers, Lake Montikata had been a favorite haunt of Jenny, Mark and Lee's. Hours spent diving off the dock, playing on the rafts and trying to catch catfish had been followed by evening fireworks on Friday nights and sing-a-longs on the beach. Nana and

Granny Bob had often brought the grandkids to this spot. It must have been the perfect place to take five rambunctious children for the day.

Lounge chairs, straightened by the lifeguards last night, stood in neat rows on the beach. Lee lay down in one and watched Charlie frolic through the water. This is where Nana and Granny Bob had positioned themselves, sentries over the grandkids while they sunbathed, read magazines and caught up on local gossip.

Lee closed her eyes and the memories were so strong, she could almost swear she was only taking a break next to Nana while the other kids played a game of Marco Polo.

One time, she remembered, her dad had come instead. Nana was hosting a colloquium at the university and the kids begged their father to take them to the lake. It was Friday after all. There would be fireworks.

Her father reluctantly agreed, leaving his usual station of Nana's upstairs den, where he spent hours reading medical journals and catching up on his continuing education credits while Mark, Jenny and Lee ran wild through Eden Grove.

It was one of her favorite times at Lake Montikata. Her father spent all afternoon shooting them through the air into the deep part of the lake and playing sea monster. He did crazy dives off the edge of the dock and let the kids cling to his back while he swam them past the buoy lines of the lake.

She remembered that she'd been so proud he was her dad that day. As she munched chips on shore and watched the other kids play, Lee felt Nana's hand on her shoulder.

"You have a wonderful father." Nana spoke after a moment. "And this is who he really is. I want you to promise me, you'll remember that."

But she hadn't remembered, Lee knew. There were too many angry words and misunderstandings between her father and her and, over the years, the memory had been lost in a hopeless tangle of hurt.

Lee sighed and stretched. Charlie lay asleep on the dock now, his thick, shaggy fur drying in the warm sun. She decided to give him a bit longer so the smell of wet dog wouldn't accompany them on the jog back into town.

Besides, thinking of her father had reminded her she needed to call him and see if he had any changes on the listing agreement. Otherwise, Nana's house would go on the market tomorrow.

She dialed his number.

"Hello, Dad, this is Lee. I was calling to see if there were any changes you wanted me to tell the Realtor before she finalizes everything."

"Glad you called. I just finished reading it late last night and wanted to let you know it looks fine."

"Oh. Good." Lee fell silent. She hadn't expected *fine*.

"How are you holding up?"

"Oh, you know." Lee shooed away a fly from her leg.

"I've...I've been talking to Jenny and she told me everything you've had to do."

"Are she and the baby doing well?"

"Yes, they're fine. But she...she actually chewed me

out a bit."

"That doesn't sound like Jenny." Lee bit her lip.

"No, but she's nine months pregnant, you know. I think her usual veneer of politeness is wearing pretty thin."

Lee laughed. "Lucky Brad."

"The thing is, Lee. I wanted to apologize for sending you down there alone. I don't think I realized just how huge of an undertaking this would be."

"That's okay," Lee said, her voice muted with surprise.

"No, it's not okay. I think I mentioned to you in one of our last phone calls that Nana's house was always a painful place for me after your mother died. Especially the front porch. That's where the two of us spent a lot of time when we were dating." His voice cracked and he lapsed into silence for a moment. "When we'd pull up in front of Nana's house, I'd see the porch and your mother felt so close again. It made me act like...well, I know I wasn't much fun whenever we went to see Nana."

Lee swiped at the tears trickling down her cheeks. "That wasn't always true, Dad. I'm sitting on the beach of Lake Montikata right now and just before I called you I was remembering the time you came. It was the most fun I ever had here."

"That was one time, Lee. That's my point."

"Well...it's better than no times." She tried to laugh, but her voice cracked.

"I'm so sorry." Her dad's voice rushed through the phone. "I've been thinking through some of my choices, the ones I've made as a father. I guess Nana's death is some sort of catalyst, but I want you to know, I've made some decisions I wish I hadn't. I hope it's not—"

"Dad?" Lee spoke into the suddenly silent phone. "Dad, are you still there? Can you hear me?"

"Sorry, Lee," he said, brisk and professional once again. "One of my patients is going into cardiac arrest. I'll call you back when I can."

The line went dead.

Lee stared at the blank screen for a minute then threw her phone into the sand and burst into tears. As sobs wracked through her body, she bent over double in the lounge chair. The loss of a mother she barely remembered and then of Nana, her fight with John Hunter and now her father's regrets fused into a searing pain in her chest.

This was why she tried to keep everyone at arm's length, she knew. To be friendly and polite, but not let anyone get too close. Loneliness was better than heartbreak and an empty house was so much safer than one filled with anger, regret and bitterness.

Her sobs slowly abated and Lee wiped her eyes and nose on the hem of her shirt. Feeling bone-numbingly weary, she stumbled as she stood from the lounger. She picked up the phone and dusted it off.

"Charlie!" She called sharply and the dog leapt to his feet. "Come on. Let's go."

Lee clipped the leash to his collar and began to run. She could sense Charlie looking up at her but kept her gaze trained to the horizon.

CHAPTER THIRTY-FIVE

Lee swallowed her regrets and tears on the jog home, tired of grieving for a past that she couldn't wait to get away from and shove back into some hidden recess of her mind. Back at Nana's house there were trucks, plants and piles of dirt everywhere. Not seeing John Hunter, she sprinted up the front steps and let herself in as quickly as possible, almost tripping over Charlie's leash in the process.

She called the U-Haul dealership to see if she could pick up her trailer today, but the earliest they could have one was first thing Monday morning.

Lee let out a frustrated groan and realized it was probably for the best, as much as she wanted to get out of Eden Grove. The painters were coming early in the morning anyway. She could give them their instructions and refer them to Granny Bob if they had any questions, pick up and pack the trailer, then drop off the keys at the Realtor's on her way out of town.

Lee glanced around Nana's house. Her mind raced with the last few details she needed to complete. Nothing of the flavor and character of Nana remained. Aside from the fancy new landscaping, the structure of the building still looked the same, but on the inside, it was evident that the home was now merely an empty shell.

Like me, Lee thought, but quickly banished the thought. She forced herself upstairs. *Only one day more,* she promised herself as she packed a box. One day.

A loud rapping awakened her later. She'd dozed off in a wingback chair going through the last of Nana's personal papers. The shadows had begun to stretch across the floor and she could see the sun sinking in the western horizon from the bedroom window. The loud knock sounded again and she ran down the stairs.

"Coming," she called. "I'm coming!"

Lee jerked open the door; it was John Hunter.

"Oh, hi. I was asleep."

"Sorry to wake you," John answered tightly. "Just wanted to let you know we're pretty much all done and I'm fixing to head home." He gestured to the front yard behind him.

Lee peeked around his shoulder and saw another freshly sodded and flowered landscape; however, she felt none of the joy and wonder she'd experienced when she'd seen a similar transformation in the backyard. Just an aching finality.

"It looks wonderful." Her voice sounded hollow, even to her.

"Thanks." John glanced at a notepad in his dirt-stained hands. "I just have a couple more odd jobs that I'll send one of my boys out to fix tomorrow. Shouldn't take long."

"Fine." Lee nodded, feeling sick at the distance

between them. “And just to let you know, I’ll probably be taking off tomorrow too.”

“Tomorrow?” John asked. His gaze darted from the notepad to Lee’s face.

“Yes, I need to get back home to work. You have my cell number if you have any questions, but I’m letting the Realtor take over the last few details of the house. It’s really just a fresh coat of paint and the house cleaners coming through at this point. I’d be in the way.”

“But...tomorrow?” John asked again, his voice louder. “Were you even going to say good-bye? To Granny? To me?”

“Of course,” Lee snapped, her head throbbing. “I was going to stop by Granny Bob’s tomorrow on the way out of town and say my good-byes.”

“But what about me?” John demanded. “Were you just going to leave forever? Without a single word? Just like last time?”

Like last time? He was the one who had left her! Hopeless resentment rose up inside of her, but she tried to hold her anger in check. “Yes, I was going to leave. Last night you made it pretty clear that I wasn’t all that welcome in your life.”

“Last night? Last night you behaved like a green-eyed monster, badmouthing a woman who’s been with me through quite a lot these last fifteen years. Unlike you.”

Lee recoiled. “Green-eyed, John? Oh wait, I get it...because you’re God’s gift to women.”

“Now wait a second—”

"I mean, we girls just can't help ourselves." Lee flung her arms wide, barely aware of what she was saying. "John Hunter steps into a room and catfights and hair pulling follow in his wake. Then the victor gets her spoils, but who knows if John will even be there the next morning."

"What in the Sam Hill is the matter with you? You're behaving like—"

"It must be so hard to handle your adoring entourage, John. I'm sure you've got a pack of girls up there in Ashville as well. Keeping them all straight must be a full-time job."

"Just stop it, Lee!" John barked, taking a step towards her, his eyes full of fire. "Don't you *dare* paint me as that kind of man, some kind of no-account philanderer?"

Lee sucked in her breath, realizing the terrible words she'd let tumble from her mouth. "John, I didn't think...I shouldn't have—"

"Do you know how much I hate the sort of man you just called me? The sort of coward that walks out on his wife and two young children because he has women waiting for him in every town this side of the Mississippi?"

Lee flinched and John's voice dropped in volume but cut her with its icy tone. "All my life I've done everything I could to be the opposite of that man, my father. To be the kind of man my son could be proud of, if I ever have one. So don't you dare go throwing that comparison in my face."

"John, listen," Lee begged.

"No, you listen," he grabbed her shoulders roughly and ignored her pleas. He pulled her to him and spoke into her ear with a fearsome intensity.

"I have loved you since before I can remember. I *lived* for those few weeks you would visit Nana each year. And then...then, you know what happened between us that last summer." He let go and Lee stumbled against the door frame. "After that, nothing. You, gone, and me, alone. My best friend and the girl I thought I loved, disappeared in one night. I know I behaved like a hormonal fool, but I tried to explain in my letters. Tried to apologize. But could you forgive me?" He shook his head sadly. "I waited Lee, but 20 years is a long time. Was I not allowed to try and find someone else to share my life with? Was I supposed to stop living until you finally decided to show up here again?"

"I'm sorry, John. I lost my temper, but what do you mean?" She grabbed at the air between them.

"No." John's voice was final. He pushed her hands away and firmly placed them at her sides. "I'm not going to that place with you again, Caralee. This week I wondered...but no. I have a chance for a life here, and I'm not going to throw that away. I've spent too many years hoping for something that will never be."

He spun on his heel and strode off without a backward glance.

"John," Lee called after him, her voice clogged with bewildered regret, but either John didn't hear her or he refused to respond.

Lee watched him walk down the street for a moment before angrily wiping her cheeks. She heard a whine and looked down to see Charlie next to her, his eyes on the now distant form of John Hunter.

"Come on, Charlie," she tugged on his collar, her voice cracking with the emotions she tried to swallow away. The empty house rattled when she slammed the front door. Charlie looked up at her and whined again, flattening his ears down and slinking around Lee's legs.

"Don't worry, buddy, everything's fine."

But it's not, a voice in her head argued. Nothing's fine. This whole trip has been anything but fine. She was even more confused now than she'd been as a 13-year-old.

Her fingers slipped from Charlie's collar, and the dog raced back to his kennel. Lee trudged wearily upstairs determined to move everything in her room down by the front door so it would be ready to go in the morning. The sooner she was in her car heading home, the better.

As I watch the delicate thing that had been growing between the two of them die, shriveling in Caralee's sarcasm and John Hunter's anger, I feel a powerful weariness fall upon me. The world keeps repeating the same old, tired stories over and over and over. Isn't there ever a chance for a different ending? I wonder.

In my day it was war and not having two pennies to rub together that kept people apart. In my grandmama's day, I know it was social status and having no independence as a woman that kept her and her love from being together—she wanted to marry a poor man from the other side of the tracks and my great-granddaddy wouldn't hear of it. In my great-great-granddaddy's day, it was the racial intolerance that kept him from marrying the Cherokee woman he loved so well.

Are we doomed to repeat the failings of our ancestors, the ones who've lived the same stories as us but in different times and with different details? Seems like, just about the time you deal with one problem that keeps people apart, ten more sprout up in its place.

I thought I had figured out why I'm still here. Maybe the Good Lord wanted some help untangling this mess Caralee and John Hunter have created, these ridiculous misunderstandings and excuses that are keeping them from each other. But if that was his aim, guess I failed him and Caralee in that too.

CHAPTER THIRTY-SIX

Lee rose early the following day, collecting garbage and setting a few more boxes on the curb for the secondhand store's last pick up. The painters had arrived early and, after discussing a few details, she left them to their work. Next, she and Charlie set out in the Jeep to pick up the trailer and buy some travel snacks for the drive home.

The angry scene between John and her replayed through her mind on an endless loop. Most of his words were a blur, but whenever she remembered him telling her, "I have loved you since before I can remember," tears would film her eyes. And what had he meant about the letter? It was only by a monumental effort of self-will that she forced herself to blot out the incident and focus on her departure.

At last she pulled onto Nana's street, trailer in tow, and eased to a stop in front of the house. Charlie pressed his nose against the window as she walked to his door. She opened it and he shot toward the front of the house.

"Down, Charlie. Down, boy."

Lee froze in her tracks when she heard the voice from the shadows of the porch. *It couldn't be*. Charlie yipped in excitement while Lee stumbled up the walk.

"Dad, is that you?" Her voice shook. The crouching form stood and turned. "Dad!" Lee shrieked and shot into his arms. "You came. I can't believe you came," she choked out once enfolded in his strong arms.

"Lee, what's the matter?" Her father's voice rumbled against the top of her head. "I didn't think you'd be this upset to see me." It had been years since he'd held her like this and Lee sensed they both felt out of practice.

"No, no. I'm happy, Dad." She pulled away and tried to control her emotions, giving him a broken smile. "I'm just so glad you're here. That I don't have to finish this alone."

"Well, you shouldn't have had to do this much alone," he said as he pulled her tight again. "I called the airline and booked a ticket out here the second after I got off the phone with you yesterday. Well, the second after I took care of that heart attack, anyway."

"Thanks, Dad." Lee pulled herself away and wiped at her tears, embarrassed now at her outburst of emotion. "I was really getting to the end of my rope."

"Well, I'm here now," he said and bent to grab the small suitcase on the ground next to him. "Let's get inside and you tell me what to do."

Lee opened the door and her father took in the empty rooms around him. His footsteps echoed as he made a circuit through the downstairs, Charlie's claws click-clacking as they followed him.

"Look at this place." His voice echoed through the

foyer. “I tried but I couldn’t imagine it without Nana. First your mother and now her. Both gone.”

Lee nodded.

“And it looks like you’ve taken care of everything. I’m sorry I didn’t get here sooner.”

“It’s enough to have you here now.” Lee led him to the kitchen and got him a bottle of water from the nearly empty refrigerator. “There’s still a few details to tie up and it’ll be nice to not have to say good-bye all alone.”

Her dad jingled the keys in his pocket and looked out the window. “The inside looks fine and the outside’s beautiful. More beautiful than I’ve ever seen it.” He paused. “John Hunter did all this?”

“Yes.”

“He’s done an amazing job,” her father said. “I told him thanks when we talked, but I’ll have to reiterate when I see him later.”

“You talked to him?” Lee said, unease filling her stomach.

“Well, someone had to pick me up from the airport and you had your phone turned off, young lady.” Her dad shook his finger at her and gave her a wink.

“It got sand in it at the beach. The ringer’s not working right.”

“No, it’s fine,” he said, and putting his arm around her, led Lee over to the couch in the front room. “I knew you were probably busy and I had John’s number from the proposal he sent over, so I figured I’d give him a try.”

Lee groaned and her father studied her face.

"It's not a big deal, Lee. I could have easily taken a taxi if I didn't get ahold of someone."

"No, it's just that he and I...we had this. Never mind." Lee patted her father's arm and searched for something else to talk about. "So, has Eden Grove changed much since you were here last?"

"In some ways yes, but in some ways it seems just the same as it ever was." A sad smile turned the edge of his lips. "John drove me by Dot's Diner. It made me remember the first time I saw your mother. She was standing in front of Dot's. It was about a hundred degrees outside and she was eating an ice cream cone. It was melting all over her hands."

The two of them spent the next few hours reliving their favorite memories of Eden Grove and Nana. Most of her dad's memories were ones Lee had never heard before and she sat in rapt attention. Her dad, like a too-full dam finally bursting, poured out story after story. Stories about falling in love with her mother at first sight, asking her to prom, and courting her throughout high school and college on Nana's front porch. Lee felt an empty part of her heart become full and she stored up these histories she'd never heard from her family's past.

Her father's watch beeped and finally pulled them from their memories.

"Two o'clock? Is that really the time?" Her father rose from the window seat. "I can't believe I've wasted the whole day with my old tales."

"Not wasted, Dad." Lee laced her arm through his and

studied the empty home around her. "Nana never had a funeral or a wake. I think this was the perfect way to say good-bye. To her, this lovely old home, and to Eden Grove.

Her dad smiled and nodded. "What did you have planned for today? Before I barged in."

"Well, now that the painters are squared away, I was going to load up the trailer with that pile of things by the front door. I thought I'd leave this evening and drive through the night."

"Now, Lee, you know that's not safe," he said, a familiar sternness returning to his voice. "It only takes one long blink of the eye—"

"I know, I know, Dad." Lee chuckled and rubbed his arm soothingly. "We can leave anytime you want in the next few days. Unless you're flying back?"

"No, I can drive with you. You shouldn't make the trip alone."

"I'd really appreciate that," Lee said. "Now what should we do for our late lunch...or early dinner? I'm not sure if there's anything left in the freezer."

"I heard a woman at the airport say something about a fair tonight when I was collecting my suitcase. That sounds like it could be fun."

"Oh shoot. I promised someone I'd go to that."

"Was it John?" her father asked. "I can't get over what a fine young man he's become. He was telling me about his doctoral dissertation on the drive over here and I couldn't believe—"

"Not John," Lee burst out angrily before she could

stop herself. "He's too busy—" The anger and pain of their last conversation left her struggling for words.

"Too busy? That's not the impression I got." Her father studied Lee's face. "In fact he seems to still...are you two?"

"No, Dad. No," Lee answered briskly, wanting to head off any more questions he might ask about John. "We just had a misunderstanding."

Her father continued to stare at her. He opened his mouth, hesitated, then finally spoke. "Lee, there's something I feel I should tell you. Should have told you, but you were only 13." He mumbled the last part to himself.

"What?"

"Raising three children without a wife was a challenge." He kept his gaze on the big picture window. "But I never struggled more than when you and Jenny were teenagers. I didn't understand teenage girls the first time around and I felt even more lost when my own daughters became them. I made a lot of mistakes, Lee. And I want to apologize for that."

"Dad, what are you talking about?"

"If your mother had been alive, she probably wouldn't have..." Her father sighed and turned toward her. "John Hunter wrote you, Lee. He wrote you a letter nearly every week for months after that summer visit when you were 13."

Lee shook her head. "But I never—"

"I destroyed them all."

"What? Why?"

"I read the first one." He reached toward Lee then let his hand fall. "I was shocked. I hadn't registered that you were on the edge of womanhood, then I read this 16-year-old boy's apology for...well, you know. He was obviously infatuated with you and I was terrified. And enraged. It sounded like he had hurt my little girl badly. I never wanted you to see him again.

"You were so moody after we came back that time, I didn't want to create more antagonism between us by telling you I'd gone through your mail. I figured we'd confront the issue on our next visit to Nana's when we saw John Hunter again. But by then he'd moved away and I thought the situation had taken care of itself. To be honest I was relieved. I felt like I was stumbling around in the dark once you became a teenager." He passed his hand over his eyes and fell silent.

He wrote me? A wild rush of relief flooded Lee's heart. *He wrote me! He* was *my friend, and he cared. But that means...*The joy departed as quickly as it had surged. This revelation had come 20 years late, and their courses were already too far apart.

"I apologize, Lee, but, again, you were only 13. He was 16. I was terrified and—"

"It's okay. I understand." Lee spoke softly.

"Do you?" His forehead was a knot of wrinkles. "I tried to do my best."

"I know." They stared at each other in silence, then Lee moved toward him and patted his arm. "I know, Dad."

Tears clogged her throat and then her father pulled her into his arms. "I hope I didn't—"

"Let's not talk about it anymore, Dad." Lee gave him one last squeeze. "Water under the bridge." She stepped back. "Now, what are we going to do about dinner?"

"Don't worry about that. You know I caught the red eye this morning to get here, and I want to be rested up for tomorrow."

"But you have to eat."

"Thought I'd walk over to Dot's Diner and have a quick meal and then check into my hotel," he said. "I figured you'd already gotten rid of the furniture."

"Well, I could come along to the diner."

"You go have fun with your friends at the fair. I insist." Her father gave Charlie a pat, grabbed his suitcase and headed toward the front door.

"At least take my car." Lee found her keys and followed him.

"I'm fine." Her father waved away the offer. "I'd much rather take my time strolling down memory lane. He paused as the two of them stood on the front porch and he took in the street before them. "Why there's that old railroad bridge everyone kept running into. I can't believe they haven't knocked that old thing down yet."

"Knock it down? It think it's kind of sweet. It's almost like a town mascot."

He chuckled. "If you say so. Well, I'll see you in the morning." He kissed her cheek. "Keep your cell phone on, sweetie, and we'll connect after I eat breakfast."

“Thanks again, Dad.” Lee hugged him tightly. “Thanks for coming.”

“I’m glad I did.” He returned the hug and then, waving, wandered down the street.

CHAPTER THIRTY-SEVEN

Lee closed the door and leaned against it, feeling as if her whole world had just been turned upside down. Had her father really taken time off work and flown here to help her? And then slacked off and told her stories all day? And then revealed that the most painful betrayal of her life was no betrayal at all?

That last one, the thought that Lee most wanted to fixate on, made her insides tremble. Maybe it changed everything, but maybe not.

Terrified. Her father had repeated the word twice. That's exactly how she felt right now.

Her phone beeped. Lee pulled it out of her pocket and saw 5 missed calls from her father and another one from a number she didn't recognize. She gasped when she registered the time. It was getting late—only two hours until Grant had promised to pick her up to take her to the fair. Her last night in Eden Grove and last chance to say good-bye to Nana.

The revelation about the letters would have to wait.

A plan had formed in Lee's mind as she listened to her father's memories and she knew she didn't have much time left. She took a quick shower and put on the only dressy thing she'd brought with her, a strappy sundress paired with a set of cowboy boots she'd found in Nana's closet when she was sorting through her clothes. Last, she pulled her still damp hair up into a messy bun with one of Nana's silver and turquoise hair clips.

"I have to go say good-bye," she told Charlie as she handed him a bone and locked him into his kennel. "And it's something I've got to do on my own."

Grabbing a pair of rusty scissors from Nana's gardening shed, Lee snipped a bouquet of late summer roses from John's newly planted bushes. She pricked the inside of her fourth finger on a thorn and held it to her mouth for a moment before wrapping the flowers in a white rag she found on the back porch. Last, she grabbed the canister the lawyer had given her at their first meeting; it contained Nana's ashes.

The sun warmed her shoulders and the cicadas screamed into the thick silence while she walked toward the old cemetery a few blocks south of Nana's house. The streets were all but deserted, and Lee guessed that almost everyone was already on their way to the fair.

The cemetery lay next to the Wachatee River that ran around the edge of Eden Grove and the closer Lee got, the more she felt like she was being suffocated by the heavy humidity that surrounded her. She opened the ancient, rusty gate and walked past row upon row of markers toward the southeast corner. Generations of Nana's ancestors lay there; she'd come here a few times with Nana to lay flowers on Papa Mardell's or other relatives' graves.

Even though the lawyer had told her of its presence, Lee still felt her eyes burn when she spied the newly erected memorial in the Abney corner of the cemetery. Lee knelt and leaned the canister against the stone. Then she studied the inscription.

Kathryn Mardell
May 30, 1920–August 15, 2012

Gone but never forgotten—
forever in our hearts

It was time. Lee stood, unscrewed the canister and gently sprinkled the ashes around Nana's memorial stone and the family that surrounded her. A gentle breeze lifted most of the ashes up over the large stones and down in the direction of the burbling river.

Lee's quiet tears broke the hushed silence of the cemetery.

"I'm so sorry I never got to say good-bye, Nana. I...I kept thinking we'd have more time. That you'd be around forever." Lee tried to explain, but her throat choked with emotion and slumping to the ground, she tucked her head into her arms for several minutes until she could breathe again.

"I'm such an idiot, Nana," she spoke as she wiped her runny nose on the rag she'd carried the roses in. "I don't seem to be able to love people right, to show them how I love them. I have these feelings inside here," Lee struck at her chest, "but every time I try to open up, to tell someone how I feel, to reach out, I get scared. I bottle it back up and hide behind the less confusing parts of life. My work, my hobbies."

Lee traced a pattern in the rough dirt beneath her. "I kept promising myself that I'd come have a nice long visit with you next year and next year and next year." Lee began to cry again. "But we ran out of next years, Nana, and I'm so sorry.

"It was hard for me to come here in the summers once I was older, but that wasn't because of you. There was work of course, but mainly it was because of John Hunter and my memories and shame over what happened between us." Lee bit her lip, hating herself for not telling Nana this when she was alive.

"I felt like he betrayed me the last time I visited and I was angry and confused for so many years. I thought he was my best friend, like the big brother I never had. Then he kissed me and...I can see what that meant, but at the time I just felt sick when I thought of him. I realize now the reason I was so angry. I thought I'd lost another person I loved. Ever since then I've barely let anyone back into my heart." Lee fell silent for several moments considering the bottled words that had just spilled from her.

"Anyway," she continued, wiping her eyes and nose again, "none of that had to do with you. I hope you know how much I loved and admired you. Seeing your house again, I'd give anything to have you in it with me, laughing and telling stories of your wild adventures. I miss you so much."

Her throat caught with tears again and instead of trying to talk she lay down in the soft grass next to Nana's marker and pretended for one last time that she was a little girl again, cuddling with Nana in her bed before she fell asleep.

As I lie here next to Caralee stroking her hair like I used to, I wish more than anything I've ever wished in my life that I could tell my baby girl that she doesn't need to apologize to me. I understand her better than she thinks because I'm just like her.

Didn't I stop knowing how to love and show love after my William died?

Haven't I felt, ever since the day I read that telegram, that part of my heart stopped working too?

Now I wish I'd been more open about William and my heartache. Maybe I could have healed if I'd shared and maybe I could have helped Caralee work through her fix if I'd told her my sad story.

But here's the thing that makes me so angry I could spit: she didn't get a telegram! I know where John Hunter is right now and I know he's dreaming and wishing for her same as she is him.

So that's why I lean down next to her ear and start whispering to her, "Caralee you're as stubborn as a mule and you never did listen to a word I said to you, so I don't know why I'm trying now. But if you ever, for once in your life, let something into that crazy thick skull of yours, listen to me now.

"Who's the woman who scurries up cliffs like a spider and drops out of helicopters to ski down mountain peaks? Who's the woman who climbs up ice sheets with a pick axe in her hands and spikes on her feet? You are. So why are you acting such a coward?

"Go grab that man right now. Explain your confusion, your daddy's actions and the damage it did to your heart, but please don't throw your chance away. I know you two can smooth things over. I promise you, John Hunter still loves you, but you've got to be brave.

"Tell John Hunter you love him. Then you hold on to him and never, ever let him go. Go now and stop being afraid.

"Stop being afraid!"

CHAPTER THIRTY-EIGHT

Lee wasn't sure how much time had passed when she became aware of the birdsong around her. She felt a tickle on her cheek and opened her eyes. A brilliantly colored butterfly flitted from her cheek to her forehead.

It took Lee a moment to remember where she was, but it came trickling back into her sleep-slowed brain. She sat up and the butterfly landed on her outstretched finger.

"Beautiful," Lee whispered as it opened its wings, allowing her to admire the full effect of its spectacular coloring. After a moment it flitted from her finger and brushed her cheek, before flying off into the dense undergrowth between the cemetery and the river.

Lee studied the place where it had disappeared and enjoyed the cool breeze that lifted her damp hair from her temples. Brushing some leaves from her hair, she spied the phone that had fallen from her pocket and checked the time. Peace evaporated.

"It's already 6:30?" She leapt to her feet, her mind racing. Grant. The fair. Her last night in Eden Grove. John Hunter. A strange sense of Nana's voice echoing through her, saying, "Stop being afraid."

She turned back to Nana's memorial and organized

the flowers before brushing a kiss on her palm and placing it on the sun warmed stone.

"I love you, Nana. Always." Her eyes began to swim with tears again and she forced herself to turn and walk away.

She broke into a run and raced through the gravestones, leaving the gate to clang shut behind her. The lower altitude of Mississippi gave her lungs an almost Olympian-like advantage and Lee sprinted the entire way back to the house. As she turned the corner to Nana's street, she saw Grant's car just pulling away from the curb.

"Grant, wait!" She ran down the middle of the street and waved her arms. "Wait!" The car paused and the brake lights came on. It pulled back to the curb and Grant got out.

"Well, I almost gave up on you," Grant drawled as she ran the final steps to his side, then doubled over, gasping for air. "Thought you got a better offer." Lee looked up and saw a glint of annoyance in his eyes.

She tried to catch her breath. "I went down to the cemetery, and I lost track of time."

"Well, that's all right, I guess. The only thing is all the good barbecue's gonna be gone if we don't hurry up."

"Your sympathies are so appreciated."

"What's that, honey? You're gonna have to speak up."

"I said, 'then by all means, we'd better get going.'" Lee walked to the passenger side, wanting only to get to the fair and find John Hunter.

Grant put the car into drive and gunned the engine.

He sped down the street in what Lee thought was a very un-policeman-like example.

Smoothing her hair back from her face, she felt a twig. As Lee brushed it from her hair, she wondered how badly disheveled she looked, thinking back to the debris around Nana's grave. The sun visor in front of her had a mirror and she flipped it down to examine the damage.

"Grant, what's the matter with you? I've got mud all over my face! Why didn't you say something?"

"'Cuz we're already late. Besides, you look fine." Grant didn't take his eyes off the road.

"Turn back right now! I need to wash this stuff off, it's disgusting." She tried to wipe the sticky muck from her face but only succeeded in smearing it around more.

"Caralee, honey, look, we're already here." Grant turned the steering wheel and careened into the parking lot. "Why don't you just go find the ladies' room and get yourself cleaned up a little. Then you can meet me at the barbecue stand."

Can you forget your stupid barbecue for one minute! Lee wanted to shout. But she bit her tongue. It might be her last night in Eden Grove, and she didn't want to create a scene in the parking lot with a police officer.

"Fine." She swallowed back her angry words. "Do you have a tissue, napkin, anything?"

Grant pulled a crumpled handkerchief from his back pocket and gingerly extended it towards her. She jerked it from his fingers and stormed off in the direction of the ticket takers, hoping they could direct her to the nearest restroom. A gangly teenage girl in tiny cut-offs and a tight tank top wrinkled her nose in disgust when Lee stopped in front of her.

"Can you tell me where the nearest restroom is?" Lee asked, burning with embarrassment.

The other ticket taker burst into giggles as the two of them eyed Lee.

"Oh, uh, yes, ma'am," one of them said, good manners finally prevailing. "It's at the other end of the fairgrounds."

"Of course," Lee muttered. She stalked through the citizenry of Eden Grove, who starred at her with a mixture of curiosity and pity. Finally, in the distance she saw a concrete building labeled *Restrooms* and let out a sigh of relief.

"Well, my lands, lookie here. I guess the Creature from the Black Lagoon came to this year's dance." Lee heard a voice that had become only too familiar.

Don't look, don't answer, a voice warned her. Just keep walking. Ignore her and get cleaned up.

"Oh, I guess we ran her off, girls. I hear these wild creatures can be a bit skittish in big crowds." The voice dissolved into grating laughter.

Lee turned and saw Kiki, surrounded by a group of friends who didn't even try to hide their gasps and giggles as they pointed at Lee. Humiliation exploded inside her and she saw John Hunter approach the group, his eyes moving from Kiki to Lee and then back again.

"What's going on here, ladies? Y'all been slinging

some mud at each other?"

"Not this time." Kiki laughed. She walked over to John Hunter and wrapped her arm around his waist. "I imagine she'd be too scared to sling any mud with me."

Her dream from the cemetery burst into Lee's mind like a shot and Nana's words echoed through her mind. *Stop being afraid.* She could almost hear Nana yelling it at her now. *Stop being afraid!*

"Scared?" Lee turned and walked up to Kiki. "I don't see anything for me to be afraid of. The only coward here is you."

"I do believe she's gone off her rocker," Kiki said, but Lee heard the uncertainty in her voice. "What on earth should I be scared of?"

"The inevitable. That soon you'll be an old, used up has-been. People will laugh behind your back and you'll keep trying so hard to be the prom queen you once were. All your glory days are already slipping between your fingers and you can't do a thing about it."

"Whoa, Lee." John moved between the two women. "Let's all just take a deep—"

"And you." Lee turned to John Hunter and poked his chest. He staggered back a step. "Good for you for settling. For not going after what you've *supposedly* wanted your entire life. For offering me one confusing glimpse of your feelings in the sycamore tree when I was 13 years old and then giving up after a few unanswered letters. Ones I never received, by the way, thanks to my dad." John's mouth dropped in astonishment.

"Now, if you'll excuse me, I've spent the last hour asleep by my grandmother's *grave,* grieving the loss of someone I loved, and I know I don't look my best. Thank you for your sympathies and kindness."

Lee spun on her heel and marched into the bathroom. Locking the stall door she leaned back against it and waited for her racing heart to slow to its normal beat. "Thanks, Nana," she spoke aloud, not caring who heard. "That felt great."

Lee emerged from the stall after a few minutes and gazed at herself in renewed despair. Telling off Kiki and John Hunter had been great, but she wished she'd looked a little better while doing it. As she tried to run her fingers through her tangled hair, a voice came from behind her.

"Now, honey, why don't you just borrow this brush and a little bit of my lip gloss."

"Granny Bob! I didn't know you were in here. Did you...did you hear what happened outside with Kiki and John Hunter?"

"Well, I wasn't there, if that's what you're asking," she said, setting the brush and the lip gloss on the counter top, "but word traveled pretty fast to where I was sitting with my chapter of the Daughters of the Confederacy. Let's just say that not all of us find Kiki quite as charming as she finds herself, so we didn't mind seeing her knocked down a peg or two.

"I also heard that Kiki tried to follow you in here, but John Hunter stopped her. She turned and shouted some particularly hateful comments about you. Then John told her to be quiet, so she slapped him and he walked off in the direction of the river."

"He walked off?" Lee asked. She tried to mask her disappointment with a broken laugh. "Well, at least Kiki's finally shown him her true colors." She wiped away the last of the mud from her face with Grant's damp handkerchief. Then, she reached for Granny Bob's brush and tried to drag it through the tangles.

The older woman rinsed out the handkerchief and worked at wiping away the smudges of dirt on Lee's arm, shoulder and dress. "You know, Caralee, John Hunter had a lot of sorrow when he was a boy and I think sometimes that bleeds over into the way he treats the people he loves the most." Granny Bob's eyes met Lee's in the mirror. "As I'm sure you understand yourself."

"Yeah, I think I do." Lee clipped her hair back into a bun and then reached for the lip gloss.

"Does that...does that change anything between the two of you, do you think?"

"I'm sorry, Granny Bob, but I don't think so. I'm leaving tomorrow and as much as I love you, this town, well, almost all of the town, I think it's too late for...that." Lee saw the older woman's face fall. "But from now on, I plan to live my life a little bit differently, and I promise to come back and visit."

"You'd better." Granny Bob collected her hair brush and lip gloss. "I couldn't stand it if I thought I'd never see you again." She reached over and grabbed Lee into a tight hug. "Now I hear the music starting. You'd better get out there and dance 'til you drop."

"Maybe I should just go," Lee said as she wiped the last of the grime off her dress and boots. "I did cause a pretty big scene just now."

"Why, honey, you're Kathryn's granddaughter! That's just the kind of entrance this town would expect. Now you get out there and dance with some of those cute boys. I know they're just dying to ask you," Granny Bob said and marched Lee from the restroom.

The relentless heat had faded and night crept around the edges of the horizon. Lee took a deep breath of the barbecue scented air and headed toward the dance floor. Her gaze traveled over the crowd, knowing she should try to find Grant. She heard someone shout her named and turned to find Tom and Emma walking her way. Davey waved from his perch on his father's shoulders.

Emma reached out and pulled her into a tight hug. "I just heard about your smack down with Kiki." She laughed in Lee's ear. "I'm so proud of you for standing up to that little hussy."

"Caralee Trenton, y'all," Tom bellowed into the dance crowd. He pulled Lee's arm up into the air. "The uncontested winner and champion." Cheers and whistles erupted and Lee collapsed against Emma's shoulder in embarrassed laughter.

"You've become the town hero." Emma winked. "It's not every day a snake's taken out."

Someone plucked at her elbow. Lee turned and found herself staring into the face of a blond man with a crooked smile.

"Caralee, Kathryn Mardell's granddaughter? Is that really you?"

"Yes," Lee answered, trying to place the familiar blue eyes.

"It's Charles Hawson. I don't expect you remember me?"

"Of course I do!" Lee pushed aside his extended hand and gave him a hug. "How could I possibly forget you?"

"Well, I know I couldn't forget the girl who smacked me in the face with a cow pie. It was one of the defining moments of my childhood."

"I had to. You told everyone I was a sissy."

"You're right. I deserved it." Charles looked over his shoulder as the music swelled and the crowd cheered. "Grant Tucker wanted me to find you and let you know he had to leave."

"Seriously?" Lee had to laugh. "First, the guy forces me to come here even though I'm covered in mud and then he deserts me while I'm in the restroom? I can't believe him."

"It is Grant Tucker, after all," Charles drawled. "But he did get a call from dispatch, so maybe you can forgive him this once."

Lee nodded and watched Tom spin Emma and Davey across the dance floor. "I guess I'll head on home then. It was nice seeing you, Charles."

"Now you just hold on a minute." Charles grabbed her hand. "I'd sure like a dance if you'd be willing to stay just a little longer."

"Really? Even with our cow pie history?"

"Well, sure." Charles led her to the dance floor, smiling. "Fearless old Bean Pole's back in Eden Grove. That's something to celebrate."

CHAPTER THIRTY-NINE

The rest of the evening went by in a whirl of remembered childhood joys and laughter. A parade of old friends and acquaintances found Lee, anxious to hear how she was handling Nana's death and about the life she'd made for herself in Durango. Many of the boys from her and John Hunter's old gang of friends had gotten married to high school sweethearts and presented the children they'd had in the years she'd been gone. Remembered escapades and shared punishments, reports of new milestones and the now full-fledged Southern charm of everyone here, soothed away the emotional turmoil of the hours before.

Lee was just finishing a dance when Tom tapped her on the shoulder. "I think this old honky tonk band's only got a few more songs in them and I had to get one more dance with the most popular girl at the party." He spun Lee across the floor. Emma and Davey clapped and waved from where they'd settled on a hay bale.

"Thanks for making this a great last night in Eden Grove. I was so busy taking care of Nana's things, that I almost didn't get a chance to see all my old friends before I left."

"I know. You've been working way too hard. When are you leaving, by the way?"

"Early tomorrow, I think," Lee answered as he danced her closer and closer to the edge of the floor. "My dad flew in to help me make the drive home. We both need to get back to our work."

"Well now, what a shame, but in that case, I think there's one gentleman here you still need to dance with." He twirled her next to a pretzel stand.

Lee stumbled as her feet came off the parquet floor and onto the grass, but a hand reached out to steady her. "Thanks, Tom. I appreciate it," a deep voice rumbled from the shadows.

"My pleasure, John Hunter. 'Night, Lee." Tom tipped an imaginary hat to the both of them and walked back to Emma and Davey.

"Hey," came John's voice after a moment of silence.

"Hey yourself."

John grabbed her hand and tugged her past the food tents and stragglers that surrounded the dance floor.

"Where are we going? Tom said you wanted to dance."

"Well, I don't," came John's tight response. He led Lee to a grove of trees next to the river.

"Fine, but I'm not going to tag along after you." Lee jerked her arm from his grasp. "What do you want, John?" she asked his back.

She saw the muscles of his broad shoulders tense as he crossed his arms. She noticed the way his wavy hair curled at the back of his neck, and when he turned she recognized the scar on his nose that she'd given him that long ago night when she threw the lamp through the window.

"I said, what do you want?"

"We'll get to that in a minute." He turned. "But what I need to know is, what do *you* want?"

"I don't understand. What are you asking?"

"I'm asking are you happy with what you've got in Colorado? Your business, your friends, your life?"

"I think I have a good life there."

"That's not what I asked," John said and stepped closer. "I asked if you're happy. 'Cuz if you're happy, I'm gonna shake your hand right now and walk out of your life forever." He reached down and gently pulled her hands into his own. "I don't want to do anything that causes you more pain or takes away from your happiness, Caralee. I hope you know that's how I've always felt, even though I seem to have failed time and time again. That last summer when I was so distant and angry—in my confused teenager brain, I was trying to protect you from something even I didn't understand."

"Which was?" Lee prompted, her heart racing.

"Well, sugar, I'm not gonna tell you unless you answer my question." John gave her a crooked smile. "Are you happy?"

Time froze in that moment and her life played out in Lee's mind as if in fast forward, slowing down as it reached her adult years. She saw glimpses of herself leading climbs or skiing down avalanche chutes, the sharp wind cutting her cheeks; Charlie and her on the front porch of her little house; laughing with her employees at work. Familiar things. Safe things.

Then she looked deep into John Hunter's eyes. What she saw there swallowed away all her fears. It was time to be brave.

"I'm content, John Hunter, but I'm not really that happy. I guess I'd say, I'm pretty lonely. Even when I thought you didn't care anymore, I never got over missing my best friend."

"Oh, darling girl." His arms reached around her and he crushed her body into his. "Neither of us has to be lonely again," he whispered. Then his lips were on hers, and the two of them poured out the passion and longing that each had stored up during the years of separation.

Lee's hands lifted up to his neck and the dark, thick waves of his hair before moving to trace the curves of his familiar face. She felt the dampness of tears and wondered if they were hers or John Hunter's or both. It was her last conscious thought before she lost herself in the love of John's embrace.

Watching those two in each other's arms is like taking a deep breath after being underwater too long. I guess I'd just about given up hope that they could finally get over their stubborn, stupid ways, work through their misunderstandings and realize they've loved each other since before they could walk. I know some people may disagree with me, but even though you get all sorts of chances for love in your lifetime, I believe you only get one chance at a grande amore. And finally, finally those two lonely souls figured it out. Bobby and I can rest easy.

I declare, now that we've got that crisis averted with a little help from yours truly, I'm not sure what I'm going to do to occupy my time. That empty house of mine is no fun. It's depressing really, to see how quickly someone can dispose of another person's life. I said my good-byes before I followed Lee down to the cemetery earlier today.

To tell the truth, the last couple of days I've felt the strangest sensation. Almost like there's this presence hovering around the outsides of my vision. I'm not sure but I think I might recognize who it is. I was scared to admit it to myself, but seeing those two young things finally let go of all their fears inspires me to let go of a few of my own. So I'll just brush one last kiss on my baby girl's cheek and then give these two some privacy.

Then I turn and a shimmering form beckons me from the bank.

"William!" I call. "William, I'm ready now."

CHAPTER FORTY

Later, after they'd wrestled through all the confusion and misunderstandings of the past, Lee and John Hunter strolled down firefly lit streets towards Nana's house. John paused to pull her yet again into the soft shadows of the trees.

"If you keep doing that, it'll take us all night to get home."

"That's the plan." John's lips met hers again.

"My dad's probably going to call me at six am tomorrow, raring to go," Lee protested, without much conviction when they broke apart.

"About that." John reached out to stroke her hair. "I assume you two will be heading back pretty soon?"

"I really need to get back to Play Harder, but now that you and I...well, I've been going over and over it in my mind."

"I know. I could tell."

"You think you know me so well."

"'Course I do, sugar. I've been studying on you for years." He leaned down to kiss her again. "So here's what I'm thinking," John spoke again after Lee had thoroughly melted into his arms. "What would you say to a road trip partner?"

"Besides Charlie and my dad?"

"Yes, besides Charlie and your dad." John kept his arm around her shoulder and they walked down the street again. "In fact, I was wondering if you'd consider moving your dog to the backseat and letting me take shotgun?"

"But what about my dad? He's sort of a front seat kind of guy."

"Don't you worry about your daddy. He and I had a nice long talk on the way from the airport and he informed me he'd much rather fly back to Colorado as long as you had someone to drive home with."

"The two of you have been conspiring together?"

"I plead the fifth."

"But what about your work and everything here?" Lee asked, serious now.

"Well, I figure I can just rent out my house again and work on my dissertation from Durango. I'm not due to meet with my advisor for another couple of months." He studied Lee's face in the moonlight. "It might get a bit complicated, but we'll find a way to make it all work out. As long as we're together. That's what matters the most.

"'Course I know this is a pretty big step. If you're not ready for something like this..." He trailed off and Lee heard the hesitation in his voice.

"How long would you need to pack up?" She laughed and he pulled her into a tight hug.

They came around the corner then and Lee gasped at the chaos: another crumpled truck, another couple of

EMTs helping a stunned driver into the ambulance.

"Is that...snow?" Lee reached out to catch one of the puffs of white that floated through the air, danced in the tree limbs and coated the street before them.

"Snow! Those are busted cotton bales, you crazy Yankee girl." John leaned down until their foreheads touched. "*My* crazy Yankee girl."

CHAPTER FORTY-ONE

A little over a year later

"Hey, Lee, how close are we to the top? I'm starting to get a little shaky." John Hunter's voice came from beneath the lip of the cliff.

"Oh come on, you big baby! You're almost here. Hurry up, the view's incredible." She took a sip from her canteen and wiped the prickles of perspiration off her forehead.

Huffing and puffing, she heard John Hunter's approach before she saw the dark mop of his hair appear. "You're going to pay for that one, Mrs. Fairchild. I don't like being called names." He jerked himself over the lip with a groan. "Even if it's by someone as pretty as you."

Mrs. Fairchild. It was still hard for Lee to get used to the new last name, even though it had been three months since they'd gotten married. She felt where Nana's ring hung on a chain around her neck next to her old sapphire drop—the place she always kept it when the two of them went climbing.

John Hunter unclipped himself from the rope and stretched. He accepted her offered canteen and took a deep drink before he spoke.

"And where do you get off calling me a *baby*? I think that's the hardest climb you've dragged me on yet, and I kept up with you just fine until that inverted part at the end."

"I was only teasing." She leaned over and kissed him. "Can you find it in you poor ol' heart to forgive me?" she said, adopting his drawl.

"You laugh at that accent now, Yankee girl, but you'll be talking like the rest of us before you know it. I think Tennessee's gonna rub off on you a lot faster than you realize." He pulled Lee into his arms and rested his cheek on the top of her head before letting out a low whistle. "You weren't kidding about that view. Takes your breath away, doesn't it?"

"Mmmmm." Lee basked in the peace of the moment. "Think I should include this in my routes for the customers?"

"Definitely. Just three more weeks until the Tennessee branch of Play Harder opens. Do you think you'll get everything done in time?"

"Oh, sure." Lee shrugged, too happy at the moment to care about the details. "And if I don't I'll just fake it."

They sat on top of a large rock and shared the lunch they'd packed earlier that morning. John's classes would start around the same time Lee's new extreme outfitters would celebrate its grand opening. She'd enjoyed the weeks they had together while John Hunter still had time to play, before the inundation of papers to grade and classes to teach would fill most of his free time.

Lee pulled Nana's ring out from under her shirt to admire it yet again. "Do you ever feel like we have Nana to thank for getting the two of us together?"

"Well, without her death, you probably wouldn't have come down to Eden Grove," John said, packing up the trash from their lunch.

"No, that's not what I mean. Don't you feel like...like there were too many coincidences and opportunities pushing us together without someone's help?"

"Like?"

"Well, like you coming back to Eden Grove at the exact same time I arrived, her yard needing landscaping and you being a landscaper. And then there were those dreams I had about Nana and the ones about you."

"Dreams about me?" John interrupted. "I've never heard about these dreams. Please go into some detail, sugar. I'm all ears."

"Stop." She shoved his playful hands away. "Now listen, there's more: the way I kept ending up in all these weird confrontations with Kiki—"

"Which only served to make her look like more of a she-devil, bless her heart."

"Exactly. And then there's the matter of this ring and the LWD."

"The LWD?"

"Yes, the *little white dress,*" Lee rolled her eyes, as if she'd always known what LWD stood for. "I mean, selling it is what made it possible for me to open the new Play Harder."

"After it had its last big hurrah as your wedding dress."

"And why on earth would Nana have something like that, an original dress from Pauline Trigère's first New York collection, still hanging in the back of her closet? She gave the rest of her things like that to the university years ago when she retired," Lee said. "At least that's what the head of the fashion department told me when she looked at the dress."

"Well, now that you mention it, I think you're right. And if you look a little further back to our childhoods, seems like your Nana was weaving our lives together even then. She'll always be with us, Lee."

The two of them sat in silence as the memories of Nana flitted through the air like dragonflies.

"Wherever she is, I hope she knows we ended up together." Lee felt tears pricking behind her eyelids.

"Even if it did take us about twenty years too long to figure it out." John pulled her into a kiss before she could get too sad.

Lee allowed his love to wash away her tears. She took a deep breath and stood.

"Let's head back home, Jon-Jon. We've got a whole lot of love to catch up on.

Granny Bob's Sweet Tea Recipe

- ¼ cup loose tea, tightly packed
- 2 cups boiling water
- 1 ½ quarts water
- 1 ¼ -1 ½ cups sugar, depending on how sweet you like it

1. Put tea in a heatproof glass container and pour boiling water over it. Let stand for 5 minutes.
2. Pour sugar into the bottom of a heavy 2-quart pitcher.
3. Pour tea and water mixture through tea strainer or fine colander into the pitcher with sugar.
4. Mix, serve over ice, and enjoy.
   Makes 2 quarts.

Granny Bob's Sweet Raspberry Tea Recipe

- 4 quarts water
- 1-1 ½ cups sugar
- 12 ounces frozen unsweetened raspberries
- 10 tea bags (Luzianne)
- ¼ cup lemon juice
- 1 cup fresh raspberries

1. Bring water and sugar to a boil. Remove from the heat; stir until sugar is dissolved.
2. Add the raspberries, tea bags and lemon juice. Cover and steep for 3 minutes.
3. Strain; discard berries and tea bags.
4. Transfer tea to a large container or pitcher. Refrigerate until chilled. Serve over ice and garnish with a couple of fresh raspberries. Makes 4 quarts

ABOUT THE AUTHOR

Kelly Baugh's adventures have taken her from the mountains of Nepal to the battlefield of the Terrible Twos, and the way she keeps herself from going crazy is to write about it. She is a native of Colorado where she resides with her husband, 2 children and 2 hyper huskies.

OTHER HOT CHOCOLATE PRESS BOOKS

HTTP://HOTCHOCOLATEPRESS.COM

Echoes

Reflections Through Poetry and Verse

By Dean K Miller

And Then I Smiled

Reflections on a Life

Not Yet Complete

Inspirational

By Dean K Miller

Planes, Trains and Chuck & Eddie

A Lighthearted

Look at Families

Essays

By Kerrie L. Flanagan

Write Away; A Year of Musings and Motivations for Writers

Essays

By Kerrie Flanagan & Jenny Sundstedt

Bobbing for Watermelons

Women's Fiction

By April J. Moore

Claire's Christmas Catastrophe

Children's

Early Chapter Book

By Kerrie L. Flanagan

The Odyssey of a Monk (Kindle)

Parable

Spirituality

By Dean K Miller

49849513R00178

Made in the USA
Charleston, SC
05 December 2015